Sacred
Celebrations

Sacred Celebrations

A SOURCEBOOK

Glennie Kindred

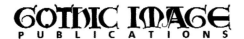

GOTHIC IMAGE
PUBLICATIONS

Published in 2001 by Gothic Image Publications,
PO Box 2568, Glastonbury, Somerset BA6 8XR, England.

ISBN O 906362 48 2

A CIP catalogue record for this book is available from the
British Library.

Illustrated and designed by Glennie Kindred

Layout by RWS Studio, Glastonbury, Somerset BA6 9DY
Front and back cover illustrations by Glennie Kindred

Printed by Hackman Printers Ltd, Cambrian Ind. Park,
Clydach Vale, Tonypandy, Rhondda, Wales CF40 2XX, United Kingdom.

Disclaimer: The author and publisher cannot be held responsible for accidents or
any harm caused due to any of the craft project ideas or herbal remedies contained
in this book.

ACKNOWLEDGEMENTS

My heartfelt thanks to:
Frances Howard-Gordon at Gothic Image for making it possible for me to fully express my understanding and experience of working with the eight Celtic festivals over the last ten years;
To those friends who contributed their poems and songs: Brian Boothby of Tomorrow's Ancestor, Vince DeCicco of Praying for the Rain, and Nicki Martin, and to my many other friends who have helped and inspired me along the way; to the Guardians, Ancestors, Spirit guides and Spirit helpers who have guided me along my path, and to all the spirits of the trees, plants and land to whom I acknowledge my allegiance, encouragement and openness to communicate; and to my family who made space and time for me to write and draw when I needed it. Thank you all for your loving support and sensitivity.

This book is dedicated to the Earth and to my children May, Jack and Jerry; to my partner Brian Boothby and my Mum; to the loving connections of true friends; the Celebrations Group and the Elementals.

Let us continue to reclaim our freedom to follow our own path and the Love in our hearts.

CONTENTS

INTRODUCTION

To celebrate the Earth's yearly solar cycle, is to take part in an ancient tradition which has been handed down to us since before Celtic times. These festivals fall at eight points during the solar year, and include the fixed points of Winter and Summer Solstices (the longest night and the longest day); the Spring and Autumn Equinoxes (day and night are of equal length); and the four seasonal peaks of Spring, Summer, Autumn and Winter. Celebrating these points is a means by which we can connect to the Earth's passing seasons and acknowledge the way this resonates within ourselves, as part of the natural world.

Interwoven in the Sun's cycles are the monthly cycles of the Moon whose influence affects all of life on Earth from the tides of the world's oceans, to the fluids within our bodies, our emotions, our unconscious, the fertility of women and their menstrual cycles.

Throughout the book I use the word 'Celtic' as a term which recognises this as a cultural lineage in the lands of England, Wales, Scotland and Ireland, as well as all over Northern and Western Europe. Many of their traditions have been lost, destroyed by the Christian religion which sought to establish a new patriarchal God, and destroy the worship of Pagan Gods and Goddesses. Much can be rediscovered through folk customs, legends and folktales. Much has been kept alive through Pagan tradition, Druidic and Bardic lore and Pictish and Celtic art. The Christian calendar, on close examination, has overlaid its own festivals to fall at the same time as the Celtic ones, but with a subtle difference of perspective. This was necessary, as part of the conversion process, which changed the whole spiritual experience of the people of these lands. The Church taught us to view Spirit and Matter as separate realms, and to fear the inner worlds. This is so deeply entrenched, that even those without any religious belief are deeply influenced by it. We also feel ourselves to be separate from and superior to the rest of nature, and that men are superior to women. This fragmented state has brought great damage to the Earth's environment and to ourselves.

In order to change this perspective, there is a need to see ourselves and our relationship to the Earth, the Moon and the Sun with new eyes. We need to re-learn what we have forgotten and re-connect to the inner realms, which are a continuous presence around and within us. We have all been conditioned for so long to only use our logical intellectual minds, it is important that we begin to become aware of, and listen to our intuitive side. It is our conferred power and inherited right.

There is no need for a hierarchy of spiritual authority. We are each able to follow our own path, to break free of outworn attitudes, damaging dogma and concepts, and to transform and change. We have to learn to be part of the natural world again. We can do this by working with the energies which are both within ourselves and all around us. Then we can feel ourselves to be part of creation and not somehow fragmented and separated. Everyone and everything is sacred. Every action has a reaction in both the inner and outer realms.

Celebrating the solar cycle of the year and the monthly Moon cycles is a way of re-connecting to the native traditions of this land. When we are freed from superstition, fear and suppression, we are once again potent and alive, and moving forward to embrace a new spiritual understanding emerging now as we enter the Aquarian Age.

This is a reference book for each of the Celtic festivals, and the Sun and Lunar cycles, as well as a source book for related activities. It is an exploration of the many aspects manifest at each festival, from the underlying energy of the Earth, and its place in the year's cycle, to the integration of the patterns and clues which have been handed down to us from traditions which have survived from the pre-christian past. By combining these different aspects, and intuitively reforming them into something new and yet connected, we can integrate what we know to create new patterns to enhance change and transformation. Thus, these festivals remain part of a living tradition which can be used as an aid to our spiritual process at this time.

Glennie Kindred

May 2000

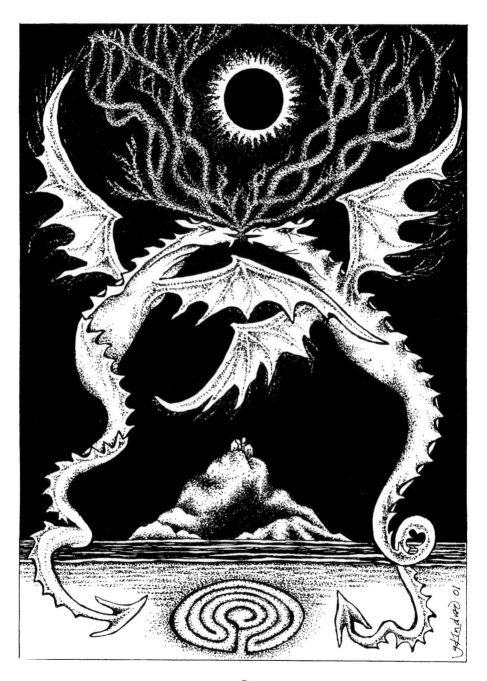

THE WHEEL OF THE YEAR

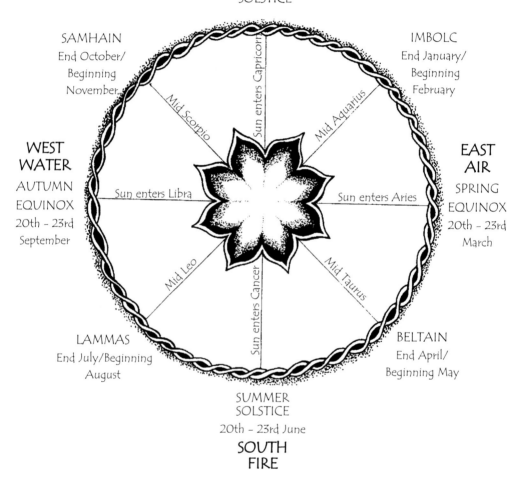

NORTH
EARTH
20th – 23rd December
WINTER
SOLSTICE

SAMHAIN
End October/
Beginning
November

IMBOLC
End January/
Beginning
February

Mid Scorpio

Sun enters Capricorn

Mid Aquarius

WEST
WATER
AUTUMN
EQUINOX
20th – 23rd
September

EAST
AIR
SPRING
EQUINOX
20th – 23rd
March

Sun enters Libra

Sun enters Aries

Mid Leo

Sun enters Cancer

Mid Taurus

LAMMAS
End July/Beginning
August

BELTAIN
End April/
Beginning May

SUMMER
SOLSTICE
20th – 23rd June
SOUTH
FIRE

THE WHEEL OF THE SOLAR YEAR

The Celtic peoples of our lands celebrated the cyclic flow of the year at eight points during the year's cycle. These festivals can be used to honour and celebrate the Earth and her seasons, ourselves and each other, our achievements as well as our losses, and to come together as a community, to share ourselves, our food and drink, dance, sing, and reflect. Each festival is celebrated with a different focus. Each can bring a structure to our lives by consciously making a connection to the passage of time and our path within it.

The wheel of the year is not just a matter of changing from one season to the next. Beneath the manifestation of seasonal change, there is also change within the subtle energies of the Earth. These energy patterns affect us all (consciously or unconsciously) so that by understanding the flow and direction of this energy, we can move with it, as true inhabitants of our planet Earth: belonging, part of and flowing with it on all levels of our being.

The Eightfold sub-division of the year is marked by the four fixed points in the year forming a cross. These are called the Quarter Points and are the Winter Solstice in the North (20th - 23rd December), the shortest day and the longest night; Summer Solstice in the South (20th-23rd June) the longest day and shortest night; the Spring Equinox in the East (20th - 23rd March), and in the West, the Autumn Equinox (20th - 23rd September) both of which are when day and night are of equal length. These are fixed points in the year, the exact day and time each year can be found in any good diary.

These Four Quarter Points are then crossed again by what are known as the Cross Quarter Festivals. These are the four great fire festivals of our Celtic past. They fall at the seasonal peaks and are used to celebrate and participate with the power of nature. They are the point at which we can connect with the developing energy of the new season ahead.

Imbolc or Imolg is in the North East and is celebrated at the end of January/beginning of February, when Winter has reached its peak and the first signs of Spring are showing themselves. Beltain is in the South East and is celebrated at the end of April/beginning of May when Spring has reached its peak and Summer is becoming apparent. Lammas or Lughnasad is in the South West, and is celebrated at the end of July/beginning of August, when Summer has reached its peak and the first signs of Autumn are showing. Finally Samhain, in the North West, is celebrated at the end of October/beginning of November, when Autumn has reached its peak, and Winter is beginning to feel that it has arrived.

7

THE QUARTER POINTS

THE SOLSTICES

Solstice means 'the standing of the Sun' (Latin) and at the two Solstice points in the year, the Sun's cycle reaches its peak, stops, and begins its change of energy. The great cosmic clock of the waxing and waning cycle of the Sun.

From Winter Solstice to Summer Solstice, the Sun is waxing, reaching its peak at the Summer Solstice, the longest day and shortest night. From Summer Solstice to Winter Solstice, the Sun is waning and the darkness reaches its peak at the shortest day and longest night of the Winter Solstice.

The Solstices then are a time to stop, and to look back on where the half-yearly cycle has brought you, and a chance to look forward and see the direction in which the next half-yearly cycle may lead you; a moment to be conscious of your life's flow and direction; a time to express your hopes and fears, your intentions; to assimilate your learnings and celebrate your achievements; a time to celebrate the light; a time to celebrate the dark; a moment to be conscious of the way this waxing and waning of the Sun affects our lives, and to celebrate this duality and what it means to us.

When the light is increasing from Winter Solstice to Summer Solstice, all beings are moving out into the light, becoming more individual and independent, expressing their own identity and uniqueness, expanding outwards into the material world. But as the light is decreasing from Summer Solstice to Winter Solstice, nature and life as a whole is integrating itself into a more social way of life, going within, reflecting and becoming more intuitive, expanding into the inner realms - exploring inner wisdom.

THE EQUINOXES

At the Spring and Autumn Equinoxes, day and night are of equal length all over the world. The focus here is the balance of light and dark, the outer world is balanced by the inner world. Both are equal.

The Equinoxes fall at the beginning of the seasonal changes: Spring with its promise of Summer, and Autumn with its promise of Winter. The new season will affect all of life and bring changes within as well as without, as well as releasing new energy patterns. Times of transition are often chaotic and stressful, but out of this chaos, new ways, new ideas and new directions can manifest. The Equinoxes are a time to take action, transform, release the past, and move forwards. Use these points as a focus for the direction you wish to go in. This means you will meet the new energy poised and prepared.

THE CROSS QUARTER POINTS

The Quarter Points of the Winter and Summer Solstices, and the Spring and Autumn Equinoxes, are then crossed again by the Cross Quarter Points, known in the past as the Four Great Fire Festivals. These were celebrated by lighting big fires on the hilltops, uniting communities by a common bond of celebration. These four Cross Quarter festivals fall at the seasonal peaks, at the point when the season is about to change into the next, and is the right time to use this developing energy. Because of this, their application during the year's cycle is of deepest and significant importance to us if we wish to work with the Earth's energies, and participate in a process of positive change both for ourselves and the Earth.

Each of the Cross Quarter festivals offers a unique opportunity for us to celebrate and be aware of the developing energy and what this could mean for us; to bring about manifestation through the power of our deepest wishes and positive intent.

IMBOLC is at the end of January/beginning of February. Winter is at its peak, but the days are lengthening slightly, and the first signs of Spring are apparent. The active phase of life is beginning as the Sun's power returns. This can be combined with the intuitive receptive energy and what has been assimilated and understood on the inner levels during the Winter months. It is a time for new beginnings, emerging ideas and the outer growth of personal seeds from their incubation period within.

BELTAIN is at the end of April/beginning of May. Spring is at its peak, the days are getting longer and warmer, and the first signs of Summer are establishing themselves. The Earth's energies are at their most active as the blending of the intuitive inner energy and the active outer energy brings manifestation and fertility. This is the life force at its most potent and powerful, and the right time to use the expansive energy to its fullest potential.

LAMMAS is at the end of July/beginning of August. Summer is at its peak, but the days are beginning to shorten slightly and the first of the harvest, the grain, is being gathered in. Here we can begin to assimilate and gather in our own personal harvest, the manifestation of our heart's desires, and the fruits of our active labour. It is a time to take a reflective look at ourselves and return to the spiritual inner world for deeper understanding of our actions.

SAMHAIN is at the end of October/beginning of November. Autumn has reached its peak now, the harvest is all gathered in. The days are getting shorter and Winter is almost upon us. We return once again to the reflective spiritual realms inside ourselves, for regeneration of the Spirit, rest, and contact with our inner wisdom.

Each of these Cross Quarter festivals is influenced by one of the four elements through the four fixed astrological signs. The fixed signs are very energetic. Their energy endures, and they propel projects to completion. Imbolc falls in the middle of Aquarius ♒, an Air sign; Beltain falls in the middle of Taurus ♉, an Earth sign; Lammas falls in the middle of Leo ♌, a Fire sign; and Samhain falls in the middle of Scorpio ♏, a Water sign.

There are some who would fix these Cross Quarter festivals by dates on the calendar: Imbolc eve on 2nd February, Beltain eve on 30th April, Lammas eve on 2nd August, and Samhain eve on October 31st. I prefer to look at the position of the Moon and any other astrological information, and choose a time when these influences are at their most potent. Celebrating the Cross Quarter Points may go on for several days.

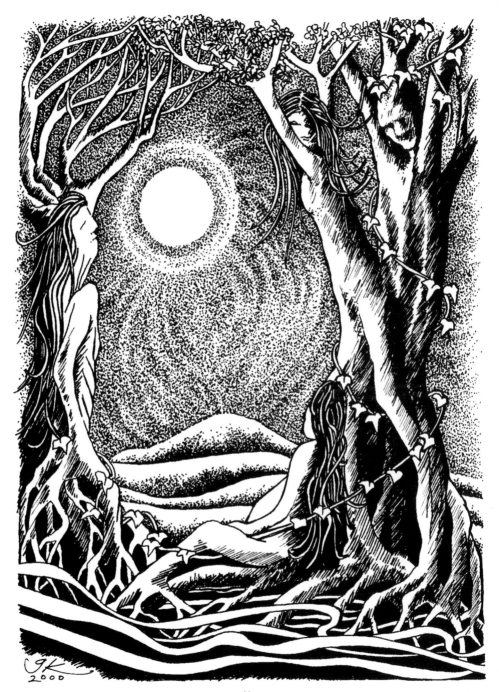

THE MOON

The Moon and Her Cycles

The Earth revolves around her axis in one day. The Moon orbits around the Sun in approximately 29 days (a lunar month). The Earth orbits around the Sun in one year. These cycles are the alternating waxing and waning rhythms of Gaia. Understanding their influence and how we can best use the energy in our lives, enables us to be integrated into their cosmic dance.

As seen from the Earth, the Moon and the Sun appear to be equal in size. The Sun is 400 times larger than the Moon, but it is also 400 times further away from the Earth. At new and full Moon, the Earth, Moon and Sun are aligned. When the Sun and Moon are diametrically opposite each other, the Moon is full. When the Sun and Moon lie in the same direction, the Moon is new.

The Sun and the Moon influence the energy cycles of all life on Earth. The Sun gives us light and warmth in an outward dynamic of manifest energy. The Moon's reflective qualities distribute this energy during the hours of darkness, bringing receptivity and assimilation.

The celebration of the eight Celtic festivals provides a connection to each phase of the solar year and its season. Within that framework, the Moon interweaves its monthly lunar cycle. The Winter and Summer Solstices and the Spring and Autumn Equinoxes are fixed astronomical points in the solar year. Using an astrological diary, you can check the influence the Moon will bring to these celebrations.

The four great fire festivals of Imbolc, Beltain, Lammas and Samhain, are not fixed points and can be celebrated when the Moon's influence most complements the energy of the festival.

The influence of the Moon was recognised and honoured by the earliest people, who noticed that the approximate 29 day cycle of the Moon's phases corresponded to women's menstrual cycles. The Moon became feminine and was personified as the Triple Moon Goddess whose unfolding cyclic phases from new to full to dark was understood as part of the cosmology and pattern of the web of life and death, representing the three great cycles of birth, maturity, death and rebirth. The Moon's aspects are personified as the Maid, emerging Moon Goddess; the Mother, abundant provider and full Moon Goddess; and the Crone, wise woman and Guardian of the inner realms, dark Moon Goddess.

The Moon is the closest celestial body to the Earth and its force of gravity is so powerful, it pulls on the oceans, causing two high tides a day. This same influence affects all the fluids on the Earth, including the underground waters, the circulation of our body fluids, the ovulation cycle, the growth patterns of plants, and the migration patterns of birds.

The Moon also influences the watery nature of our unconsciousness, our emotions, our moods, feelings and perceptions. She is reflector and shadow, and the cycles of her three aspects influence us more deeply than most of us are aware. Keep a Moon diary and watch how closely your patterns are connected to the Moon's outward and inward flow. The alternating waxing and waning of the Moon's cycles when understood, can enhance and balance the way we choose to live our lives.

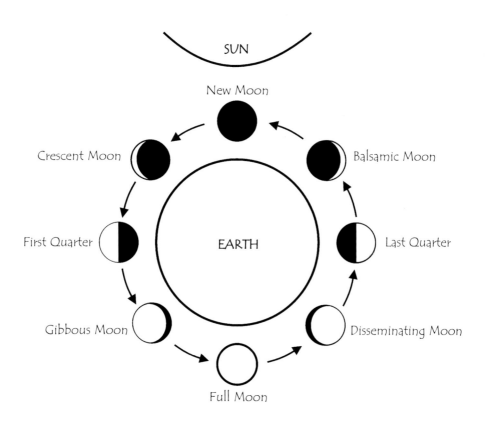

THE PHASES OF THE MOON

New Moon

The Sun and the Moon rise together in the East. The Moon is invisible because it is hidden by the Sun's brightness. The new Moon is sacred to the Maid aspect of the Triple Moon Goddess, bringing inspiration and intuition. It is like a new seed, full of potential and energy. The new Moon is the time for new beginnings, the time to begin new projects, new directions, new resolutions. It is the best time for invocation and speaking out your intent.

Crescent Moon

The Moon rises mid morning and sets after sunset. She can be seen in the western sky in the late afternoon. The rising waxing energy of the Moon brings growth to all ideas and plans. In nature, foliage, fruit and seeds develop when the Moon is waxing.

Waxing Half Moon

The Moon rises about midday and sets about midnight. She can be seen from soon after she rises until she sets. This is a period of growth and activity on all levels.

Gibbous Moon

Visible soon after she rises just before sunset, to when she sets just before dawn. From here to full Moon, make the most of her abundant waxing energy. It is a time of activity and expressing yourself through your feelings.

Full Moon

Rising at sunset, and setting at sunrise, the Moon is visible throughout the night. The Sun and Moon are opposite each other in the sky and the Moon is reflecting all of the Sun's light. This is the time for celebration and outward expression. It brings change, revelation and emotional peaks. Sacred to the Mother aspect of the Triple Moon Goddess, it brings abundance and the blending of Spirit and Matter. This is the peak of psychic power and heightened energy, sometimes causing us to feel unbalanced and crazy (lunatic). This is the time of culmination, fruition, and completion. The Moon is so bright she can light the night and cast Moon shadows. This brings a period of increased light which is sufficient to assist photosynthesis in plants, and thereby increases growth.

Disseminating Moon
The Moon now begins to wane. She rises mid-evening and sets mid-morning (one hour later after sunset each night). The waning Moon brings self-assessment, looking within, and reflection. In nature, the waning Moon cycle promotes root development.

Waning Half Moon
The Moon rises around midnight and sets around mid-day, and is visible from when she rises to when she sets. The Moon continues to wane, bringing inner reflection, transformation and change.

Balsamic Moon (Waning Crescent Moon)
The Moon rises before dawn and sets mid-afternoon. This is the very last sliver of Moon seen in the eastern sky in the early morning. The waning Moon is sacred to the Crone or wise woman aspect of the Triple Moon Goddess, bringing inner wisdom and entry into the dark inner mysteries and knowledge. This is the time for banishing rituals, to let go of things no longer helpful to you, to break psychic links.

The Dark of the Moon
The Moon is said to be dark for three days before the new Moon when it has waned so far that it is no longer visible in the sky. Waning and dark Moon rites are for guidance and understanding, and for assimilation of wisdom on inner levels. It is a time for quiet inward reflection, reaping the fruits of our wisdom and experience.

THE MOON AND THE SUN-SIGNS

The Moon passes through a different Sun-sign every two and a half days. When she reaches the sign the Sun is in, it is the new Moon. When the Moon is full, she is in the opposite sign from the Sun.

Integrate both the outward manifest qualities of the Sun-sign, and the inward reflective qualities of the Moon's cycle to understand the way this affects our lives.

Moon Qualities

The Moon brings us closer to our emotions and feelings. She is receptive, soaking up and assimilating, adapting and changing. She influences the way we nurture ourselves and others. We are more likely to sense what's going on rather than to consciously know. She brings us intuition and reflections from within.

Moon in Aries ☽ ♈

Aries is a Fire sign and will act directly and instantly, a natural starting point for new projects and plans. It is the right time to channel all that 'me-first' energy to initiate change, and to act on impulse. Ruled by Mars ♂ it brings assertiveness and courage to express your feelings. Be aware of selfishness and impatience.

Moon in Taurus ☽ ♉

When the Moon is in this fixed Earth sign, a calm stability will settle around you. Ruled by Venus ♀ you feel sensuous, secure, solid, unhurried and earthed. You may also feel possessive and stubborn.

Moon in Gemini ☽ ♊

Gemini Moons bring stimulation and activity, spontaneity, communication, conversation and a myriad interesting ideas and connections. Gemini is a mutable Air sign ruled by Mercury ♀. Moon in Gemini is the time for communicating your feelings, and making connections within and without. It may bring great restlessness and scattered emotions.

Moon in Cancer ☽ ♋

This Water sign is ruled by the Moon ☽ herself and this is a highly emotional time when tears can come readily and there is a tendency to become over-sensitive, dependent and needy. Memories are strong, and the home, family and mothering are important. It is a good time to look after family and friends and make time for your home.

Moon in Leo ☽ ♌

This fixed Fire sign, ruled by the Sun ☉ demands attention on all levels. It is a time for magnanimous gestures of creative celebrations. Be generous with your feelings and your enthusiasm in sensitive and thoughtful ways.

Moon in Virgo ☽ ♍

Virgo, mutable Earth sign, ruled by Mercury ☿, asks us to look at what needs to be taken care of. Moon in Virgo is the patterning seer, arranging, categorising and tending, until every meticulous detail has been integrated and understood. There may be a tendency to lose the overview, and become over-critical of yourself or others.

Moon in Libra ☽ ♎

A harmonious and romantic phase for family, friends and lovers to relax and appreciate each other. Libra is an Air sign, ruled by Venus ♀ and will restore balance to the emotions through diplomacy and the refining of ideas and ideals. Use this time for making things beautiful and harmonious. You may be indecisive and extremist.

Moon in Scorpio ☽ ♏

Scorpio is a fixed Water sign ruled by Pluto ♇ and Mars ♂. When the Moon passes through this sign, feelings are intense and deeply felt, sometimes to the point of obsession. During this time you delve into your unconscious and come face to face with the dark shadowy side of yourself. You may have to look at your fears and deal with the emotions which this brings up.

Moon in Sagittarius ☽ ♐

Now is the time for optimism and a relaxed easy-going phase. Ruled by the benevolent Jupiter ♃, the Moon in Sagittarius connects us to our inner wisdom and prophetic truths, allows us to be spontaneous and to seek adventurous solutions. It can be a restless time bringing an inner need to throw off all responsibility.

Moon in Capricorn ☽ ♑

This Earth sign is ruled by Saturn ♄ the great teacher, and will bring strength and inner wisdom, and a desire to organise yourself, set down some rules and guidelines. Find ways to help yourself deal with your emotions, but avoid becoming too pessimistic or rigid.

Moon in Aquarius ☽ ♒

An Air sign ruled by Uranus ♅, the Aquarian Moon brings a love of personal freedom and individuality. There is an ability to detach yourself from old emotional patterns. Be idealistic, challenging, unpredictable, and see what is revealed.

Moon in Pisces ☽♓

This Water sign, ruled by Neptune ♆ will bring dreamtime into your waking life, and magic into all possibilities. Moon in Pisces will bring intuition and receptivity, and a place from which to wish all your dreams into reality. Spiritual awareness and meditation are the highest use of these energies. Celebrate the irrational and the Spirit paths; leave the rational mind behind.

At the same time as combining this intergrated Sun sign with Moon qualities, remember to also weave in the energy inherent in the Moon phase, and the direction in which the Moon is moving. Keeping track of this brings a connection to the natural energy flow and means you can make the best use of it in your daily life.

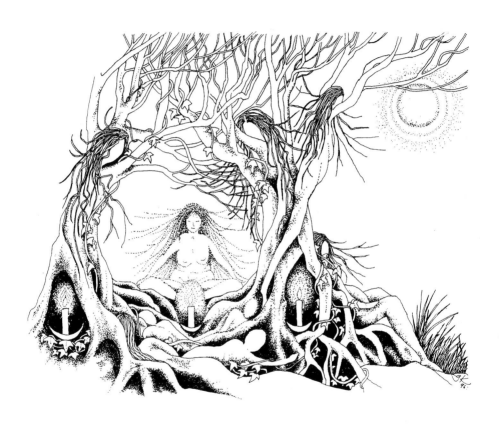

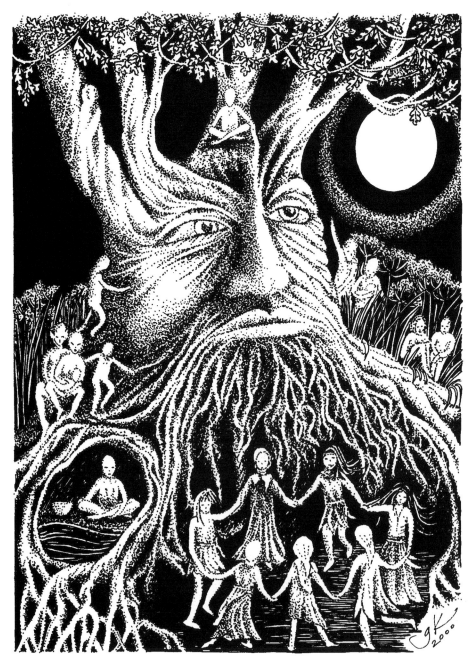

20

CELEBRATION, CEREMONY AND RITUAL

The way you celebrate the Celtic festivals is a matter of choice and experiment. What matters most is the experience of communicating with the outer world, bursting with created abundance, and connecting to your inner levels and spiritual path. The changing year provides a wealth of experiences through the cyclic ebb and flow of the Sun's energy. Interwoven with this, are the monthly cycles of the waxing and waning Moon, and the planetary influences.

Each festival is a chance to feel yourself as part of the whole, and also to connect to the moment, the here and now. From this point of being you can look back on what you have been doing, feeling, thinking; on your health, and on your spiritual journey. You can also look forward with an understanding of the Earth's (and your) inherent energy flow, to where you wish to go, how you may best use the oncoming energy for your greater good, the greater good of the Earth, and all those around you.

It may be that you wish to celebrate these festivals on your own, or with a close friend; it may be that you prefer to gather with a group of friends and explore the possibilities of creating ceremonies and rituals together. You must work at the level you feel most comfortable with. Touching your deepest feelings and expressing the sacred will bring with it a connection to the inner core of your being. If you are with friends, inevitably you will become closer as a result of this sharing.

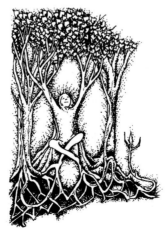

THE FIVE ELEMENTS AND THE CELTIC TRADITION

Central to any ceremony or sacred space are the four directions and their corresponding four elements of Air, Fire, Water and Earth. The fifth element, Spirit or Ether, is said to give birth to the four, and is everywhere and nowhere, within and without. It is both immanence and transcendence. It is interwoven and interlocking. If you were creating a sacred circle to include all the elements, Spirit or Ether's place would be at the centre, and it would also be the circumference. On the pentacle, Spirit is the top point with the four elements making up the other points. The four quarters linked with Spirit make the pattern of a cross within a circle, a symbol which predates Christianity.

The five elements can be used to create a temporary or permanent sacred area. This may be done in a room, a garden or amongst a group of trees. You may wish to create a large outside sacred space, large enough to include the whole group of friends taking part in the celebration. If you have a large garden or a piece of land, you may wish to set up five permanent shrines to each of the elements. This may be used as a force-field or protective circle around the whole area.

Most of us lack the space within our homes to have a room put aside as a permanent sacred space, but if you have a spare room or attic which can be created for this purpose, it is a wonderful asset. It can be used for group meetings, meditation, healing, and any time you need to connect deeply to your inner world. Weather conditions, especially during the Winter, make it difficult to celebrate the festivals outside, and so there is a need to create a sacred space inside. You may want to celebrate on your own, and therefore need only a small space. You can set up the five elements by invocation and the placing of something to represent each element. Hang an elemental hanging on the wall using coloured wool or painted material. You might do a painting which summons the power of each element visually. Decorate a stick with coloured wools and threads, hang things from it which suggest that element, and place these in each of the directions as you visualise their inherent energy. You may wish to make four shrines in the four directions, placing appropriate things in each. The seasonal changes bring fresh things to add and new understanding. Always remember to include Spirit, by honouring it in some way at the centre and the circumference. This may include flowers, a candle, a gift, a figurine, a flat stone or tray on which are placed small representations of each of the elements.

Stand at the centre. Use a standard compass to establish where the four directions lie. Turn it until the red arrow settles on North. This fixes the position of the four directions. Central to creating a sacred area using the five elements, is visualisation. You must visualise the five elements strongly in your mind's eye in order for their energy and power to become manifest. By doing this, you are creating links and connectors for the energy to travel through.

Air in the East

The Sun rises in the East, and so it is the place of new beginnings. Visualise the wind, the flow and patterns of air; the sky with the birds gliding and travelling along the air currents; gales and strong winds, gentle balmy winds; visualise sounds travelling, your voice and its power, the power of song, music, your breath. Air brings the power of thought and communication. Use your voice to speak out a welcome, to honour the presence and the power of Air, to thank the Air for its gifts to humankind. Place a feather, hang a bell or mobile or windchime in the East.

Fire in the South

Visualise the heat of the mid-day Sun, flames of Fire consuming, transforming and cleansing. Fire brings passion, power, change and creativity. Fire connects us to our life spirit, sexuality, expansion, our vital energy. It can be creative or destructive. It represents transformation. Its colours are red, orange and gold. Light a candle here, or burn some incense or herbs. Welcome and give thanks for the active vitality of the spirit of Fire.

Water in the West

Visualise waves, the sea, flowing streams, waterfalls, rain, tears, the Moon. Water reflects our emotions flowing through us, the pull of our hearts, our deepest feelings, our unconscious, our imagination and our intuition. Here is love, compassion, receptivity, mysteries, the soul. Place a bowl of spring water in the West. Give thanks for the life-giving element of Water and the receptivity this element brings.

Earth in the North

Visualise the material world, trees, plants, rocks, soil and animals. Visualise the mountains and the caves, the roots, the minerals and crystals beneath the surface of the Earth. The North is the place of our inner wisdom and ancient knowledge. It brings containment, fertility, abundance and experience. Place a stone or a crystal in the North to represent the Earth. Welcome the nature spirits, the plant and tree devas, the Faerie and other elementals. Give thanks to the Earth for its supportive energy.

Spirit

The fifth element, Spirit, is all around us, above and below, within and without. It connects us to the unseen world, our Guardians, guides, and our spiritual path. It is at the centre of our being. It cannot be seen, cannot be named, but it is always with us, connecting us to a universal energy and power, Unconditional Love, connecting us to what has been and what will be and yet it is always in the present moment.

With each season you will find new ways of representing the five elements, and each season presents a new opportunity to creatively express each of them. This is the most powerful way of understanding how these forces work within us. The enjoyment is in the making, and you will almost certainly surprise yourself and produce something you are very pleased with.

Creating an impermanent outside sacred space is much the same as creating one within a room, except it is useful to have much larger things to represent the elements as outside things need to be visually stronger.

A large stick put in the ground at each of the four directions, with coloured ribbons or streamers made from crepe paper, is a quick and effective way of marking the directions if a large group of friends are gathering. Coloured scarves are also effective hung from a tree or tied to a stick.

If you want to be more ambitious, make a large hoop (one metre in diameter or less) from a freshly cut Hazel rod (approx. five foot long). Bind the ends together with string and then, using material and paint or wool and threads, create a sacred hoop or shield for each of the directions. This can then be brought out and hung up in the appropriate direction, inside or outside (see pg. 96 for how to make a sacred shield).

Semi-Permanent Shrines for the Five Elements

Freshly cut Hazel rods can be used to create outside areas, arches or bowers where each of the elements may be represented. They are not completely permanent, but they will last for a few years before the wood eventually becomes brittle.

Four rods create a much stronger archway than two. Make four holes in the ground with a metal spike and embed the thick end of four freshly cut Hazel rods into the ground. Cross them over in the middle and tie them together with strong string. This creates an area where you can add things to suggest each of the elements. You may wish to have them high enough to hang an elemental shield in, or much lower and more enclosed, where candles can be lit. The bower can be decorated with greenery, flowers, grasses, twigs, woven with Willow, and hung with relevant items. Each new season brings different things to decorate them with - these may not be permanent either. Coloured wool, material and threads quickly fade in the sun and the rain.

AIR IN THE EAST

Wrap the Hazel rods in thin gauzy material and nets and scarves. Windchimes may be hung up inside. Tie on feathers and streamers of wool and threads to catch the breezes. Thin silvery things are good. A nest with eggs represents new beginnings and the spiral pattern the eddies of air currents. Its colours are white, pale purples and pale yellow.

FIRE IN THE SOUTH

Use materials, ribbons, scarves and wool of oranges, red and golden yellows. Use gold material to catch the light, red geraniums and marigolds. Light candles, burn incense and herbs. Representations of the Sun may be hung in the middle or round the edge.

WATER IN THE WEST

Use Willow to wrap around the Hazel rods, along with coloured ribbons and wool of every shade of blue. Hang painted fish made out of salt dough or felt, hang shells and use shells for making patterns on the ground. Make a pond in a glass bowl.

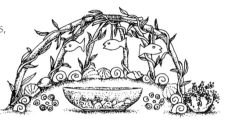

EARTH IN THE NORTH

Wrap evergreens around the bowers such as ivy and yew. Leafy beech twigs make a quick fill-in. Weave in any flowers of the season, wheat or grasses. Place in potted plants or trees, herbs, or a vase of flowers. Add crystals, rocks, pieces of wood, fruit, nuts, bones, Earth Goddesses and Gods etc. Its colours are black, purple, dark greens and browns.

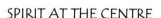

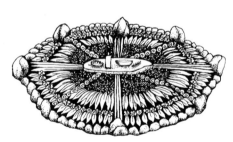

SPIRIT AT THE CENTRE

Create a mandala using natural materials beginning with a flat round stone, a round of wood, or something similar at the centre. Radiate the pattern out from the centre using leaves, stones, flowers, earth, any available material. Each of the elements can be represented here as a focus for the whole. Circle the whole thing with nightlights and another at the centre.
Sometimes it is appropriate to place an offering at the centre.

Permanent Shrines for the Five Elements

If you wish to create a permanent place in your garden or on your land for the five elements, you will need to use materials which will endure. Material and wool quickly lose their colours and eventually rot. Rock, stone and well-oiled wood may be used; plants which are permanently growing there, or in pots, especially herbs, are good. Many herbs and trees have traditional associations with the five elements and the Celtic festivals (see page 58)

Clay is another permanent material if it has been fired and glazed. It will get dirty in the wind and the rain, but can be washed easily enough. Other less durable items can be added to your outside areas at the time of the celebration, and taken inside afterwards.

Working with and understanding the five elements is to make a connection to the Earth and all its aspects. These elemental energies are to be found within ourselves and within our lives. They can be consciously worked with, like any other system. Choose an element to work with when their qualities are uppermost at a particular time of the year, or because you feel you need to connect and communicate with that particular energy.

Once you have set up the four directions, light a candle in the middle for the fifth element and walk around, or sweep around the outside forming a circle, burning incense or herbs, and perhaps stating your intent or asking for protection or the presence of your Guardian spirits and guides. The words you use are a personal choice, reaching out or reaching in. The important thing is that they make a connection which brings a change within your consciousness. Words are power. Use them wisely. Only say what rings true.

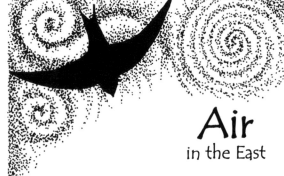

Air
in the East

the intellectual and mental processes ◇
light ◇ elusive and uncontainable ◇ communication ◇
new beginnings ◇ knowledge ◇ inspiration ◇ renewal ◇
ever-present ◇ formless ◇ breath of life ◇ rebirth ◇
inner wisdom ◇ new skills and fortunes ◇ ideas ◇
invocation ◇ messages

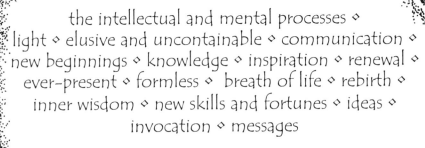

sound ◇ voice ◇ song ◇ music ◇ Dawn ◇ Spring ◇
sky ◇ air currents ◇ flight ◇ birds ◇ butterflies ◇
dragonflies ◇ moths ◇ bees ◇ clouds ◇ gliding ◇
hovering ◇ movement ◇ wind ◇ gales ◇ storms ◇ spirals

Mercury ◇ Venus ◇ Uranus
Gemini ◇ Libra ◇ Aquarius

harmony of the mind

Tarot swords

white ◇ pale purple ◇ spring yellow

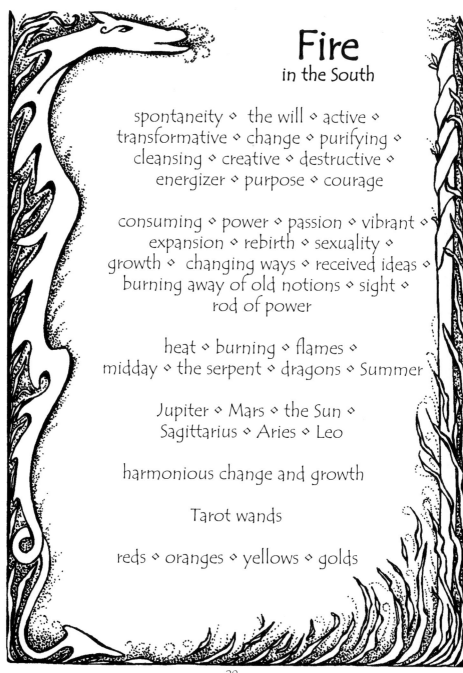

Fire
in the South

spontaneity ⋄ the will ⋄ active ⋄
transformative ⋄ change ⋄ purifying ⋄
cleansing ⋄ creative ⋄ destructive ⋄
energizer ⋄ purpose ⋄ courage

consuming ⋄ power ⋄ passion ⋄ vibrant ⋄
expansion ⋄ rebirth ⋄ sexuality ⋄
growth ⋄ changing ways ⋄ received ideas ⋄
burning away of old notions ⋄ sight ⋄
rod of power

heat ⋄ burning ⋄ flames ⋄
midday ⋄ the serpent ⋄ dragons ⋄ Summer

Jupiter ⋄ Mars ⋄ the Sun ⋄
Sagittarius ⋄ Aries ⋄ Leo

harmonious change and growth

Tarot wands

reds ⋄ oranges ⋄ yellows ⋄ golds

Water
in the West

emotional side of our natures ◇ change ◇
subtle energies ◇ imagination ◇ receptivity ◇
the soul ◇ moods ◇ Love ◇ psychic perception ◇
compassion ◇ inner purpose ◇ mutable ◇ wisdom ◇
trust ◇ still ◇ deep ◇ flowing ◇ mysticism ◇
enchantment ◇ the heart ◇ currents ◇ cleansing ◇
fertility ◇ immersion ◇ spirals

sacred wells ◇ sacred springs ◇ the source ◇ the sea ◇
waves ◇ tides ◇ rain ◇ Autumn ◇ twilight ◇
lakes ◇ rivers ◇ streams ◇ gushing ◇ meandering ◇
ice ◇ fish ◇ dolphins ◇ whales ◇ shellfish ◇ boats ◇
waterfalls ◇ mermaids ◇ undines ◇ flow forms

Pluto ◇ the Moon ◇ Neptune ◇
Scorpio ◇ Cancer ◇ Pisces

harmony of the emotions

Tarot cups

all shades of blue ◇ purple ◇ turquoise

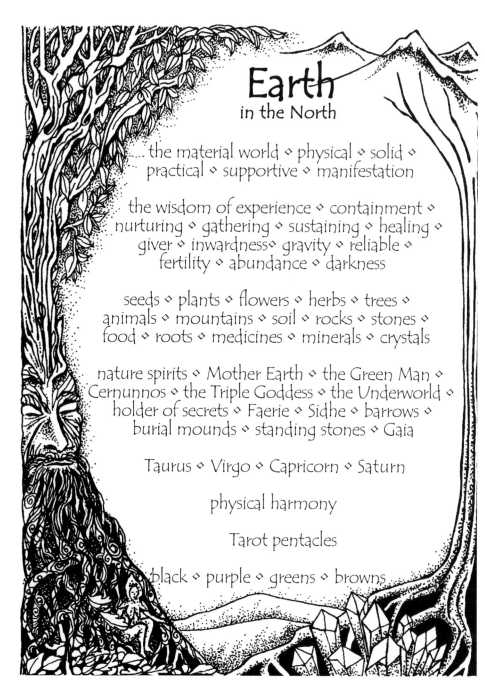

Earth
in the North

the material world ◊ physical ◊ solid ◊
practical ◊ supportive ◊ manifestation

the wisdom of experience ◊ containment ◊
nurturing ◊ gathering ◊ sustaining ◊ healing ◊
giver ◊ inwardness◊ gravity ◊ reliable ◊
fertility ◊ abundance ◊ darkness

seeds ◊ plants ◊ flowers ◊ herbs ◊ trees ◊
animals ◊ mountains ◊ soil ◊ rocks ◊ stones ◊
food ◊ roots ◊ medicines ◊ minerals ◊ crystals

nature spirits ◊ Mother Earth ◊ the Green Man ◊
Cernunnos ◊ the Triple Goddess ◊ the Underworld ◊
holder of secrets ◊ Faerie ◊ Sidhe ◊ barrows ◊
burial mounds ◊ standing stones ◊ Gaia

Taurus ◊ Virgo ◊ Capricorn ◊ Saturn

physical harmony

Tarot pentacles

black ◊ purple ◊ greens ◊ browns

Spirit

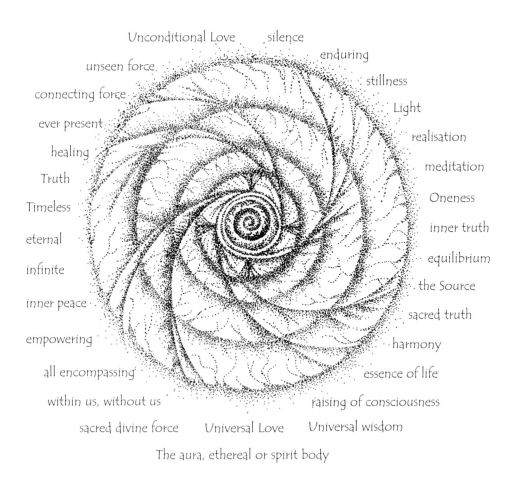

Unconditional Love   silence

enduring

unseen force

stillness

connecting force

Light

ever present

realisation

healing

meditation

Truth

Oneness

Timeless

inner truth

eternal

equilibrium

infinite

the Source

inner peace

sacred truth

empowering

harmony

all encompassing

essence of life

within us, without us

raising of consciousness

sacred divine force   Universal Love   Universal wisdom

The aura, ethereal or spirit body

MANIFESTATION THROUGH THE FIVE ELEMENTS

Metaphysics has brought us to understand that all physical matter is alive with energy and that we, as part of that energy, do have influence over the flow and direction it takes. All thought is manifest. (Therefore be careful what you think.) We are, each one of us, responsible via our thoughts for what we have drawn into our lives, the circumstances we find ourselves in and our health.

The five elements form the whole and can be seen as the variant parts of the process of manifestation.

WATER is the element of the emotions. This is where our desires and needs swim around in our unconscious mind. At each of the festivals we celebrate, we have the opportunity to become more aware of our emotional desires. Our emotional energy is very powerful and needs to be directed consciously.

AIR is the element of thought and it is here in our minds that the process takes shape. We are often at the mercy of our thoughts which can be likened to a runaway horse. Through meditation there is more control over the thought processes and it provides us with a greater awareness of where our thoughts are taking us. Meditation also brings a greater ability to concentrate. With practice, an image, desire or a mantra may be held in the mind to create a positive thought-form. Each of the festivals provide us with the opportunity to work consciously with our thoughts through the application of meditation, positive affirmations, and visualisation.

FIRE is the element of transformation and creativity brought about by the power of the will and intent. Your passions, beliefs and desires bring changes often beyond our control.

SPIRIT The province of the Spirit realms stands outside time and space. The outcome of your desires manifest here first, and their ultimate manifestation in the physical world will come after. Edward Bach's pioneering work with illness has brought us to the understanding that illness is a direct result of negative emotions and thought-forms, that illness first manifests in the aura, ethereal or Spirit body and can be treated by addressing the negative aspects which caused the problem to begin. Spirit is the connecting force, the hub of life itself, within us and outside of us. Through it we are part of all life and all of existence on all levels, seen and unseen.

EARTH is the element of the physical world and is where everything eventually becomes manifest. This endless process is continuously happening whether we are conscious of it or not.

By choosing to be aware of this dynamic, we can use the eight Celtic festivals as reference points, to enhance the flow of our most positive intent, to bring healing and positive manifestation for ourselves and the Earth.

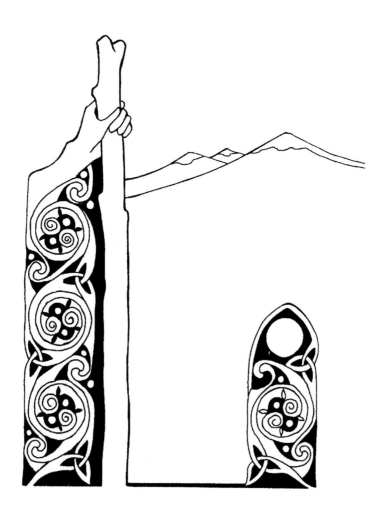

MEDITATION

Meditation is an ancient technique and one which is important to master. It is based on the mind's ability to stay concentrated upon a given stimulus in a poised and relaxed manner. The mind is then able to make a shift in consciousness from the babble of everyday thoughts to another level. The benefits of meditation go way beyond the time spent in actual meditation, bringing greater relaxation and tranquility, improved concentration, and more control over the thought processes. It also brings improvement in memory, improvement in creative thinking, enhances self-understanding and aids spiritual development

Meditation is a huge subject in itself and there are many many different techniques. Buddha, one of the earliest recorded meditation teachers, taught his followers to concentrate on their breath and made it clear that all benefits of concentration can be gained from this method alone. This is therefore a very good starting point.

To begin, your body needs to feel relaxed. There are many variations, but sitting with a straight back and crossed legs is a good position to start with. Consciously explore your body from your head to your toes, checking all parts are without tension. Generally, people's awareness is centred too high. Relax and sink. Feel your roots going down into the Earth and let the Earth's energy flow through you.

Begin to focus on your in and out breath from the nose, but do not let your attention follow the breath into the lungs. Feel the cool air on the inbreath, and the warm air on the outbreath. Awareness should always remain at the nostrils. Inevitably, thoughts will come crowding in, but look upon them as people trying to distract you and simply take no notice of them. Each time you find your mind has drifted away from your breath, just gently bring your focus back to your breathing.

A mantra, which is a word or phrase, is another focus for meditation. Choose any positive affirmation you feel is helpful to you. Say it quietly on the outbreath, leaving the inbreath free, as empty space (or vice versa). Eventually do not say it out loud at all, but only in your mind. Each time you find yourself following your thoughts, come back to your point of concentration. Thus the mind circles round and round a key point or idea, and in the process, will bore a 'well' down through layers of thoughts, until a breakthrough is made onto another level.

With practice you will be able to hold an image strongly in your mind without the interference of mundane thoughts. This is essential for all shamanic work involving visualisation, for inner journeys and many healing techniques.

CREATING A CEREMONY

Observing the eight Celtic festivals creates an opportunity for participation in a continuous ongoing cyclic process where we can consciously become connected to our own and the Earth's energy. Through them we can touch our innermost feelings and awareness which allows us to express the sacred in our lives.

If these ceremonies are to be effective and powerful, they must help us find spiritual awareness, and the source of our personal power. This is the life-force, the power of Universal Love which remains the same through all the ages, and is to be found in the teachings of all the great spiritual masters.

The ceremonies must bring the spiritual and physical worlds into balance. They need not be complicated. In fact, the simplest things work the best as they can be interpreted on many different levels by everyone.

In my experience, a bit of pre-planning and a few special things gathered together before a ceremony will help to make it both meaningful and special. Go out into nature, even if it is only into your garden, and gather a bunch of flowers if you can find some. If not, sprigs of different leaves are as beautiful and, even in the depths of Winter, there are twigs with buds forming, and evergreens. Creating a seasonal shrine is a lovely thing to do and helps make your connection to the Earth's cycle.

Bring together the things you will use for the five elements: a crystal or stone for Earth, a feather or mobile for Air, a new candle, for Fire, a special bowl for water (spring water if possible), something for the centre to represent Spirit. This is part of the build-up to the actual celebration and connects you to your innermost sacred world. Perhaps a chant will come to you now.

Go for a walk if you can. Really feel the moment within the Earth and within yourself.

Make time for meditation before you start so that you are open to your intuition and free from mental clutter.

Get some food and drink together, ready for the end of the ceremony, as food is always good after opening up to the inner levels, to 'ground' the experience and yourself. The food and drink can be blessed and eaten as part of the celebration. Seasonal food is best.

If you are celebrating with a group of people, it is good to take it in turns to choose the venue, decide how to represent the five elements, plan the flow and content of the ceremony, and let the rest of the group know the time and place and any special things to bring. In this way the ceremonies are varied, and everyone gets a chance to be creative working together. This leaves the rest of the group to be completely free to get totally involved in the ceremony. There should be at least two people who are 'holding' the energy of the ceremony, who know what's going to happen next, and keep it flowing. Everyone can bring food and drink to share, and something for the shrine. Decorations, incense, candles, greenery, flowers, all help to add atmosphere to the moment. It is good to dress up and make the moment special, even if it is only by wrapping a coloured scarf around your waist, hair or shoulders.

When planning a ceremony, take into account the season, the venue, its size, whether it is indoors or outdoors, whether there is room to dance. Is it alright to make a lot of noise like drumming? How can you help everyone to get the most out of it? How can you engage and include the children? How will you include and express the five elements? How will you bring the group together to begin the celebration? How will you close it?

I particularly like creating ceremonies which give the whole group the greatest freedom of expression, and a chance for everyone to share themselves and speak from the heart. For example: if there is room, the whole group can gather at each of the directions. One person can welcome the power of that element, but the whole group can speak their thanks and connection as they feel moved to. It doesn't matter if things get repeated. The important thing is the speaking out as this makes the connection so much stronger. There may be a group activity planned for each element. For example: at Earth in the North, planting the feet firmly on the ground and feeling your roots going down into the Earth, or for Fire, dancing and springing about like flames. Alternatively, five people may be chosen to represent and speak for each element. They may read a poem or speak from the heart, invoking for all who are present, the spirit of the element.

Opening and Closing Ceremony

You should always have an opening ceremony at the beginning of your celebration, to welcome all the Spirit guides, helpers and Guardians, to honour the five elements, the Ancestors and the nature spirits. Stand at the centre. Using a compass, find the four directions and place something in each direction to represent their elements. Mark an outer circle by burning incense or herbs as you define its perimeter and light a candle in the centre of the circle to honour Spirit.

Speak out any invocations of intent as you do these things to help focus the energy of your celebration and your circle.

If you are celebrating in a group, the opening ceremony should unite the whole group together. Holding hands in a circle completes a circuit of energy. Sing a chant together, walk a spiral in and out again, a circle dance, anything which helps create a mesmerizing trance-like atmosphere. A steady drumbeat will immediately invoke a sense of ceremony. What you bring, through the power of your intent, will reverberate through all you do and say. Feel your power and the power of the life-force within. Feel the presence of the Spirit world so close to ours. Feel alive...and in the moment!

At the end of the celebration, it is equally important to have a closing ceremony. Bring the group back together by making a circle, holding hands again. If you are on your own, come back to the centre of the circle again. Thank each element in turn, thank all your Spirit guides, Guardians and helpers for their help and involvement in your celebration. Thank the elemental beings of the Earth who, unseen to you, may have drawn nearer. Thank each other. Appreciation lifts the spirits and opens the heart.

CHILDREN

It is very important that our children learn to acknowledge and express their inner world, to balance the over-emphasis in our society and their education on material achievements and status. Taking part in ceremonies will help them to make connections to the natural world and to their creative and intuitive processes, as well as giving them an opportunity to explore their subconscious and the inner levels of their minds. It is a time for parents and children to be together, for people without children to get to know friends' children, for relaxing and playing together, to talk about belief systems, and the understanding of life's mysteries. It is an opportunity for all ages to come together and learn from each other. It can be helpful for children approaching puberty to be welcomed into the adult world. Young girls are welcomed into womanhood as they begin menstruating and young boys are able to take their place amongst the men. This is the old tribal way and there is much value to be gained from it.

If you are celebrating with a group of friends, there are often children of different ages. This, of course, makes it hard to involve all of the children all of the time. It is better that they can engage in what interests them, and be free to disengage if it doesn't. This respects their freedom to do only what they want to do. It is equally important that the children respect the activities of the rest of the group. For example: not running around and making a lot of noise where people are meditating, and not disrupting a ceremony.

Often children will want to be involved in only some parts of the celebration, such as drumming or singing and chanting, or dancing. Lighting the candles and incense, collecting greenery and flowers, making a special nature shrine, are all activities which children love to join in with. It makes them feel a part of it right from the beginning. Children learn best from adults who talk to them as if they matter. Children will become involved if that is the group's intent, and their opinions, choices and needs are listened to within the context of the opinions, choices and needs of the rest of the group.

Children's imaginations are very vivid. They like to take initiative and be active. With this in mind, it is not hard to help them become involved. Stories are a wonderful way of bringing them together. Telling and re-telling the myths and legends and folk stories of our lands are wonderful for the whole group, as well as the children. Storytime, with mugs of cocoa around the camp fire, is an enjoyment for all ages, a chance to snuggle up together and gaze into the fire.

Most children love to perform and, with the help of sensitive adults, they can be encouraged to put on plays or dance performances which explore the theme of the festival being celebrated. Rehearsing can absorb them totally while the rest of the group is involved in a quieter activity which may not interest them. The whole group can come together for their performance.

Craft Activities

A craft activity at each celebration usually appeals to the children and creates another opportunity to be pleasurably involved together and for shared discussions. Making things which are relevant to the season, using natural materials as far as possible, is as liberating an experience for the adults as it is enjoyable for the children.

The choice of activity and where it will happen requires some consideration. Often it is easier to work on the floor inside or outside. Put an old sheet or blanket down first. This can be gathered up at the end, keeping all the mess in one place. Use masking tape or string or glue sticks, and avoid using pots of glue or paints which may be tipped over. If these are to be used, it is better to have them on a separate table covered in newspaper or plastic sheeting. The adults can then keep an eye on it and any spills can easily be cleaned up if accidents happen.

A box of useful art and craft materials may be gathered together, providing a basis for the art and craft activities. A small amount of money from the group members could set this up, and then sharing in the cost of new materials when needed. The box should include:

a few pairs of child-friendly but sharp scissors (round-ended),
a pot of felt-tip pens,
a pot of pencil crayons, a box of wax crayons,
acrylic paints in tubes,
glue sticks, PVA glue, tubes of Copydex,
masking tape, Sellotape,
paintbrushes/different sizes and types,
coloured wools and natural sheep's wool,
embroidery threads/silks,
cardboard,
coloured sugar paper, white drawing paper,
tissue paper, crepe paper,

leather, leather thong, chamois leather,
ribbon, scraps of material,
needles for sewing, bodkins for wool,
string,
sticks of all sizes from cocktail sticks to natural sticks and twigs,
driftwood,
seed cases,
leaves,
beads,
shells,
feathers,
dried flowers,
basket-maker's willow,
and many other natural materials.
All can be used in many different creative ways.

A set of acrylic paints in tubes is a great asset as small amounts can be squirted out at a time. They are water soluble and yet once dry, will not smudge or come off. They dry quickly, can be used thickly or thinly (mix with water), and work well on all kinds of different materials. It is also worth investing in a few good paintbrushes for careful work as well as some cheaper ones for the younger children. If some different materials need to be bought for a special activity, most people are happy to pay a share of the costs, and you can check this beforehand.

Modelling natural clay is a potent and powerful medium which spans all age groups and abilities. Children abandon themselves to it, forming and re-forming it in a timeless primal transformative process which spans back over the aeons. It is wonderfully pleasurable and deeply absorbing even if the finished model isn't kept and the clay is squidged back into a ball. It doesn't require any special skills although, of course, skills will be learnt.

Put a piece of plastic sheet or plastic tablecloth down first. Sharpened sticks make good modelling tools. Wooden boards or cardboard pieces are ideal for putting your models on while you work, and stops the models sticking to the plastic. If you want to join two pieces of clay together, roughen both surfaces and press them together. Try to avoid using water. It's a lovely sensation when clay gets really wet and slippery, but models will disintegrate and your work area will get really messy. Partly dried-out clay (it is called 'cheese-hard') is wonderfully easy to carve with a vegetable knife.

It is possible to buy small bags of clay through a craft supplier, or ask your local potter to sell you some. It's very cheap. Once opened, keep the clay wrapped up in a damp cloth and wrap the whole thing in plastic. It will keep for years like this. Any dried clay can be wrapped up separately from the main piece in a wet rag (cotton T-shirt material is best), then wrapped in a plastic bag. In less than a week it will be soft enough to squeeze back into a useable lump again.

One of the main problems with clay is that the models become brittle as soon as they dry out. They need to be fired, which effects a chemical reaction and hardens the clay. Nowadays this is done in a kiln, but in the past clay was hardened in the fire or an earth kiln. If you are having an outdoor fire as part of your ceremony, you can dry the models out on the edge of the fire or in the sunshine. The models should be dried out properly first. Then put them in an old biscuit tin (make sure it is tin, including the lid) and place this right on the edge of the fire, turning the tin frequently, being careful to use thick oven gloves. At the end of the evening, pile the hot ashes around and on top of the tin, and leave until morning. This is a very simple way of firing clay, but it works sufficiently well to be able to harden the models. They can then be painted with acrylics or rubbed with shoe or furniture polish.

Other modelling materials can be used which will dry hard in the air or can be baked in an oven. None of them have that raw earthiness or tactile quality of natural clay, but they are still fun to use and easily bought or made. Making your own modelling material is easy and inexpensive. I include here a couple of my favourite recipes:

Salt Dough
300g plain flour
300g salt
1 tablespoon oil
Approx 200ml water
Mix ingredients together in a bowl. Add more water if necessary.
Turn onto floured board and knead.
Better if made the day before.
Keep in fridge in plastic bag. Keeps indefinitely. If it goes soft, knead in more flour.
Knead in food dye to colour, or paint or glaze with egg before baking.
Bake for 20 mins on gas Mark 4 or 180°C.
Make sure everything is dried out completely before baking or cracking will occur.
An oven which is too hot will also cause cracking.

Play Dough

2 teaspoons cream of tartar
1 cup plain flour
Half a cup of salt
1 tablespoon vegetable oil
1 cup of water
Mix in a bowl to form a smooth paste.
Mix in food dye to colour.

Cook the mixture in a non-stick saucepan. Cook slowly stirring all the time until the mixture eventually forms a stiff ball. Stop cooking at this point and knead the ball as it cools on a wooden board, for at least 5 minutes. Stored in an air-tight container, it will last several months.
If you wish to bake items hard, dry out well first, then bake in medium-hot oven for 15 - 20 mins. Can be painted and varnished afterwards.

Guided visualisation/Inner Journeys

Guided visualisation journeys are a great favourite with children of all ages. Let them choose a crystal to hold, and have some light blankets or scarves for them to lie on, or put over themselves. Cushions help them to be comfortable. Begin by asking them to focus on their breathing and then tell them you are going to help them go on a journey in their minds. The nature of the journey may be worked out beforehand. It may be into a garden, or through the woods, through a hole in a tree; it may be out into space; it may be flying on the back of a bird, or a mythical animal, or under the sea, or a journey to meet their animal guide or helper. The possibilities are endless. Speak slowly, leave plenty of space for their minds to fill in the details. In fact, it is important not to put too much detail in, and to encourage them to look around them in their mind's eye. It is especially important with younger children to make short journeys (about five minutes), and leave plenty of time for hearing all about what happened to them, what they saw, and how they felt on their journey. This sharing is a very pleasurable part of the experience and they look forward to telling the rest of the group what they saw and where they went. Drawings or paintings can be made of a special part of the journey that they wish to remember.

Forums and games

Different members of the group may have skills and knowledge which they can share with the children. There could also be a time put aside for a special focus (a forum) in which the whole group is invited to share and discuss what they know on a given subject. Subjects could include: the Moon, stone circles, labyrinths, Earth energy, ley lines, crop circles, the chakras, the aura, crystals, astrology, the Green Man, herb lore, tree lore, animal symbolism, and many more related subjects. The children will choose subjects which they wish to discuss. The introduction of a talking stick may be used sometimes. This is a stick which is handed round the group. The person holding the stick is the only person who should be speaking at any one time.

Games are also a good way to involve children. There are many new non-competitive games which can be played and shared with the whole group, providing fun and interaction on many levels. Be inventive and creative, make up new games which can become favourites; encourage the children to make up games; encourage the adults to join in and abandon themselves to their child within.

MASKS AND HEAD-DRESSES

Putting on a mask or an elaborate head-dress can transform the wearer into another person, another being, or to another level. They can provide an opportunity for the wearer to enter another world which can be liberating and deeply moving, sometimes even frightening. They can help a person enter into the spirit of a part of themselves which they wish to explore. They can also simply be great fun and add an extra dimension to a celebration. They are a way of connecting to the moment, capturing everyone's imagination in ways previously unexplored. Afterwards, when your mask or head-dress is hanging on the wall, they are a great memory of that celebratory moment, and are waiting for the next occasion to come to life.

Through the choice of mask you wish to wear, much can be learnt about yourself and your need to express that particular part of yourself. You might wish to take on the role of a particular archetype in a shamanic sense, to share and connect to an energy, such as a moon mask, or an animal mask or a mythical being. This may release a whole range of qualities in the wearer which may go beyond the actual time spent wearing the mask.

When you put your mask on at the beginning, the moment should never be rushed. Feel the presence of what you are now a part of. This needs your full attention. Masks and head-dresses invite an exploration of imaginative ways to move, taking on a particular rhythm or pulse. This may be enhanced through dance. Uttering sounds will also help you to feel the spirit of what you are becoming. Once you have become engaged with yourself, you can then begin to interact with others within the context of ritual, ceremony, plays or narrative story.

We have a wealth of myths and legends which have been handed down to us from the Celtic tradition. They represent the most accessible way we have of touching our native Celtic wisdom. Many old teachings are to be found within them. Tell them and retell them, and each time new things will be revealed. Masks may be used as an aid to storytelling through the medium of narrative plays. Performances can include dance and music. Processions take on new energy and excitement when everyone is masked or in elaborate head-dresses.

If you are using masks to conjure up an atmosphere, remember to make the most use of silence and the power of the mask's presence. Make the most use of lighting if it is dark. Candlelight always adds atmosphere. Use candle lanterns if you are outside, or small table lamps which can be switched off or on, if you are inside. Torches can be elaborated by adding coloured tissue paper cones, and these too can be switched on and off when needed. Candlelit processions are always a wonderful sight, and very powerful.

Masks or head-dresses may be worn to invoke the five elements. If a big mask is made, it will need an ally to move with the person carrying it, and to speak for it, as sound can become muffled from behind a mask. Head-dresses work well here as they leave the face free. Face paint can be used on the face for added effect.

One other point is to be aware that perhaps your mask may frighten or un-nerve other people, especially younger children, and this needs to be sensitively dealt with. If you are aware that your mask may appear to be a bit frightening, then establish with the children who it is underneath the mask, and please don't be tempted to feed that fear by acting fiercely or chasing them. Masks have very powerful energy both for the wearer and the observer. They should always be worn with a sense of ceremony, and an awareness of the deeper energy behind them.

Making Masks

There is a deeply absorbing connection made as you create your own mask or head-dress. Ways to make them are too numerous to describe here, but if you want to make a mask, here are some clues and starting points:

One of the quickest and easiest ways to create a mask is to go to a fancy dress shop, buy a cheap moulded plastic mask, and then go to an art shop and buy some PVA glue and some coloured tissue paper sheets. Tear the tissue up into small pieces and with slightly watered-down PVA, paste them all over the plastic mask, overlapping them several times and building up the colour variations. Cover the whole thing with a layer of glue and leave to dry overnight. If you want to elaborate the shape of the plastic mask, use glue-soaked tissue paper or attach cardboard shapes first using masking tape. Pipe cleaners are also useful for added extras and, once twisted into shape, can be covered in the glued tissue paper.

If you want to paint your mask or build the surface and shape up a bit, use torn newspaper strips instead of coloured tissue paper. Give it a coat of white emulsion paint when it's dry. You then have a really good surface to paint on your design. Acrylics are the best paints to use, eliminating the need for varnish.

If you want to make a mask which will fit your face exactly, the following method is the most successful I have found. You will need to buy a roll of old fashioned brown paper parcel tape, the kind which needs to be wet to become sticky. This can be bought in various sizes from art shops and some stationery shops. Cut the tape into lots of strips, approximately 1-2 cms x 3-4 cms. then you will need someone to help you. Lie on your back with your head on a towel. Place a thin plastic sandwich bag or piece of tinfoil over the upper part of your face, up to the tip of your nose. **Be very careful not to cover the nostrils so that breathing is not impaired**. Then, with a bowl of water and the piles of cut strips, ask your helper to wet the strips of parcel tape quickly, and lay them over the plastic on your upper face, moulding into the shape of the forehead, cheeks, round the edge of the hairline, down the nose, keeping holes around the eyes. Try not to get it too wet. By building up the layers, the mask will take shape quite quickly and will dry and keep its shape in 5-10 minutes. Take it off the face, peel off the plastic, and there you have a perfectly moulded impression of your upper face. This mask is light and comfortable, leaving your mouth free for talking and eating. (The lower face can be face-painted for added effect.) Once dry, go over the edges with masking tape to make them strong. Additions such as beaks, horns, ears etc. can be added using cardboard and masking tape and then finish with a layer of torn paper strips, and leave to dry out completely. Finish off with a coat of white emulsion before painting with acrylics or covering with coloured tissue paper. Final embellishments with gold or silver paint always look great in candlelight. When the mask is dry, make holes in the side and attach elastic.

Making head-dresses

Head-dresses can be made using an existing hat as a base, and then adding things. Pipe cleaners, wire, tissue paper, cardboard, can all be used as well as natural materials, greenery and dried flowers.

Another technique is to sew things on to a sturdy material headband which is elasticated at the back, or inside the headband itself. Add felt shapes, ribbons, or other material (shiny material works well). Pipe cleaners can be twisted this way and that and will add height to the head-dress. Very large sparkly pipe cleaners can be bought and used very effectively. A good haberdashers has all kinds of wonderful paraphernalia which can be creatively used to great effect.

Finally, if you want to make a head-dress out of greenery, begin by twisting some long thin whips of Willow over and over each other to make a circle which is a little bit loose on your head. This provides the base for other greenery to be attached to it and wrapped around it. Once you have got your main shape, extras can be poked in the gaps and tied in using green garden wire.

1 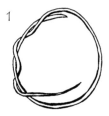 Choose a long whip of Willow to begin your circle. If you use fresh Willow, be aware that it will shrink as it dries out and the whole thing will become looser and bigger. If you are using basket makers Willow, the variety which has the bark removed needs to be soaked in the bath or a stream for about 3 hours before you use it. The variety which has the bark on, needs to be soaked for 3 days before use.

2 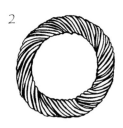 Use only the thinnest whips. Attach the thick end by poking it in the circle and weave with the thin end of each whip. It is better not to end and begin in the same place on your circle, so vary the length of the Willow whips that you use. A pair of secateurs is essential for this activity. Trim loose ends.

DANCE

Dancing is part of all of us and is a direct link to our inner levels and emotions. The Dance of Life is all around us, and we can link in with the Earth's energy and feel the pulse of her rhythms resonate at the core of our deepest selves. Dance is an opportunity to connect and express yourself, to let yourself go. There are many ways it may be used as part of a celebration or ceremony.

If you are celebrating on your own, you might want to put some music on which helps connect to your mood and the festival, or you may find that a chant you are singing becomes the starting point for movement and rhythm. Explore this connection between the sounds you make and the different ways in which your body can express itself. Feel your power and abandon yourself to the dance.

If you are planning or including dance in group celebrations, there are many different themes and methods to explore. A simple drumbeat is all that is needed to begin movement. Dancers may have bells or shakers or sticks by which they can add rhythms while dancing. If someone can play a whistle, this simple instrument can cut through all other percussion. Clapping and vocalizing sound all add to the build-up of energy created by improvised focused dancing. Explore each of the five elements in turn, express yourself, become one with them. Dance yourself as Sun or Moon, an animal, an archetype. Take off your shoes and touch the Earth. Express her pulse, her place in the cycle of the year.

Dance can be used at the beginning of a celebration as a way of bringing people together. Here the group could be led into a spiral and out again, or into a weaving pattern to connect and create a web of energy and intent. Other patterns of flow could be explored. Use the power of movement to raise the energy and connect the group to each other.

Circle dance and folk dance are more formal, but also bring the group together. Someone will need to teach the steps and provide the appropriate music. Keep the dances simple and, once the dance is learnt, the movement and energy changes from one of concentration to one of 'flow', a pulse of rhythm through which the whole group is connected, and the mind can slip into a meditative state. Here lies the ancient source of its power. These dances have been handed down to us from the past and perhaps had a deeper meaning and purpose which we can try to understand. Perhaps it is time to re-invent new dances which have significance and power for us now, and which can aid and enhance our re-connection to the Earth's solar and lunar cycles?

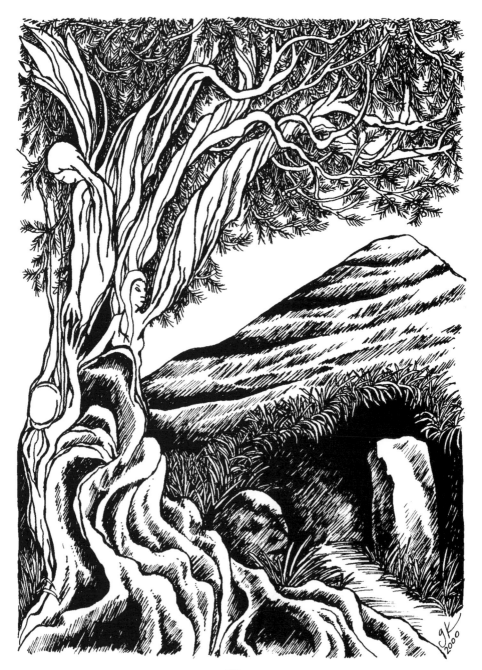

BETWEEN THE WORLDS

The Celts believed in three parallel universes which co-exist with this, our own, three dimensional world (Bith) which is governed by time.

The Celtic **Otherworld**, Annwn, is a place of rebirth, inspiration and life renewal. It is the home of powerful deities. It can symbolically be thought of as a place above this one, but it lives within us. It is a place of Angels, Spirit guides, animal guides, Guardians, the Ancestors, loosened from earthly desires and living outside of time.

The Otherworld can be entered from this world, accessed through dreams, trance, meditation, altered states of mind. It is close to this world but beyond it. It can be reached through hidden doorways in the land and when the veil between the worlds is thin. We can find these doorways and strengthen them by use and acknowledgement of their existence. These doorways into the Otherworld can be found by springs, wells, sacred groves, sacred hilltops, caves and other natural places. The stone circles, barrows and burial mounds of the past may also have been built on sites which access and amplify this energy, and can be used as places to enter into and communicate with this Otherworld.

The Celtic **Underworld** is the hidden doorway into the Faerie Realms. Hard to enter and even harder to get out of again, folk stories tell us that time runs differently here. Peopled by a race apart, beyond our normal sight, beyond our control, but co-existing with us and ever-present, if we take the time to make contact. Their presence can be felt in the wild places of moor and mountain where they have retreated from humankind. But they are just as likely to be found by hearth and home, in the garden or by sacred springs, perhaps willing to communicate with us again if we respect their existence.

Finding places of power in your locality will greatly enrich your life, especially if you work with the Earth energies there, trusting your intuition to guide your actions. It could be that our participation and the rituals we use could stimulate the flow of the Earth's life-force, increase the energy and health of these power places so long neglected. Dowse any area you feel is important, mark with a stone, bury crystals, release the energy. The nearest living parallel from which we may learn about this is through the Aborigines in Australia. They speak of 'dream-time' and the 'spirit-tracks' which connect the power centres of their land. These power centres they call 'places of increase'. These are the places of pure immanent energy where visions can be dreamed into reality.

There are many places we can go to make this kind of connection. Standing stones, stone circles, dolmens, burial mounds, barrows, tumuli, sacred wells and any sacred place of the ancients. We can also sometimes come across it unexpectedly in a wood, by a spring, in the high places. There is no mistaking the feeling as you find yourself slipping out of time and normal reality. In those special places where the veil between the worlds is thin, we can slip from an everyday state of mind into something dreamy and altered in some way. Vision hazes and a faraway look comes into the eyes. Here is the interface between the worlds. Here we can feel the timeless presence of past and future, receive visions and insights, travel out of time and place.

Dragon Paths and Leylines

Geomancy is the art of tuning into the vibration of underground currents of Earth energy. This may be made up of underground water currents, veins of minerals and streams of electromagnetic energy - all of which can be dowsed. These energy paths were known in the past as the dragon paths or the serpent force and more recently as leylines. They can be found by connecting stone circles, burial mounds and other ancient sites. Burial mounds were called dragon hills and the dragon was their legendary guardian. They may have been built on Earth faults where the underground radiation from the Earth may cause altered states of consciousness necessary for shamanic journeying. The slaying of the dragon may have been an ancient system of geomancy where the dragon paths were staked to release these energies in a similar way to acupuncture, as a means of keeping the Earth healthy. By the same token, modern dowsers have noticed that people living directly on underground currents, known as 'black water', will become ill, and they can redirect these harmful energies by staking the ground with metal pipes.

The dragon paths or leylines which connect the power places can be found by using an Ordnance Survey map and connecting up the ancient sites, springs, wells, tumuli, burial mounds, churches (especially where they are dedicated to St Michael, the dragon-slayer). But you will need to dowse the land to find the twists and turns of the serpent force. This may lead you to find the 'places of increase', the power places where Earth energy is potent and concentrated, especially where the lines of energy meet and cross. Much has been lost, but with a new awareness, some of it is now being re-found. It is up to us to find and strengthen these ancient connections and old knowledge, and to work with the Earth energy in new intuitive ways.

Stone Circles

Megaliths, dolmens and stone circles, dating from 5000-500BC, are found to be all over Western Europe, the British Isles, Scandinavia and the Near East. These are fantastic feats of engineering and skill. Many of them were built as huge cosmic calendars, aligning not only the Earth's energies but also measuring the planetary cycles of the Sun and Moon. They provided a focus for interaction with these energies as well as connecting the power and flow of the Earth's energies through the dragon paths. Thus the whole system is a web of interconnecting energy flow. The stone circles continue to draw us. We go there seeking some kind of communion with the Earth, Earth energies and our Ancestors. We walk about them, perhaps following hidden pathways of energy and feel drawn towards sitting in certain spots, or towards certain stones. For myself, I understand their energy to be for manifestation, outward expression and activation - for bringing out what is within, for celebration and ceremony, for dance, movement, and aligning with the potent life-force energy. But this is only my understanding at this point in time. You may have your own.

Burial Mounds, Dolmens and Barrows (Tumuli)

These are large man-made mounds from the Neolithic and Bronze Age, dating from 4000 to 700BC. They consist of a stone box chamber which was covered with earth. They sometimes have elaborate entrances which may or may not have a

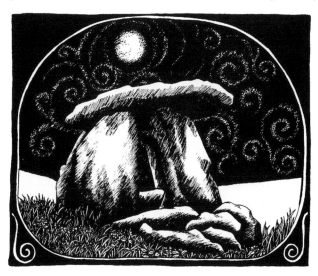

blocking stone across it. They are Earth wombs and perhaps never were used as tombs to bury the dead. More likely, in the light of recent understanding of the Earth energy found there, they were places to communicate with the dead. They may have been used by the shaman for inner journeying or for holding the power objects of the tribe, skulls of previous chiefs and shamans through which communication could be invoked. They were called dragon hills and were said to be guarded by dragons. In Ireland they were called hollow hills and were said to be entrances to the Faerie realms. They are certainly places of powerful Earth energy and part of the network of dragon paths which link potent places together.

It has been found that many of these sites emit an increase in natural radioactivity (is this the same as the 'places of increase' of the Aboriginies?). This can bring drowsiness and altered states of consciousness. They are places to gain inspiration and insight, to meditate and to go within. Accoustically, they may be used for interesting ventures into sound, resonant healing and chanting. They are places to go to make contact with the Earth, for inner journeys, for healing both the Earth and ourselves, and working with the energies present in creative and intuitive ways.

The Spiral
The spiral is one of our oldest symbols, representing eternal life, unfolding growth within and without, Spirit and Matter, death and rebirth, continuous creation. At the centre is the point of complete balance, a stillness within, around which all things revolve.

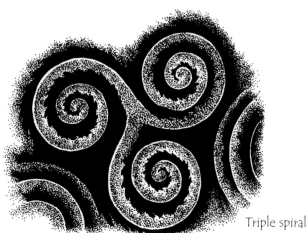

Triple spiral

54

A spiral path can be made permanently on the land using stones, turf, Willow or herbs. This can then be accessed whenever you wish to walk its energy flow. The ebb and flow of its energy pattern make it a perfect tool for walking meditation, making your way to the centre to meet your own still point within, before coming back out again having gained insights from within. It can be walked out anywhere and it doesn't need to be marked out on the ground first.

In Celtic art it is found as the single, double and triple spiral. It can be used as a symbol in decoration wherever its intrinsic properties need to be recognised and invoked.

The Labyrinth

Labyrinths are part of a similar processional path as the spiral, creating and protecting a still point at the centre. They can be used for inner journeying, to contact the power within, for initiation. It is also said that spirits travel in straight lines, and the labyrinths may have been used as a device to shake off unwanted spirits which may become attached to a person in the course of shamanic journeying. They can also be seen as a device to enhance the flow of left brain/right brain activity. A labyrinth is a continuous path which, when followed, leads a person in and out again.

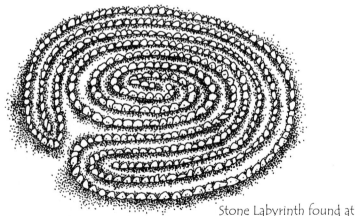

Stone Labyrinth found at
St Agnes, Isles of Scilly

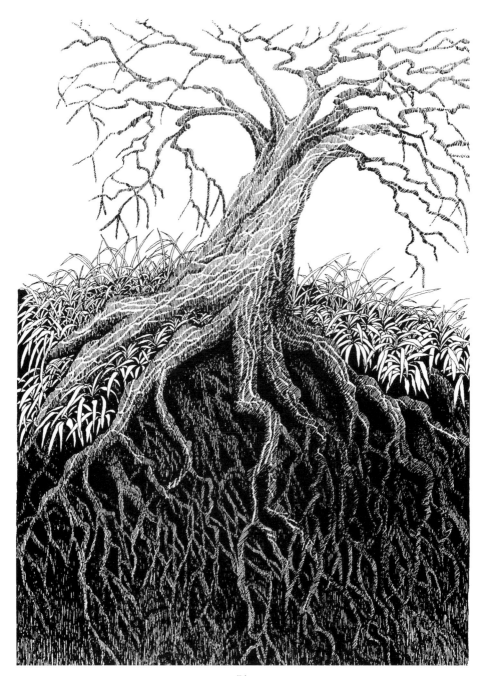

THE TREE OGHAM

THE 20 OGHAM FEDHA OR FEWS
(READ FROM THE BOTTOM UPWARDS)

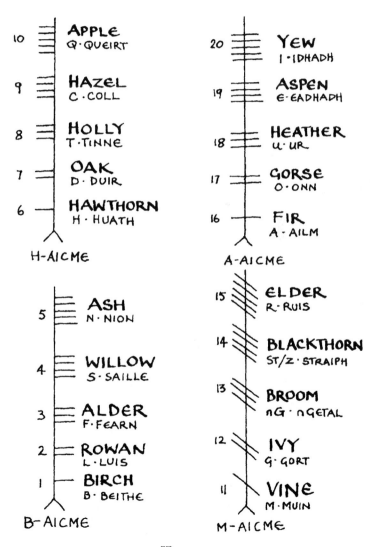

10 — APPLE
Q·QUEIRT

9 — HAZEL
C·COLL

8 — HOLLY
T·TINNE

7 — OAK
D·DUIR

6 — HAWTHORN
H·HUATH

H-AICME

5 — ASH
N·NION

4 — WILLOW
S·SAILLE

3 — ALDER
F·FEARN

2 — ROWAN
L·LUIS

1 — BIRCH
B·BEITHE

B-AICME

20 — YEW
I·IDHADH

19 — ASPEN
E·EADHADH

18 — HEATHER
U·UR

17 — GORSE
O·ONN

16 — FIR
A·AILM

A-AICME

15 — ELDER
R·RUIS

14 — BLACKTHORN
ST/Z·STRAIPH

13 — BROOM
nG·nGETAL

12 — IVY
G·GORT

11 — VINE
M·MUIN

M-AICME

57

THE WHEEL OF THE YEAR
WITH RELATED TREES AND HERBS

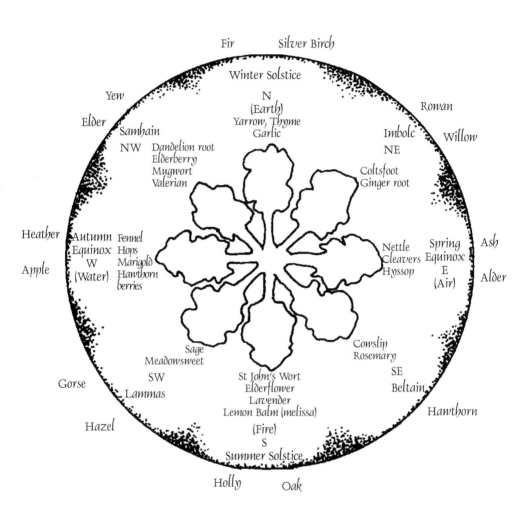

Fir   Silver Birch

Winter Solstice

Yew

Elder

Rowan

Samhain   Imbolc   Willow

NW   NE

N
(Earth)
Yarrow, Thyme
Garlic

Dandelion root
Elderberry
Mugwort
Valerian

Coltsfoot
Ginger root

Heather

Autumn   Fennel
Equinox   Hops   Nettle   Spring   Ash
W   Marigold   Cleavers   Equinox
(Water)   Hawthorn   Hyssop   E
berries   (Air)

Apple

Alder

Cowslip
Rosemary

Sage   SE
Meadowsweet   Beltain

SW   Hawthorn
St John's Wort
Lammas   Elderflower
Lavender
Lemon Balm (melissa)

Gorse

Hazel   (Fire)
S
Summer Solstice

Holly   Oak

58

THE EIGHT CELTIC FESTIVALS

The following section charts the progression of the year's solar cycle and the eight festivals which have been used since Celtic times to honour and celebrate the changes of energy which this brings to the Earth and ourselves.

Each festival looks at the way this energy was used and interpreted in the past, as handed down to us from Pagan and Druid tradition, and folk customs which have survived the passage of time.

Each festival looks at the underlying energy of the Earth, how this energy affects us, and how we can use this in new and relevant ways.

Preparations for each festival include ideas for things to do before the festival to bring a deeper connection to these developing energies. Choose to do what you are most drawn towards, and find your own ways to make these connections. Similarly with celebrating the festivals, I offer clues and ideas, most of which I have used either on my own, with a small celebrations group and sometimes with larger gatherings of 50 - 100 people. You will find many more ways of your own. These celebrations lend themselves to gathering with kindred-spirits, sharing and expressing yourself and your feelings, but to celebrate them on your own is an empowering experience as you listen to the guidance of your inner wisdom. However you celebrate them, the important thing is to mark the occasion in some way, touch the sacred and potent part of yourself, your own sense of the spiritual, following the path of the heart, respect for the Earth and the unseen spirits of our land.

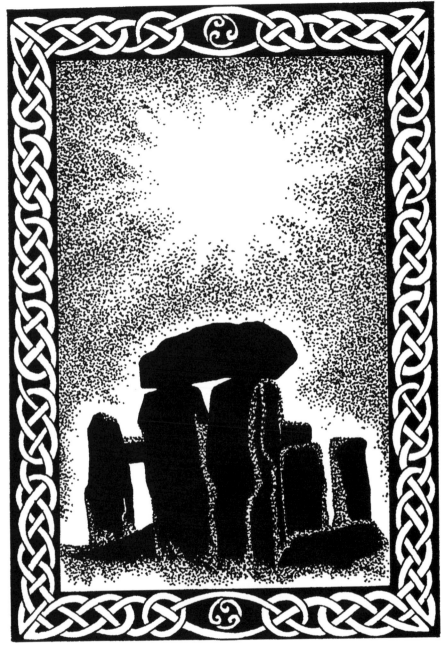

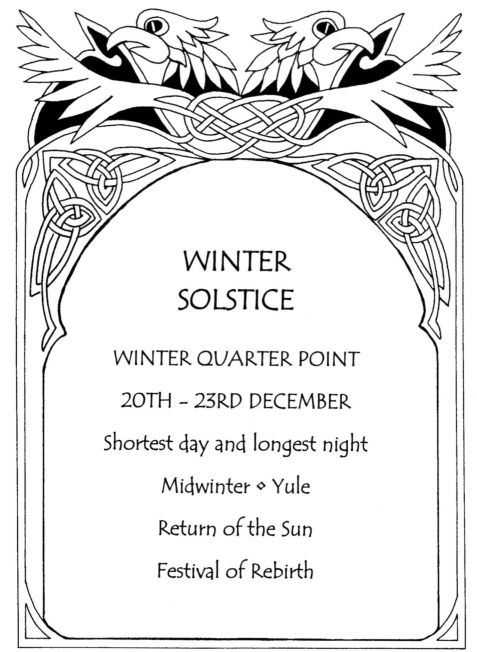

WINTER SOLSTICE

WINTER QUARTER POINT

20TH - 23RD DECEMBER

Shortest day and longest night

Midwinter ◆ Yule

Return of the Sun

Festival of Rebirth

WINTER SOLSTICE

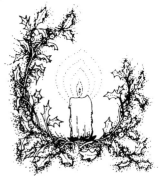

The Sun enters the sign of Capricorn ♑ as her rays shine directly at their southern extreme for the year. This is the shortest day and the longest night of the Northern Hemisphere. In the Southern Hemisphere they celebrate the Summer Solstice at this time.

The great cosmic wheel of the year, the fiery hub of the universe, the symbolic wheel of Time, is acknowledged here. Jul or Yule means wheel in Norwegian. Northern Europeans of our Celtic past believed this mystic wheel stopped turning briefly at this crucial point as one cycle ended and a new cycle of the Sun began. It was taboo to rotate any wheels at the Winter Solstice, from cartwheels to butter churns, as they waited for the return of the Sun. The Solstice was a moment to stop, to look backwards in inner reflection and to look forwards to a new active season as the Sun's returning power brings increased daylight, growth and activity. From now on the days will lengthen and the warmth will come again. This was an important moment in our Celtic past. Megalithic monuments acknowledged this return of the Sun. The outer Sarsen ring of Stonehenge is orientated to the Mid Winter Solstice sunset. Newgrange in Ireland is aligned to dawn on the Winter Solstice when a shaft of light pierces a long tunnel deep into this burial mound to illuminate an inner chamber. It is possible still to be one of a handful of people who experience this moment standing deep inside this earth-womb chamber.

To understand this moment, it is important to realise that this festival is not the beginning, in a linear way, of looking at things, but a rebirth within a cycle in which the starting point chosen here is part of a vibrant whole. Therefore it is necessary to make a connection to what has gone before. Since the last festival at Samhain, the Earth has been withdrawn within itself. The darkness of the receding daylight hours has been felt by all of nature and humankind. Root energy has been strengthened, the dreamworld explored, mysteries understood. The deep wisdom of the unconscious has brought spiritual insights. The old year has died and, through reflection and assimilation, the way is now prepared for rebirth of the active principle. The 'cauldron of regeneration', as this process was known, was central to Celtic and Pagan understanding. Something old must die in order for something new to be reborn. The period of rest and darkness is a vital link in the cycle of life.

Homes were decorated with evergreeens, Holly, Ivy, Mistletoe, Yew, all of which had magical spiritual significance representing the cycle of everlasting life. The Church tried to stop these old customs but they have endured. Other traditional customs for the Winter Solstice included yule logs, door wreaths to symbolize the wheel of the year, feasting, gifts, dancing, masks, mystery plays, mummers' plays, processions, decorated trees, and candlelight. These were to honour the return of the Sun and the return of the dynamic, creative, active phase of life.

The Pagan tradition tells of a Sun King who ripened the harvest at Lammas and was sacrificed back into the land within the seed. This is the sacrifice of the active principle as the Sun loses its power and the energy turns within. He stays underground as the Dark Lord of the Underworld, Satan, Pluto, Hades, the Grim Reaper, Lord of Death. At the Winter Solstice he is reborn as the Lord of Light, the Sun King, the Sun God. This is one interpretation of the Winter Solstice.

The Christian church adopted this time to celebrate the birth of the 'Son of God', Jesus, the newborn King, on the 25th of December, just a few days after the Winter Solstice. The Mithraic religion had a similar saviour, Mithra, who was also born at the Winter Solstice after his death and conception nine months earlier on the 25th of March (Spring Equinox/Easter). He too was called the Light of the World. Norsemen celebrated the birthday of their Lord Frey at the Winter Solstice. A similar story is the one of Heracles, a Greek saviour, also born from a virgin. His twelve labours symbolized the passage of the Sun during the year through the twelve signs of the zodiac. After this journey, he was clothed in scarlet robes, killed, resurrected as his own Divine Father, to marry the Virgin Mother Goddess and be reborn all over again at the Winter Solstice. The ancient myths and legends have many stories and versions of wheel kings who were wrapped in fiery cloaks or fiery wheels. Divine Fathers and Divine Sons were one and the same person, cyclically alternating and uniting through marriage with the Virgin Mother Goddess to be reborn as new again.

Although we have a tradition of the Sun being a masculine, active, outward, creative energy, there are older traditions which celebrated the Winter Solstice as rebirth of a Sun Goddess. Anastasia was one of Rome's great Goddesses. Her holy day was that of the Sun's rebirth at the Winter Solstice. This festival began with its eve called 'matrum noctem', the night of the mother. There were many earlier Goddesses, all systematically destroyed, turned into devils or demons, masculinized or turned into saints to be incorporated into the Church. Another interpretation of this part of the year is explained through the story of Demeter and Persephone who was abducted by Pluto and taken into his Underworld for the Winter months. But Persephone was queen of the Underworld long before there was a Pluto, and Pluto was an earlier female deity, a daughter of the Cretan Earth mother Rhea. Pluto became masculinized in Christian times and given the qualities of the devil. Other female Goddesses include Epona, Macha, Artemis, Astarte, Blodeuwedd, Kali, Demeter, Diana, Branwen, Creiddylad, Cerridwen, Morigan, Ceres, Grain, Brighidh, Kore - to name but a few.

Celtic understanding interpreted the cyclic nature of the Sun's passage year through a Triple Goddess. This included the virgin Goddess of the Spring, the Mother Goddess of the Earth's abundant growth period, Summer and harvest, and the Crone who represented the wisdom within during the Winter months. This triple deity is found all over the world and is understood as three aspects of the same energy. The Winter cycle belongs to the Crone. During the Christian era, she became the dark witchwoman, the object of fear and superstition. Her connection to the inner world of wisdom, intuition and insights from within, almost became lost to humankind. As the Sun is reborn at the Winter Solstice, she becomes her virgin self again, echoing the virgin birth of the Sun king. It is interesting that at the time of the Winter Solstice, the constellation of the virgin rises in the East.

But times are changing and an even bigger cosmic wheel is turning as 2000 years of the Piscean Age give way to a new 2000 years of the Aquarian Age. Now at Winter Solstice let us acknowledge not a Sun God or a Sun Goddess, but celebrate the return of the Sun's energy and the active dynamic outward creative expression of self-knowledge that this generates in all of us, whether male or female. Let us celebrate the rebirth of the balance of power to humanity as a whole, healing the wounds of separation, fear and dominance. A new cycle begins.

THE UNDERLYING ENERGY OF WINTER SOLSTICE

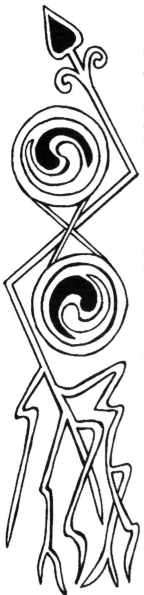

The Earth has been withdrawn inside herself. Winter brings the hardships of cold and shortness of daylight. Very little outer growth has happened, but deep within the Earth, roots have been growing, bringing stability and nutrients to the plants and trees. New buds are slowly forming on the trees and bushes and deeply buried bulbs are beginning to send up their first hardy shoots. All of nature has slowed down, waiting for the energy to change and for warmth to return.

Due to the restraints of Winter, we too have slowed down and have been conserving energy. We have spent time withdrawn within ourselves. The time between Samhain and Yule is the dark time of Winter, and allows us to enter into dreamtime. As the outer world is darkened by shorter days and cloudy cold weather, the inner realms can expand. This has been a great opportunity for us to experience this world within, to get in touch with our dreams and to make inner journeys for wisdom and understanding. It has been a time to assimilate our experiences and an incubation period for our own personal seeds, plans and ideas. Now with the return of the active outward energy that the Sun brings, all of this can slowly begin to manifest.

This is the Sun's birthday and a celebration of its rebirth. Life will become active again from now on. Being part of this cycle means that we too are reborn at this time. We bring the wisdom of our inner journeys out into the world, to grow with the increasing light from the Sun. It is a time for birthing our visions and naming the dreams that we have been incubating so that we can assist their manifestation consciously in our lives. This is the time to celebrate the active principle whose positive qualities of intellectual and rational thought, determination and assertiveness bring independence and purpose to our lives.

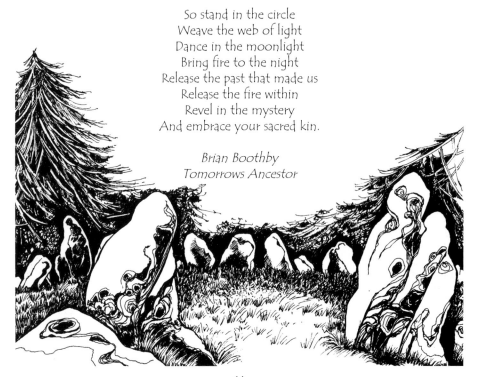

Standing in the circle
Beneath the web of light
Dancing in the moonlight
On a cold new year's night
And it seemed we were lifted
Flown across the years
Power-circle shifted
By power-circle seers

And the Goddess and John Barleycorn
Will put flesh upon the bones
Fly ribbons round the barrows
Plant footprints round the stones
The Goddess and John Barleycorn
Will keep the spirit strong
For those who remember
For those who sing the song

So stand in the circle
Weave the web of light
Dance in the moonlight
Bring fire to the night
Release the past that made us
Release the fire within
Revel in the mystery
And embrace your sacred kin.

Brian Boothby
Tomorrows Ancestor

PREPARATIONS FOR
WINTER SOLSTICE

VENUE ◇ EVERGREENS ◇ WREATHS ◇ SOLSTICE BUSH
◇ GIFTS ◇ BOWER ◇ CANDLES ◇ YULE LOG ◇
MYSTERY PLAYS ◇ CARNIVAL ◇
HERBS: YARROW ◇ THYME ◇ GARLIC ◇
TREES: SILVER BIRCH ◇ FIR ◇
THE BEAR ◇ THE WOLF ◇ THE EAGLE

◯Traditionally the Winter Solstice is a time to
gather with family, friends and kin, but few of us have the space for
bringing lots of people together. It is possible to hire a village hall or
similar space for the day, sharing the cost amongst everyone. This
gives you practical facilities and a space large enough for
dancing and feasting. Decorating a big space will need some
planning but much can be done with evergreens, the four
directions and the five elements, coloured hangings and side-
lighting (table lamps or candle lanterns).

◯Evergreens

Evergreens are brought into the home at this time to represent
everlasting life. They are hung around the doorways and the
windows and each area of the country has its own customs,
inclusions and superstitions. Each of the different
evergreens has a deeper symbolism and inherent energy
which can be consciously worked with as you make
your Winter Solstice decorations. Take time to make
contact with the tree or plants you wish to use.
Greet it, appreciate it and ask for some of its leaves
or twigs for your Solstice decorations. You will know

in your heart if it is alright to cut. It usually is, but sometimes it isn't. Respect that. Thank the tree or plant afterwards. It creates a loving energy-field which is beneficial to both the plant and yourself.

Holly
Holly is sacred to mother Holle or Hel, the Underworld Goddess. Holly is one of the native trees favoured by the Druids, and part of the Celtic Tree Ogham. The Holly symbolizes everlasting life, recovery, goodwill and potent life energy. A tree of death and regeneration, it unites past actions with present actions and restores direction in your life. It also helps the heart open to Unconditional Love. Red Holly berries of Pagan Solstice decorations represent the red female blood of life, while the white mistletoe berries represent the white semen drops of the life-giving male. Holly and mistletoe are displayed alongside each other to represent the sacred marriage which brings forth new life.

Mistletoe
At Midwinter mistletoe was ceremoniously lopped from the Oak tree, caught in a cloth so that it did not touch the earth, and laid on the Solstice altar to represent fertility (hence kissing beneath it).

Ivy
Ivy is another plant commonly used for solstice decorations and represents the search for the self and the search for enlightenment through the freedom to follow your own path. The Ivy is about finding your own inner resources and acting upon them. All evergreens link to the concept of everlasting life and rebirth so central to Celtic spiritual understanding.

Yew
The yew tree is revered throughout the Northern Hemisphere as a tree of regeneration and rebirth. It provides a direct link to the spirit realms and the Ancestors. The ancient Yews to be found in churchyards were there long before the churches. In the Celtic past the Yews provided contact with the old wisdom hidden deep inside the Earth and ourselves. **The bark, leaves and seeds within the fruit are poisonous, so use with care.**
           After the festivities are over, keep all the cuttings you have used as decorations for special sacred fires, or lay them back on the Earth with thanks and respect. Some say to burn them at the Spring Equinox. Some of the wood can be used for making a wand, Ogham stick or Ogham key, or a talisman.

The special qualities they have can be accessed by contageous magic, that is, by contact with the wood. Carve or whittle the wood with a penknife, then use rough, medium and finally smooth sandpaper. Finish by oiling the wood to protect it from drying out and becoming brittle.

☉Wreaths

There is an old tradition of making wheels of evergreens as we celebrate the wheel of the year turning once again towards the Sun. It may take the form of a wreath to hang on the door, or it may be lain horizontally with places for candles to be lit.

Begin with some long thin whips of Willow (at least 4 ft lengths if possible), wrapping them into a circle (1). Always use the thin end for the weaving. Continue by anchoring the thick end of a new piece of Willow on the circle you have made and, using the thin end to weave, wrap it over and over, round and round several times until a thick base has been made (2). Weave the evergreens around this base (3), using it to anchor in the ends. Green garden wire is useful for tying in loose ends, creating hooks, fixing in candle holders etc.

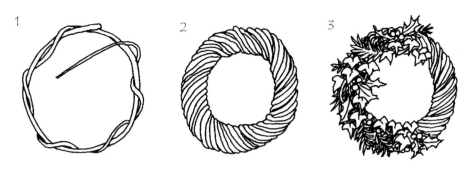

☉Bower

In the garden create a bower of evergreens using a Hazel arch as a base (see page 25). Light candles here for the returning Sun. A permanent Winter Solstice bower could be created in the North by planting evergreens around the Hazel arch and weaving them around each other as they grow. Placed facing the Sun at dawn on the Winter Solstice, it can become a wonderful seating area for generations to come.

○Solstice Bush

Having rejected the idea of bringing a cut tree into the house for decorating, our family has had much enjoyment on Solstice morning, going out to gather greenery to make a Solstice bush. You will need a few sturdy branches (preferably evergreen) to give it form, anchoring them into a pot of wet soil with rocks around the base. All other greenery can be poked into the wet soil to bring a richness and variety of different leaf shapes, dried flowers, fruits and berries. Small natural decorations and sweets can be hung from it.

○Yule Log

This is traditionally a log of Oak, a sacred tree with connections to the Sun king. It is a very slow burning wood which gives out great heat. Traditionally it was placed on the fire with much ceremony, the ashes were kept for fertility and the half-burnt log as a protection from lightning. You can use the log for absorbing and clearing energies, thoughts and feelings you wish to purify, transform and release into the fire. Releasing old energy opens the way for new energy to come in.

○Candles

Lighting candles for the return of the Sun is an old tradition at this time. Buy plenty of them so that you can light your space with their flickering light. Buy a special one for special wishes and hopes. Make some candles of your own. Dipped candles are the easiest and most satisfying to do, especially with children. You will need coloured wax, wick, an empty food tin can, an old saucepan and plenty of newspaper on the table. Break the wax into the tin and stand in gently boiling water until the wax is all melted. Take the tin out of the water and stand it on the newspaper. **Do not let the children boil the water themselves and warn them to be extremely careful with the tin of hot wax.** Using a length of wick each, dip the wick in the wax, pull it out to dry, dip it in again, pull it out, and so on. Gradually the wax builds up layer upon layer to make a candle. The wax needs to be melted to about a depth of 7 cms in the tin. After a while the wax begins to cool and is used up on the candles, so the wax in the tin gets very low. Return the tin to the pan of boiling water, add more wax and re-melt. Do this as often as needed.

Creating enough light for an evening celebration in the dark of Winter is another consideration. Plenty of table lamps and subdued lighting adds atmosphere, but nothing beats large amounts of candles burning. Candle lanterns are excellent and very safe. Night-lights in jam jars are also very safe, but you need a lot of them to create a good light. Paint the jam jars with glass paint (another activity which everyone loves to do), and use green garden wire to wind around the top of the jar for making long carrying-handles for processions.

Handguards can be made for household candles if they are to be carried in procession or as part of a ritual dance. Using any stiff card, cut out a circle of 15 cms diameter. In the centre, slice a star-shape with a sharp knife. The candle can then be poked through here. **Please be extremely careful when using a naked flame**

◎Herbs of Winter Solstice

Yarrow - *achillea millefolium*

One of the best fever remedies, producing copious amounts of sweating and lowering the blood pressure. Drink a wineglass full of the infusion hourly until the fever subsides. Pour one pint of boiling water on ½-1 ounce of dried herb. Leave covered for ten minutes. (Especially good combined with elderflower and peppermint.) It will speed up the clotting of blood and can be used on all wounds, old and new. Use the crushed fresh leaves or soaked dried leaves directly on cuts, for nosebleeds or earache. Chew them to relieve toothache. The Druids used yarrow to divine the weather. In China, yarrow stalks are used with the I Ching oracle system. Yarrow will strengthen the etheric body (our spirit body) as a protection against the influence of others, and also radiation.

Thyme - *thymus vulgaris*

A valuable tonic herb for the whole system and antiseptic. It stimulates white blood cell production to help the body resist infection. Useful for all digestive complaints, inflammation of the liver, nervous indigestion, flatulence, bad breath and hangovers. It will promote perspiration in fevers, lowering the temperature and quickly cleansing the body. Use for dry irritating coughs, sore throats and ear infections. It will relieve insomnia and calm night fears. Thyme brings courage, inner strength and a stronger sense of purpose. Pour one pint of boiling water on ½-1 ounce of dried herb and leave covered for ten minutes. Drink a wine glassful three times a day.

Garlic - *allium sativum*

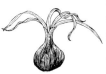

A powerful antiseptic useful for all viral and fungal infections, colds and fevers. Also for all respiratory problems, circulatory and heart problems, causing blood pressure to be lowered and helping reduce blood cholesterol levels and angina. It is a good external rub for arthritis and rheumatic pain when used hot. The juice diluted with water can be used as an antiseptic on wounds. Garlic makes it easier to transcend the physical plane, thus aiding astral travel and even the transition of death. Eat raw.

○Trees of Winter Solstice

Silver Birch - *Betula pendula*

The first tree of the Celtic Tree Ogham. BEITH B. The Silver Birch is the first tree to colonize new ground, dropping its leaves and twigs to enrich the soil so other trees may follow. It is thus a tree of life-giving properties, vitality and nourishment, signifying a new start, a new beginning, birth, rebirth, inception, new opportunities. The Celts used the twigs of the Birch for driving out the spirits of the old year and considered the Birch to have great powers of purification and renewal. Link with Silver Birch to prepare yourself for new journeys, spiritual or physical. As the Birch sheds its bark, let go of any unhelpful influences and clear the way for the new active phase of the year to begin. The wood from the Silver Birch is very good for carving and was traditionally used for babies' cradles.

Fir and Pine trees - Scots pine - *Pinus sylvestris*

Originally Pine groves were part of temples to the Goddess or Great Mother. Roman priests called 'dendrophori' or 'tree bearers' on the eve of Midwinter Solstice, would cut down one of her sacred Pines, decorate it and carry it into the temple. The Fir is the sixteenth tree of the Celtic Tree Ogham, honoured for its ability to help us develop the perceptions, insights and wisdom to see far beyond the present. It indicates strength and healing learnt from past experiences. From this viewpoint, farsighted actions can be undertaken, great things can be done, new objective insights acted upon. Bring a spray of Pine into the house as part of your evergreen decorations or Solstice bush. Thank it for its gifts. Afterwards, make a wand or Ogham key from the wood.

○Power Animals

The Bear

Throughout the Celtic lands there is evidence of Bear cults. They were revered and honoured for their strength and great reserves of power. Bears are not aggressive, but if provoked, could be deadly. Celtic warriors going into battle may have invoked the strength and wisdom of the bear. Votive statues of bears and ritual jewellery have been found throughout the Celtic lands. Bear's teeth were prized as talismans. Bears' pelts were prized as clothing and for sleeping on. The Bear goes into its cave in the Winter, representing the power of introspection and inner wisdom. The Bear teaches us to go within in order to digest our experiences, to become a spiritual warrior by integration of intuition and inner wisdom with strength and purpose.

The Wolf

Wolf wisdom brings guidance in dreams and meditation. Here intelligence is linked with instinct. The Wolf is free to explore alone or be with the rest of the pack for companionship, strength of numbers, nurturing. When exploring hidden paths alone, we may discover new truths to share with the rest of our family and kin. Wolf brings strength and courage to be who you are, to face the cycles of death and rebirth and to learn from them.

The Eagle

From earliest times there was the belief that souls could become birds. Latin 'aves' meant both bird and Ancestral Spirit. Eagles were said to bring messages from the Gods to foretell the future. They are known as symbols of death and rebirth, associated with the Sun God, Fire and lightning. The Eagle was thought to be a passing spirit, the soul of a God returning to heaven after an earthly incarnation as a king. It is linked to solar mysteries and initiation rites. The Eagle was often identified as a firebird or phoenix, representing a shamanic 'baptism by Fire' that could bring transformation and rebirth from the ashes. Shamans were said to be able to transform themselves into Eagles.

○Winter Solstice is traditionally a time for mystery plays and carnival. The Midwinter carnival of medieval times included the story of Saturnalia as King Carnival, who was killed with the old year before the new Sun rose again.

73

Consider performing a piece of drama, dance or masked play which helps to illuminate the message of the Winter Solstice. Look for old folk legends with richness of symbolism and imagery. Make the most use of colour, light and masks, exploring ways to go beyond words to conjure atmosphere and deep connections.

○Clear the way for changes and new beginnings. Cleanse your aura and that of friends and family by burning dried sage in a small pottery dish and 'bathing' in the smoke. Visualise a spiral of bright light around yourself and visualise your aura bright and sparkling. Clean your room(s). Cleanse everything by washing it all in salt water. Give away as presents what you no longer need and is cluttering up your space. Create a sacred shrine area where you can light a candle, and keep a few things there which will help keep your spiritual focus.

○Cleanse all your crystals by washing them in running water and putting them outside for a while. Let them bathe in the Winter Solstice Sun, in the moonlight, in the rain, the frosts and the snow. Let them regenerate through the power of the elements. Any crystals which have been used a lot for healing and psychic work, bury in salt for twenty four hours before washing in running water and leaving outside.

○Celebrate and salute the Sun. Make a large Sun out of basket-maker's Willow or cane, creating a space inside for a night light in a jam jar. Use masking tape to hole the shape together by taping the joins to make them strong. Cover with yellow tissue paper leaving a hole top and bottom. Stiffen the tissue paper by giving it several light coats of watered-down PVA glue, letting it dry well between the coats. Use it during your celebrations. It can be hung from a stick or string.

○Nothing beats watching the real Sun break free of the horizon on Solstice dawn. Plan how and where you can do this.

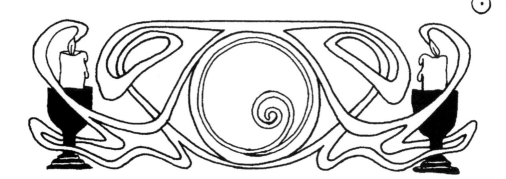

WINTER SOLSTICE CELEBRATIONS

⊙The eve of Winter Solstice is a special night to be out under the stars, to connect to the wisdom within and that of the mystical wild part of yourself which links with the Earth at this, one of the most ancient rites of transformation and rebirth.

⊙Stay up all night, tell stories of power and reconnection to the mystical energies, the magical world, whose vibrant and vital dance is all around you. As the Solstice Sun dawns, what will you take with you as the Earth's energy turns once again towards expansion, creativity and manifestation?

⊙If you can't stay up all night, then get up early before dawn. Go to a special high place and watch the Solstice sunrise. If you live in the East near the sea, watch it dawn over the sea. Make a pledge or a wish. Affirm your dreams and visions, prepare yourself for changes and new beginnings.

⊙This is the time to celebrate your friendships, family and sacred kin. Experience belonging to a tribe. Focus on the spirit of generosity and let your heart open in gratitude for all you have in your life. By feeling thankful for what you have in the present, you open the channels for your own abundance.

⊙In the heart of Winter, when we can sometimes feel a bit isolated and low, celebrating the Winter Solstice will bring a real heart-warming connection to the Earth and like-minded friends. It can bring deep spiritual connections which the commercial and religious aspect of Christmas may not. Invite friends to spend Solstice eve with you.

⊙Find a venue which is large enough to bring your local like-minded community together to celebrate the Winter Solstice in true tribal fashion. A village hall can be hired for the day. Ask everyone to bring special food to share and have a feast. Celebrate the Earth's abundance and the friends and family with whom you can share it. Book a good band for dancing to. Ask everyone to bring a gift, a present – the same number of presents as there are in your family – labelled adult or child. These can be put into adult or child labelled baskets as people arrive. (It's a good idea to have a few extra presents to save any disappointments.) These presents need not necessarily be bought, but something of yours which you no longer need or use. This is the spirit of the 'give-away'. Later, after the feast, the presents can be distributed by the children or put in the centre of the circle so that each can go and choose a present from the basket.

⊙Begin the gathering with an opening ceremony focusing on the rebirth of the Sun and what this means for all of us. Light candles in the middle of the room and circle the light, holding hands and chanting. Put out all the other lights so that the candles become a meditative focus. **Be careful not to dance too close to the naked flames.**

⊙Represent the four directions with each element. Light candles at the centre to represent Spirit. Create four wall hangings or large elemental masks which can be carried in and hung on the wall or placed in each of the directions. Ask five people to speak for each element, invoking the qualities they bring to this time.

Earth in the North

We give thanks to the Earth for this period of rest and darkness which has led us to explore the deep wisdom inside ourselves. Like the Earth, we have strengthened our roots by understanding ourselves and our experiences better. Through this inner exploration we can contact the source of our being, find spiritual meaning in our lives, find healing and clarity. Now as the Sun is reborn, we begin to make ready for a new phase of life, to manifest a new set of possibilities and experiences in the material world.

Air in the East

Give thanks for the Air, for inspiration and inner knowledge which brings us new ideas and creates new beginnings. Give thanks for the power of our voices in song and sound, and for the movement of our thoughts which allows us to explore new levels of understanding. Communication on all levels is the gift of Air. Here at Winter Solstice, with the first new breath of the new cycle, we ask that our communications be direct and clear, that we listen to the messages we receive from within, and act upon them during the active phase of the year.

Fire in the South

Give thanks for Fire, the vital energy source, creative life-force reborn now as the Sun. Fire brings spontaneity, expansion, growth, passion and active energy. We can begin to express ourselves in the world again, bringing what we have learnt from our time of rest in the darkness out into the light. We are cleansed, changed, transformed by our contact with the spirit realms, free to begin again a new cycle of the Sun.

Water in the West

We thank the gift of Water which has brought us contact with deep mysteries, subtle energies and inner perceptions. During the Winter darkness we have touched our souls and the deep emotions hidden inside ourselves. Now, with the rebirth of the Sun can come release through outward expression, through art, poetry, music, dance and fertile currents which lead us to follow our hearts, love and compassion. Our imagination and receptivity can work together with the active phase of the Sun so that we merge and follow both aspects of ourselves.

Spirit

Spirit within and without and ever present. We give thanks for this vital connection to this essential part of ourselves which cannot be seen and cannot be named. We reach out and in, connecting to our source and the guidance from within. We touch the sacred, the still point of power at the centre of our being. Through it we are a part of all life and all existence on this Earth and beyond it.

The words I have written here are intended as clues, pathways to understanding how each element can be expressed and understood at this time. When speaking for the elements, it is important to speak from the heart and with power, so that you help to make the connection strong for all those present. Begin by visualising the element to build up a presence. Create a visual picture of words, so that all those present have strong imagery for each element. Use the elemental charts on pages 28, 29, 30, 31 and 32 to help you.

○ Be still. Experience the stillness of Midwinter. Be aware of where you are physically, mentally and spiritually. Meditate for a while on the direction you wish to be going when the time for movement comes.

○ Each light a candle for something you wish for with the return of the Sun. Have a bowl of sand in the centre of the circle to plant all the candles in. Let them burn right down. By naming your wish out loud, you create energy. The possibilities you dream will become your reality. Be part of the mystery of the Winter Solstice. Allow the miracle of transformation to emerge from the darkness. Aspire to do what you most wish to do.

○ Bring something out from the dark into the light – something which needs honouring, reclaiming, examining, blessing, or thanking. Share with each other the wisdom and understanding which has been gained.

○ Make some resolutions to help you as you begin the new cycle. (New Year resolutions grew out of this Winter Solstice custom.) Share your hopes and intentions with each other. Speak them out. Give them power. Feel the strength of your intent.

○ Dance a spiral dance, sing a chant, hold hands, beginning as a circle and then gradually begin to spiral into the centre. When the person leading the spiral reaches the centre, stop and let the spiral catch up with itself and then with everyone close to each other, begin to intone 'Om'. Let each person intone 'Om' until they have no more breath, take an in-breath and begin again with any note you wish, harmonizing with each other so that the sound becomes a continuous wave of harmony which should last for at least ten minutes as it swells and merges with power and sound. Being so

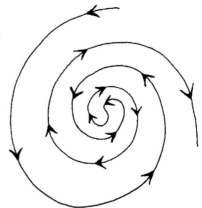

close to each other, the sound vibrates through each other's bodies until it gradually subsides. The 'Om' is a sacred word sound. The Celts called their moon-mother 'Omh' meaning 'She who is'. After this wondrous sound bath, take up each other's hands again and turn back on yourselves to come out of the spiral back into a circle again.

⊙Celebrate and salute the Sun. Switch off all the lights and bring in the Sun you have made, lit up with night-lights inside and hanging from a stick. Let each say whatever comes to them to honour the return of the Sun and its rebirth day. Give thanks for the positive active power, for assertiveness, determination, for our intellectual and rational thought. These qualities will bring independence and purpose to our lives. Through this dynamic expansive power, the seeds of our deepest longings can become manifest.

⊙Ask everyone to bring drums and percussion. Feel the sense of a tribal gathering as you drum and dance together. Release the old year. Release the restraints of Winter. Open your energy to possibilities unlimited and magical as you feel your emergence into the new active phase of the year.

⊙If possible, have a fire and a yule log of Oak. Use the log to focus what needs to be changed and purified by fire. Release old patterns. Leave behind what is no longer helpful to you. Put the log on the fire with ceremony and intent. Let each person call out what Fire will purify and change. Celebrate the release of energy that this brings by drumming and dancing. Let out any sounds, words, chants you need to express. Vocalise the power you feel. Support each other by echoing back the sounds, joining in with the chants. Celebrate and move forwards free of the restraints which were holding you back.

⊙Tell stories round the fire in an age-old tradition of shared vision and teaching. Choose the old legends and folk tales which reflect and help us understand the power of the Winter Solstice, of rebirth and transformation. Connect to the magical and the mystery which can spin us out of time, bring illumination and insight.

⊙ Poems can be read, mystery plays or dance-drama can be performed. Follow the Winter Solstice themes of returning light. Make the most use of subdued light, candle lanterns or torches with tissue paper lightly wrapped around the ends to disguise them.

⊙ Have a candlelit procession. If possible, walk out into the night. Enjoy the darkness and the lights of all the candles. Take a circular route to end at where you began as your path recreates the wheel of the year turning. These are magical moments which will be remembered for years to come.

⊙ Bless the food and drink everyone has brought to share. Be thankful for your abundance.

⊙ Book a good band to play. Party, dance, celebrate, interact with friends and family.

⊙ Circle dancing brings a gentle reconnecting energy at the end of the evening and brings the group together before leading into the closing ceremony.

⊙ The closing ceremony is an important focus bringing the group close together again. It renews and acknowledges the sacred as important in our lives. It is the moment to give thanks for each other, the moment, the forces that be, our Guardians and Spirit guides, the five elements, the energy they bring us, and the deep connections we have made. It will bring a celebration back full circle and invokes a sense of completeness - a powerful reconnection to take out with you into the world. An uplifting chant is always appropriate at the end, uniting the energy and providing a focus which can be rekindled during the coming weeks.

By the Earth which is her body
By the Air which is her breath
By the Fire which is her bright Spirit
By the Living Waters of her womb
The circle is open
and yet unbroken
Merry meet and merry part and merry meet again!

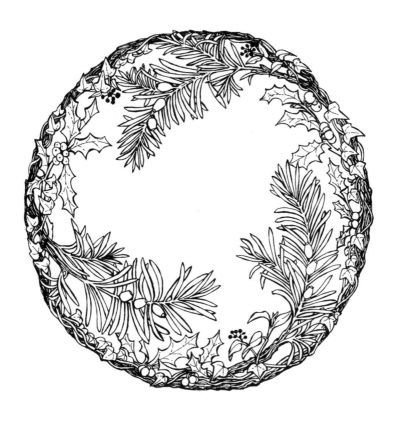

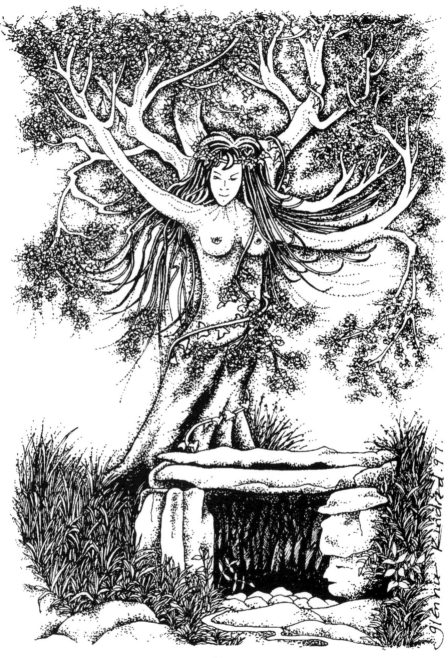

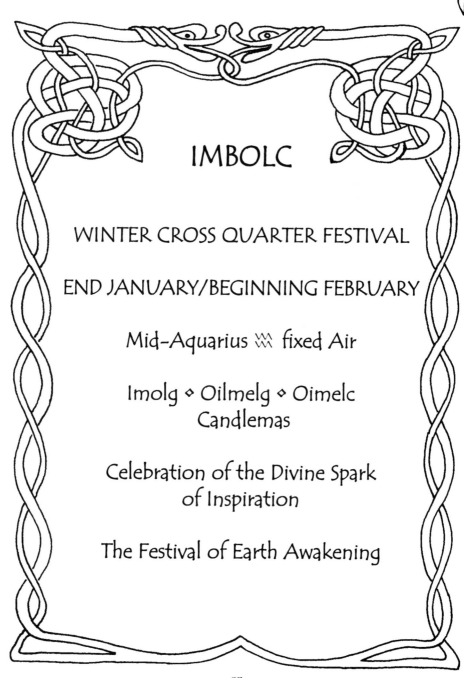

IMBOLC

WINTER CROSS QUARTER FESTIVAL

END JANUARY/BEGINNING FEBRUARY

Mid-Aquarius ♒ fixed Air

Imolg ⋄ Oilmelg ⋄ Oimelc
Candlemas

Celebration of the Divine Spark
of Inspiration

The Festival of Earth Awakening

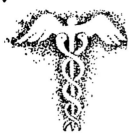

IMBOLC

This festival celebrates the reawakening Earth and the potential of manifestation inherent at this time. The Cross Quarter festivals are an opportunity for us to use the developing energy of a new season. Here it is important that we remember to use our intuitive unconscious energy, the inner wisdom we have gained during the Winter months, and bring it out with us into the active phase of the year. It is this union of the two aspects of ourselves which is the power and magical alchemy of Imbolc, bringing fertility and manifestation. Candles are lit at this time to represent the return of the light as the Sun's energy begins to increase. Candles also represent the divine spark of creativity which comes from within and the intuition from which new ideas become manifest.

In Celtic tradition, the Triple Goddess has become her virgin self again, known as Bride, Brigid, Brigit, the Maiden. Her attributes are intuition, inspiration, divination, keeper of the sacred Fire, the spark of life. Her life-giving waters are the sacred springs and holy wells of our land, and were honoured at this time. She is the preserver of tradition through poetry and song. In Celtic countries, poetry was understood as channelled ancestral memory. It was seen as sacred, as an aspect of clairvoyance, vision and divination. English, Welsh, Scottish and Irish mythology are rich with legends of the beguiling Spring Maiden who is called Olwen, Niwalen, Gwenhyver, Blodeuwedd, Brigid, who initiates the young king in a deeply spiritual sexual experience. Hidden in these tales of love and sexual initiation lies the secret alchemy of Imbolc. The power of the unconscious represented by the young female is the spark of intuition from within as it joins with the intellect of consciousness (represented by the young Sun King). It is this union of these two aspects of energy which brings about manifestation and growth on all levels.

Other ancient myths reflect the same process in action. Persephone returns from the Underworld (the inner world) as herself made new, the young Spring Maiden. Before this, she sits in her cave and spins a web of a great picture of the universe which 'the Mother makes into reality'. Northern Europeans worshipped the Great Goddess Freya, the virgin aspect of the Triple Goddess who, in Nordic myth, are the Three Fates who stood at the foot of Odin's tree of sacrifice. The constellation of Orion was called the distaff of Mary, but previously it was called the distaff of Freya who spun the fates of men (humankind). Freya represents sexual love, her alternative name 'Frigg' became slang for sexual intercourse. Clotho in Greek myth was known as the fate virgin, the fate spinner, the first of the Moerae (later called Mary) who spun the thread of destiny. Roman Pagans worshipped Juno Februata, the Goddess of the fever (febris) of love, later replaced with St Valentine by the Church. Athene, Isis, Minerva, Diana, Aphrodite - are all similar versions of this aspect of energy.

The early image of the Virgin was very different from what we now imagine. She was seen as being full of her inherent ability to be fertile. She was honoured for her vibrant sexuality. In pre-Christian Rome, the 'Virgines' were unmarried women. They combined a natural abundant sexuality with the potential of motherhood and procreation. These free young women must have presented as much a threat to the new patriarchal Church as the old matriarchs. A marriage system was introduced which harnessed women's natural nurturing caring instincts to serve men. Her sexuality became feared by the Church and by men for its potential power over them. Virgin became synonymous with purity.

The worship of the Goddess was channelled by the Church into the worship of the Virgin Mary. It is interesting that virginity is the most emphasised aspect of her, not her motherhood, even though it was wildly inexplicable. They were well aware that the Goddess worship they sought to suppress could re-establish itself through the worship of Mary, so they had to diffuse and debase her power and the power of the female. Mary became passive, meek, subordinate, without sexuality, successfully removing her previous attributes. This complex reversal of women's natural instincts, as a method of control by the Church has, of course, had the most dramatic and far-reaching psychological and sociological effects throughout the Christianized patriarchal world. Inner reflection, the unconscious, the intuition, receptivity, the inner voice – all became synonymous with everything female and was also denied, suppressed and feared. This has meant that men as well as women have been cut off from this vital aspect of themselves.

The Church incorporated this festival into their religion as Candlemas, celebrated on the 2nd February. Candlemas is known as the festival of the purification of the Virgin Mary, a time which, according to Judeo-Christian rule, a woman must be purified forty days after childbirth as she had been made

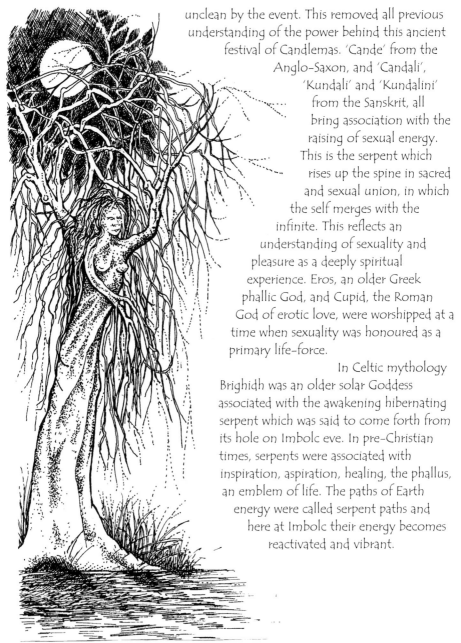

unclean by the event. This removed all previous understanding of the power behind this ancient festival of Candlemas. 'Cande' from the Anglo-Saxon, and 'Candali', 'Kundali' and 'Kundalini' from the Sanskrit, all bring association with the raising of sexual energy. This is the serpent which rises up the spine in sacred and sexual union, in which the self merges with the infinite. This reflects an understanding of sexuality and pleasure as a deeply spiritual experience. Eros, an older Greek phallic God, and Cupid, the Roman God of erotic love, were worshipped at a time when sexuality was honoured as a primary life-force.

In Celtic mythology Brighidh was an older solar Goddess associated with the awakening hibernating serpent which was said to come forth from its hole on Imbolc eve. In pre-Christian times, serpents were associated with inspiration, aspiration, healing, the phallus, an emblem of life. The paths of Earth energy were called serpent paths and here at Imbolc their energy becomes reactivated and vibrant.

THE UNDERLYING ENERGY OF IMBOLC

The days are beginning to lengthen. It is still cold but buds are forming on the trees. Sap is beginning to rise and the bulbs are pushing through the Earth. Everywhere there are signs of the Earth stirring. Dryads and nature spirits are waking up now. The serpent life-force is ready to be reborn. Our acceptance of Winter is giving way to an urge to move forwards into Springtime energy. Now is the time to prepare inwardly for the changes which will come. Plant your ideas and leave them to germinate. Bring forth your visions and inner understandings through poetry, song and art. Divination and clairvoyance are potent now as the link with the dark inner realms is strong.

At Lammas, opposite Imbolc on the wheel of the year, consciousness began its descent into the inner realms and the dark, to find inner wisdom and regeneration. Here at Imbolc the unconscious is emerging from the inner realms, revitalised, potent and fertile. The unconscious and the conscious join and unite to bring about growth, fertility and manifestation.

Imbolc is the time for initiation and healing, for reclaiming what has been forgotten. It is a time for invocation of the life-force and working with the dynamics of its potency. The intuitive flashes, the sparks of inspiration are needed more than ever to complement the active rational approach which dominates our western life-style. The returning active phase of the solar year brings with it an opportunity to use the Fire from within, to combine the dynamic inner power with the dynamic expansive energy of the year's cycle.

We are trying in our own way to live the dreams and visions of a New Age, but we are still connected to the old ways. We each carry the seeds of a new vision, a new way of being. Each time these visions re-emerge after the incubation period of Winter, they are stronger and we are surer.

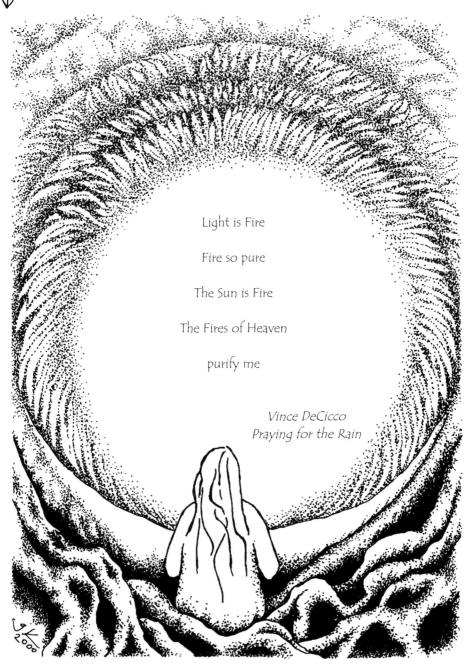

Light is Fire

Fire so pure

The Sun is Fire

The Fires of Heaven

purify me

Vince DeCicco
Praying for the Rain

PREPARATIONS
FOR IMBOLC

CLEARING OUT THE OLD ◇
WELLS ◇ DIVINATION ◇ POETRY ◇ ART ◇ CANDLES ◇
BRIGID'S CROSS ◇ SERPENTS ◇ SNAKE STICKS ◇ GARDEN PROJECTS ◇
FREYA ◇ ST VALENTINE ◇
PERSONAL SHIELD–MAKING ◇
HERBS: COLTSFOOT ◇ GINGER ROOT
TREES: ROWAN ◇ WILLOW

◊ Decide where and when to celebrate Imbolc. The new Moon would enhance the energy of new beginnings. Plan an evening celebration and invite friends. Ask them to bring wool and special things to make Brigid's crosses, their poems to read, or pictures to share, candles, something for the shrine and food and drink to share.

◊ Look for ways to express Imbolc. White and yellow hangings, muslin or scarves, spring flowers, bulbs in pots, twigs in bud. Make night-light lanterns using a willow frame which is covered with coloured tissue paper and coated with watered-down PVA glue spread very thinly. Weave a place to hold a jam jar for the night-light, leaving a gap to get new ones in and out.

◊ Buy plenty of candles for lighting and some special ones for ritual, invocation and wishes.

◊ Look for any local old wells and sacred springs. They were previously honoured at this time as the lifeblood of the land and worshipped as the source of our wellbeing. Hellywells and Hels wells as they were known, were associated with the Goddess Hellenes, but later they became known as Holy wells. Many became connected to the Church and many fell into disuse and were forgotten. If you find a well site, tend and care for it. Plant Spring bulbs around it. Bury crystals, invoke your commitment to working with the Earth and restoring love and respect to our Earth which has been so thoughtlessly abused. Bless and give thanks for pure Water.

Create a shrine to Imbolc. Bring back something from your walks. Establish the five elements by representing each one on the shrine. Pick a vase of early Spring flowers, budded twigs or bulbs in flowerpots - anything which suggests the awakening Earth. Light a candle at the centre, as you focus on your inspirations, aspirations, dreams and visions.

Clear out the old and make way for the new. Clear and clean your space. Give away unwanted possessions along with their associations. Wash all your crystals and leave them out in the sunlight or moonlight to recharge. Re-examine the resolutions you made at the Winter Solstice. Seek clarity and wisdom to help you find your way.

Make time for meditation, writing poetry, drawing and painting. Create simple new chants and new tunes. Pick up an instrument, even if you think you can't play. Begin simply with three or four repetitive notes and see what words come to you.

There is still time to plant new trees and bushes and to create magical areas in your garden. Plant a Willow archway at the bottom of your garden by cutting Willow twigs and planting them straight into the ground. Within a few weeks they will be growing and can eventually be trained and twisted to form a Willow archway or a seating area, a place to sit and contemplate. Interweave with honeysucke, clematis or winter-flowering jasmine. Plant herb seeds indoors now so that you have lots of herbs to plant out when the time comes.

Find ways to celebrate and revive women's arts and crafts such as needlework, weaving, beadwork, macramé. Get together and work on a group project such as making a large quilt which can be hung and displayed. Decide on a theme and decide the size of the square everyone must use. Get the children involved and the men, and create something of great inspiration. The squares can be sewn together and backed. Loops can be sewn onto the top enabling the whole thing to be hung from a pole.

◊ Brigid's Cross

Traditionally made to hang on the door or in windows at Imbolc (similar to God's eyes). Traditionally woven out of grass, straw, rushes or vines. If you are using dried materials, soak them in hot water first to restore their flexibility. You can also use wool. Natural woven wools are the most interesting, but children like to use bright colours.

1

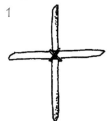

2

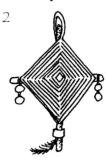

1. Begin by binding two sticks together which are of equal length as in fig (i). Silver Birch sticks, Willow, or Rowan would all be appropriate wood for the symbolism and significance they represent.

2. Tie on the first piece of wool, straw etc., wind it over the first twig, wrapping it round the twig once before moving on to the next twig. Wind it over and round this twig in the same way. Continue round and round in the same pattern, tucking in the ends. These beautiful weavings represent the all-seeing eye of Brigid, to watch over you through the coming year. Shells, beads, tassles or feathers can be hung from it or woven in as you go round. You may try tying three or four sticks together to make them more elaborate and experimental. Old crosses from last year should be ritually burnt to release the old year and open the way to moving forwards.

◊ Snake sticks

Another relaxing and focusing activity which can be done alone, with children or a group of friends, is to paint snake sticks, serpent sticks or dragon sticks. Driftwood is particularly good but any dried stick will do. Check first that it is strong and will not break easily. Chip off any bark which may be left on, and sandpaper if necessary. You may like to whittle a simple face at one end and the 'tail' at the other end. Paint it with acrylic paint to represent a snake, serpent or dragon. As you work with this ancient image, unravel what you know and understand about it. True to its own nature, it has many layers and levels of energy. Its early pre-Christian meaning of health, healing and potent energy has become obscured and reversed in our minds. Share with each other what you know, think, understand. Share any experiences you may have had working with this symbol of power.

∮ Plan a new outdoor project on your land or in your garden, if you have one. If not, plan a window-ledge project or something to grow outside your door. Let your imagination run wild. Plan to create something unique and inspirational. One big plant pot can become a mini-world with rocks, crystals and wood placed amongst miniature alpine and dwarf varieties of plants. Solar fountains (with a backup system for dull days or nightime) can be used to create a very special place, with a seat nearby planted with sweet-smelling herbs. Represent each of the five elements with appropriate plants, colours and atmosphere. The list is endless. An outdoor project will bring you connection to the Earth both in the doing and the end result, satisfying many aspects and levels of your being.

∮ Write poetry, indulging in your imagination, releasing your hidden or pent-up feelings. Let it all pour out. It doesn't have to be 'polished' or 'finished'. You don't have to show it to anyone or even keep it. Just do it for yourself; see what comes out. If you like it or like some of it, share what you want to with friends, write it in a special book. Above all, you will find understanding and your own wisdom hidden within it. From your unconscious many things will be revealed to help your understanding of yourself. Bringing things out from the unconscious is the special energy of Imbolc and may help you to find your way forward.

∮ Herbs of Imbolc

Coltsfoot - *tussilago farfara*

In February the coltsfoot flowers appear before the large leaves which can be used throughout the Summer. 'Lago' in Latin means 'I carry' (away) and holds a clue to its inherent energy of moving emotional and physical stagnation. It is a primary lung remedy, expelling phlegm from the lungs and easing irritating coughs. It will also help expel tar, dust and other pollutants from the lungs and has unique properties as a herbal tobacco which can be safely smoked (previously the main component of 'country tobacco'). The flowers and leaves can be made into herbal tea. Pour 1 pint of boiling water onto ½-1 ounce of the dried herb, cover and leave for ten minutes. Drink a wineglassful three times a day. Keep in the fridge and drink cold or gently re-heat, but do not boil. Add honey. Drink to relieve any lung congestion, coughs, asthma, drink after walking or cycling in traffic. Drink or burn as an incense, to clear the psychic channels for clairvoyance, visions and inner clarity.

Ginger root - *zingiber officinale*

A good herb for this time of year as it will help revitalise and stimulate the Fire within (ginger has long been associated with dragons). Use where the cold and damp of Winter has caused problems such as head colds, catarrh, poor circulation, chilblains, digestive sluggishness, menstrual cramps, and for people who continually feel the cold. Use whenever you need to increase Fire in the body and get things moving.

      Boil 2 ounces (50gs) of ginger root with 1 pint or ½ a litre of water and the thinly peeled rind of a lemon for ½ an hour or so. Strain and, when cold, keep in the fridge. Add a tablespoon of this liquid to a cup of hot water and sweeten with honey. Drink as needed. (**Warning: Do not use if there is high blood pressure, stomach ulcers or inflammatory bowel conditions, as it will aggravate them.**)

◊ Trees of Imbolc

Rowan - *sorbus aucuparia*

Rowan is the second tree of the Celtic Tree Ogham - L. LUIS. It has long associations with the Maiden aspect of the Triple Goddess, is ruled by Mercury, the principle of communication between the worlds and is also associated with serpents. Rowan is also known as Quickbeam or the Quickening tree. It will help 'quicken' your psychic abilities and connections. It has a beneficial protective energy which will help increase your abilities to receive visions and insights and will help increase communication with the spirit realms.

      Spending time with the Rowan will strengthen your positive life force energy so that your personal power is so strong, it can withstand any negative influences. This is why in the past it was used for protection and to ward off evil. Sprays of leaves were hung in doorways, worn in the hat, carried as a talisman.

      Rowan is linked to the Norse word 'runa' and Sanskrit 'runa' meaning magician. Rune staves, the sticks on which runes or the Ogham symbols were inscribed, were traditionally made of Rowan wood. A Rowan wand will enhance clairvoyance, bringing greater clarity in interpreting the messages we may receive. A Rowan walking stick is particularly potent and is good for night walking.

Plant a Rowan tree near your house or by your gate. This small beautiful tree is ideal in a garden. It has starry white flowers in the Spring, sparce light foliage in the Summer, and the leaves turn bright red and orange in the Autumn along with abundant clusters of bright red berries which attract the birds. The berries can be used for sore throats and hoarseness and as a mild laxative. They can also be made into a jelly (jam) by mixing them with crab apples and also wine.

To make a Rowan wand or walking stick, you will need to spend time with the tree first and ask the tree before cutting. Respect the tree at all times. Thank the tree for its gift. Take the bark off as soon as possible, if you want to get down to the wood. Leave the wood to dry out for a while a few days inside, a week or two outside. After it has dried out, carve it and sand it using a rough sandpaper first, then medium, then fine. It is a beautiful wood to carve. Lastly, oil it to preserve the wood. Teak oil will darken it slightly, but not as much as linseed oil.

Willow - *salix alba/salix nigra*

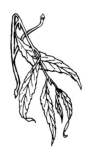

This is the fourth tree in the Celtic Tree Ogham - S. SAILLE, also long associated with the Maid aspect of the Triple Goddess. The word saille became anglicised from the Latin 'salire' - to leap, and old French 'saille' meaning to rush out suddenly. This became 'sally' meaning a sudden outburst of emotions, action or expression, as in 'sally forth'. Known in Celtic myth and folklore as a tree of enchantment and dreaming, it was associated with poets, the Moon and Water. It greatly enhances confidence to follow your intuition and inspired leaps of the imagination; it puts you in touch with your feelings and deeply-buried emotions. The Willow helps us express these, letting them out and owning them. The twigs of the Willow are flexible, teaching us to move with life rather than resist what we are feeling.

The Willow's essential energy is this power to help things move from the emotional unconscious level to the surface, conscious level. Whether you are over-stimulated by your feelings or cut off from them, spending time with a Willow tree will help heal the imbalance. Taking the flower essence will help in the same way. It has long been used as a symbol of grief and those who have been forsaken in love. Deserted lovers would wear 'the green Willow' to share their heartache with others. Our deep unconscious thoughts speak to us through our dreams. Sleep with a Willow wand under your pillow and your dreams will become more vivid and meaningful.

Willow whips are used for binding magical and sacred objects. The Willow will always enhance inspired leaps of the imagination, and is recommended to be used when seeking to assimilate ancient teaching or any inspired teaching.

◊ Freya

A Great Goddess of Northern Europe who represented sexual erotic love. Her sacred day was Friday and considered to be the best day for weddings. The Romans re-named this day 'dies Veneris' after Venus, their own version of this Goddess. In pre-christian times, Friday was a holy day dedicated to Freya. Fish were eaten as symbols of fertility. Later, of course, Friday was called 'unlucky' and doubly unlucky if it fell on the 13th as it combined the Goddess' sacred number (the number of lunar months in a year) and her sacred day.

◊ St Valentine

February has long associations with sexuality and love. Juno Februata, the Roman Goddess of love, gave her name to the month, and the festival of Lupercalia on the ides of February included a tradition of exchanging small papers or 'billets' on which partners were chosen for erotic games. These forerunners of our valentine cards were discouraged by the Church who tried to replace them with short sermons. But the love notes survived, although changed from their original meaning. The Church replaced Juno Februata with St Valentine, a mythical martyr who was said to be executed at the very moment he received his billet of love from his sweetheart. Despite all efforts of the Church, this festival remains dedicated to lovers. Eros, Cupid, Kama, Priapus and Pan are all Gods of erotic love from pre-christian times when sexuality as a primary life-force was worshipped. Renaissance art depicted Cupid as a small winged baby, but ancient talismans of Cupid were winged phalli made in bronze, bone and wood. Cupid was the son of Venus and Mercury, the Goddess of Love and the God of communication between the worlds and serpent energy (in Greek myth Aphrodite and Hermes). Their child Eros, God of erotic love, was an herm-aphrodite, combining opposite qualities in sexual union.

◊ Personal Shield Making

Make a personal shield to hang in your sacred space. The Celts would have used their shields to identify themselves through symbol. It is an outer manifestation of the inner spiritual warrior, and the making of a shield brings the inner and outer person into a balanced whole. It is also a way of connecting to the rich heritage of symbolism which has been handed down to us through the ages from the Pictish symbol stones, animal and bird totems, symbols of power, balance and energy, symbols of healing and clan affinity.

1. Begin by making a hoop from a freshly cut straight Hazel rod. Bind the two ends together with strong garden twine or leather, and leave to dry out for a week or two so that the wood can shrink. You may add strength to the frame by binding on a cross of Hazel (1).

2. Traditionally the hoop would have been covered in a piece of hide, but good strong cotton, sailcloth or calico is more practical for most people. Make holes around the edge at regular intervals and thread a length of twine or leather thong through them. This pulls the material or hide tightly round the frame. Knot firmly (2).

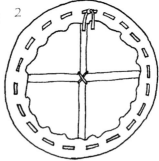

3. An alternative method is to use strong twine or leather to lash in the central material. Material needs to be turned in and sewn to make the edge strong (3).

Don't worry about making a perfect circle. It is the process which is important and your technique will improve with practice.

4. You may need to have several meditation sessions before you are clear what images you wish to depict, or you may already be clear about it. Make some drawings on paper and then decide on your background colour. Paint the material with emulsion or acrylic paint. This stiffens it up a bit and provides a good base on which to paint your design. Acrylics are permanent and waterproof. If you are using a piece of hide, paint directly onto the hide. Create a power song as you work, breathe life into your ceremonial power shield.

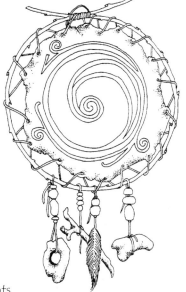

5. Alternatively, sew your design on, using different materials (appliqué) or buy a circular embroidery frame, and using a free style stitch, embroider the images and colours you want to depict. This can then be put into a Hazel hoop by either of the above methods.

◊ Explore and research serpents and dragons. Two serpents entwined around a central rod is an ancient pre-christian symbol representing physical and spiritual health, as in the Greek caduceus. We understand the double spiral to represent the genetic double helix, the DNA. The serpent was seen as an emblem of the life-force, intrinsically linked to the power of sexuality, the phallus and inner wisdom.

◊ Begin a Moon diary. Working with the cycles of the Moon brings a deeper understanding of the duality of light (waxing Moon) and dark (waning Moon). The Moon puts us in touch with our emotional receptivity and unconscious selves. This will help balance our solar rational minds. Receptivity is a state of attentive listening, focusing inward rather than giving out. It means being tuned in to yourself, ready to receive inner knowledge or inspiration from within.

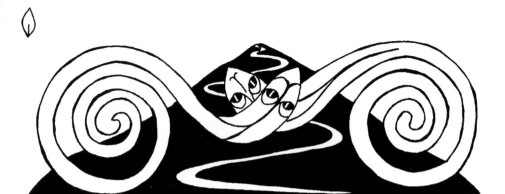

IMBOLC CELEBRATIONS

◊ Spend time outside, feeling the emergence of the life-force.
Talk to the trees, welcome the awakening Dryads and nature spirits. Pick some
snowdrops and other early Spring flowers for your Imbolc shrine. Cut some twigs of
Willow, forsythia, winter jasmine, almond and cherry blossom. Weave them into a circle
the same as you did with the Winter Solstice wreath, but this time place it in a wide
shallow bowl of water. Keep the water topped up, and during the next few weeks the
twigs will begin to root and the leaves and blossom will come out. Place moss, a stone
or a crystal in the centre of the circle and leave on a window ledge. Arrange any twigs
left over into a vase of water. If gathering with friends, this could be something you
make together at the beginning or the end of the celebration.

◊ Place on the shrine any methods of divination you may wish to
use, such as Ogham sticks, Tarot cards, Runes, I Ching. Now is a good time to use any of
these systems to help you see the way forward.

◊ Burn dried coltsfoot as an incense, or drink as a tea to help
focus and clear channels so that messages, intuition and clairvoyance can come through.

◊ Make time for visioning. Candle-gazing, scrying (gazing into a
flat dish of water, especially good in the moonlight), staring into mandalas (circular
patterns radiating from a central point), or fixing your gaze on Celtic knotwork
patterns, are all aids to allowing the intuitive process to unfold. Staring into nothingness
and daydreaming are very good for you and can open the doorway to receiving
messages from the Otherworld and our Spirit helpers and guides. Sit with trees and
'receive' impressions from them. 'Read' the patterns in the clouds, see pictures in the fire.

Use this relaxed state of mind for making inspired drawings.

◊ Gather with friends or put aside a special day and evening to spend by yourself. Celebrate and honour your inner intuitive reflective qualities. Follow your intuition and inner voice, understanding that your spiritual path embraces both the dark and the light, the unconscious and the conscious. Let your rational mind go, follow what you 'feel' is right and not what you 'think' or 'ought' or 'should'.

◊ It is good to have a fire outside if the weather is fine. Failing that, find creative ways to light your celebration space with candles to celebrate the return of the light and the kindling of the inner Fire. Symbolically cleanse and purify by Fire what you wish to clear away and leave behind. You could write this down on a piece of paper to burn in the flame, or visualize it and give it to the fire symbolically, or vocalise it, saying "I leave behind..."

◊ Burn dried sage and use the smoke to cleanse each other's aura or spirit body which exists around the physical one. This is a Native American tradition, but it has become very popular in ceremonies here. Waft the smoke with a large feather or bird's wing, if you have one.

◊ In the light of Imbolc, invoke the five elements as an opening ceremony. Gather the group together in a circle. If you are on your own, sit or stand inside the circle created by the four directions.

Earth in the North

A powerful surge of new growth is now stirring in the depths of the Earth. The life-force is now potent again. The serpent awakes. Seeds germinate. Plant the seeds of future actions and manifestations. Welcome the nature spirits waking from their long Winter sleep. Welcome all of Nature as it begins to stir. Thank the dark for its nurturing regenerative qualities. Honour the part this still has to play.

Air in the East

Celebrate the intuition, inspiration, the unconscious, clairvoyance, messages from dreams and the Spirit realms. Value your transformative visions and act upon them. The spiralling of light energy from the dark creates new beginnings, new ideas, new directions.

Fire in the South

Thank Fire as it emerges now. Light the inner Fire. Rebirth the Spirit into the conscious realms and notice the upsurge in personal energy this brings. This is the spark of the life-force, the spark of sexuality. Fire dragons and serpents awake. This is the time to manifest your visions, a time of initiation, expansion, transformation, creativity and dynamic expressive power. Release!

Water in the West

Give Thanks for the Water of Life. May our actions be guided by the reflective, feeling, nurturing side of ourselves - the path of the heart where we follow our dreams and deepest wishes. Imagination is the spark of creativity from within. Love is the great healer and guiding star.

Spirit

Within and without and ever present. We give thanks for this vital connection to this essential part of ourselves which cannot be seen and cannot be named. We reach out and in, connecting to our Source and the guidance from within. We touch the sacred, the still point of power at the centre of our being. Through it we are a part of all life and all existence on this Earth. Past, present and future are linked in a timeless connection and sacred truth.

⟡ Spend time in meditation. Reach out and feel the stirrings of the Earth and oneness with the germinating seeds deep within the still cold ground. Ask for guidance to help you move forwards, and for directions which will serve your greater good and the healing of the Earth. Meditate on your reflective intuitive qualities and how you can use them and enhance them in your life. Meditate on your sexuality and ask for guidance and direction.

⟡ If you have gathered with friends, make a circle, holding hands together and focusing inwards. Bring that energy outwards by singing a chant, building an energy matrix which flows through you all. Sing the chant for ten minutes at least, giving the power a chance to build, reach its peak and subside.

⟡ Pass around seeds or crystals and each imagine what you wish to grow, what you wish to bring forth from within. Later plant the seeds or bury the crystals.

◊ Walk a serpent path together. Lead the circle into a tight spiral and imagine yourselves to be the Earth dragon or Earth serpent asleep, curled up tight for the Winter. Gradually feel yourself waking up as part of the energy of the re-awakening Earth.

◊ Each light a candle for the positive qualities you value about yourself. Share these with each other and how you hope to use these in the coming active phase of the year's cycle. Plant the candles in a large bowl of earth in the centre of the circle and let them burn right down. Use the soil for any growth rituals you have in the future.

◊ Light a candle for those you love and their positive qualities you value. Light candles for healing, for friends, family and yourself. Light candles for the Earth. Light a candle to celebrate the activation of the inner Fire, for the Fire of inspiration, for illumination, for the spark of sexuality and attraction.

◊ Symbolically clear away the dross and dormancy of Winter. Cleanse and purify what you wish to leave behind by giving them to the flames to transform.

◊ Make a pledge to honour and listen to your intuition, your inner voice, your inner wisdom. These inner qualities are vital links to our spirituality and understanding of ourselves. Doubt destroys your intuition. Don't let it! Now we can be released from the fear, the superstitions, the propaganda which controlled our emotions, inner consciousness and spiritual wellbeing. The beginning of this new journey of discovery and joy lies here with this pledge. Choose from a bowl of small quartz crystals, open your inner self and embrace your pledge.

◊ Many folk dances still follow the retrograde motion of the Moon (widdershins) instead of the clockwise motion of the Sun. The Church reversed the directions of all circular walks, ie. around boundaries and wells, as well as charms. Explore the energy inherent within Sun-wise or Moon-wise rituals.

◊ Chanting enhances power, energises the body and stills the mind. Incantation is a means of gathering energy from within. Enchant comes from 'incantre' – to sing over, and women's singing was particularly feared for its power to charm. Explore ways to use your voice and simple chants to energise and focus your intent. The use of chanting in ritual helps to bring altered states of mind, releasing the mind from the confines of conscious reality, opening the way into and out of the inner realms. The chant should consist of a short memorable phrase. It is better if it is no more than two or three lines long. It is repeated over and over again until the energy and power have built up and shifted on to another level of consciousness. Bring in harmonies, experiment, be creative with it.

◊ To banish Winter and welcome Spring, ritually burn the evergreens which were brought into the house for Winter Solstice. Scatter the ashes under fruit trees.

◊ Symbolically plant ideas, seeds of ourselves which we wish to germinate and see grow. Share these with each other.

◊ Plant seeds to grow on windowsills which can then be part of future celebrations. If you are celebrating with a group, ask everyone to bring one packet of seeds each and then share them.

◊ Imbolc is a time for any initiation ritual or rite of passage. It should have a three-fold nature. The first is separation from the old. The second is transition, and the third is integration into the new.

◊ Imbolc is a time for transformation and change. We can move on from old outworn ideas and attitudes and reintegrate into new patterns and ways of being which will serve us better.

◊ Share with each other the poems, chants, music and songs you have been creating. Inspire each other with your visions and creativity. Share with each other your accomplishments of all kinds, celebrating the re-emergence of the self as you step out into the active phase of the year.

◊ Sit together and make Brigid crosses or wands of Willow or Rowan. A Willow wand can be put under your pillow to enhance your dreams. Rowan will enhance divination and clairvoyance. Both will help you make a connection to your intuition and unconscious. The twigs should be cut with the blessing of the tree at least a week before you need them, to give them a chance to dry out a bit. Peel off the bark, shape the ends, carve if you wish, and then sandpaper, beginning with rough, then medium, then fine.

◊ Pass a Willow basket of emotions around the circle. Honour your feelings. Write on paper, stone or wood and place in the basket.

◊ Weave circles of fresh Willow whips to wear on your head, to signify and amplify being in touch with your emotions. Look for ways to help yourself deal with your feelings and emotions. How can you bring them out in positive expressive ways? Share these thoughts with each other. Drinking sage tea will help release stagnant emotions. Sage works on the throat and will help to release emotion through the use of sound. Let out how you feel. Let it all out and express yourself. Vocalise!

◊ Dance together in a circle or on your own. Weave a circle of energy, a circle of change and transformation. Weave into the dance everything you wish to change, what you want to begin, and how you can connect more fully to your intuition. Weave new dreams to take hold and grow. This is the spark of power which initiates their becoming. Dance to celebrate being free of Winter. Dance to be free of old outworn restrictions. Release words of invocation for a new direction. Dance to activate the Fire within. Dance to release negative attachments. Dance to let go of the old and embrace the new. Dance your dreams awake!

◊ Bring the group together for a closing ceremony by holding hands in a circle. If you are on your own, come to the centre of your circle. Thank the Guardians, Angels and Spirit guides, for their presence and help. Thank the Elements for their guidance and thank each other. End on a chant which carries forward the energy of Imbolc in everyone's heart - something to take with you into daily life, to remind and connect you to the sacred in yourself.

◊ Bless the food and drink to share.

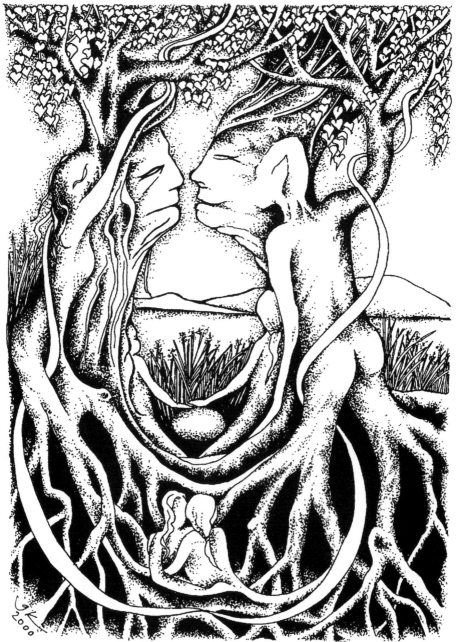

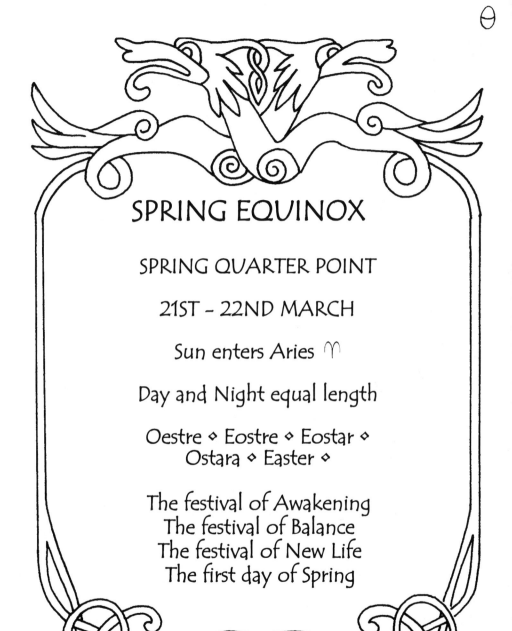

SPRING EQUINOX

SPRING QUARTER POINT

21ST - 22ND MARCH

Sun enters Aries ♈

Day and Night equal length

Oestre ⋄ Eostre ⋄ Eostar ⋄
Ostara ⋄ Easter ⋄

The festival of Awakening
The festival of Balance
The festival of New Life
The first day of Spring

SPRING EQUINOX

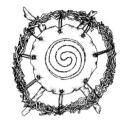

Day and night are of equal length all over the world. In the Northern Hemisphere we still celebrate it as the first day of Spring. The days are getting longer and warmer now, and the nights shorter. This is the festival of balance: the balance of light and dark, the balance of the Sun's active energy in the day and the Moon's receptive energy at night, the balance of the inner world and the outer world, the balance of the conscious Fire energy with the forces of the watery unconscious. Here at the Equinox, we can look at and work towards this balance within ourselves. This will bring change and healing as we move forwards into new understanding and new actions.

The Celts understood that the physical, mental and spiritual levels were so interlocked and perfectly balanced, that whatever is done on one level will inevitably affect the other two. Every action has a reaction. Your spiritual understanding constantly affects your decisions in your everyday life. Your mind affects your Spirit, your health and what you attract into your life. Here at Equinox, make time to understand this balanced flow of energy we are part of.

The Spring Equinox is often represented by the beguiling Spring Maiden with a Willow basket of eggs. The female is represented because from her new life comes. The egg symbolises the rebirth of nature, the fertility of the Earth, creation. The cosmic egg contains male and female, light and dark, expansion and contraction, conscious and unconscious, continuity and balance. The egg is potential life, full of promise. The plans which have been incubating on the inner levels since the Autumn, can now hatch out onto the physical plane. Both the Spring and the Autumn Equinoxes have a long history of dragons. Here at the Spring Equinox the dragon energy both within ourselves and the Earth is waking up.

Oestre, the Goddess of Light, brings fertility with the Spring. This is the root of the word 'oestrus', the time in an animal's sexual cycle when it is fertile, and oestrogen is the hormone stimulating ovulation. The Church overlaid this festival with Easter and its theme of rebirth and resurrection from death. Its timing is based on the old lunar calendar: the first Sunday after the first full Moon after the Spring Equinox, formerly the pregnant phase of Oestre passing into the fertile season.

The Pagan tradition celebrates the union of the Spring Maiden with the young ardent male. Their union makes all of nature fertile. The sexually potent young woman of the Spring Equinox is balanced with the sexually potent young man. Here we can make contact with their archetypal energy within ourselves. The sexually beguiling Spring Maiden is a ready image for us to understand but it may deny her potential power by focusing on her physical beauty alone. In the West many women are breaking free of the restraints of the sexuality which has been imposed on them from the past. They are balancing their male and female sides within themselves and looking for the same balance in men. The ardent young man who is non-aggressive, in touch with his instincts and can show his feelings, is a precious image to hold. The Greeks gave us Pan with horns and hooves. The Celts gave us Cernunnos or Herne, also with horns, in touch with his animal instincts, wise, magical, the master of the three levels of existence, playful, sexual, sensuous, spiritual. He was outlawed by the Church who changed him into the Devil, the root of evil, thereby denying men an essential part of themselves. We need to reclaim him. Men need to connect to his life-giving instinctive nature. Women need to find him in the men they know. Here lies the spark, the power of their potential.

Beyond this, we need to balance these energies within ourselves regardless of gender. It is the energy and power of the rational conscious mind when joined with the energy and power of the intuition and inner wisdom, which brings fertility and manifestation. This is the union which brings forth new life on many levels.

As we step into the active phase of the year, remember to balance the rational logical mind with instinct and intuition. We have laid such importance on our logical minds, that we have become used to ignoring our intuition. Learn to listen, to trust, and to act on your inner wisdom and bring your whole self back into balance.

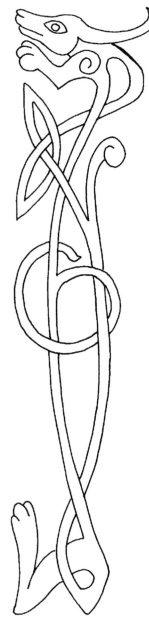

THE UNDERLYING ENERGY OF THE SPRING EQUINOX

Everything in nature is coming alive and awakening. The Sun is gaining strength, the days are longer and warmer. Blossom and catkins are on the trees, buds are bursting, seeds are germinating, Spring flowers appear, eggs are hatching and all the animals are preparing to have their young. Everywhere is evidence of life's ability to regenerate.

The energy is turning from the dark depths of Winter and the inner world, to an outward manifestation of the conscious world. It is time to throw off the restraints of Winter and the cold, and reach out for what it is we want for ourselves and the world.

It is a time of rain and sunshine, the mingling of the elements of Fire and Water, Spring gales, high tides, feelings of wildness and chaos. Run wild in the wind and celebrate life's fertility. We are breaking out and moving forwards. We feel empowered to take risks, strike out on our own, make things happen. It is a time to begin new ventures, make plans, journey.

An egg can be balanced on its end today. The balancing of the Earth's energy is now blended: light with dark, conscious with unconscious, Fire with Water. Here is the union of power which brings fertility and manifestation. This is the spark of the life-force. This is the Dance of Life – interdependent complementary parts of one energy system which we can embrace on our journey to become whole.

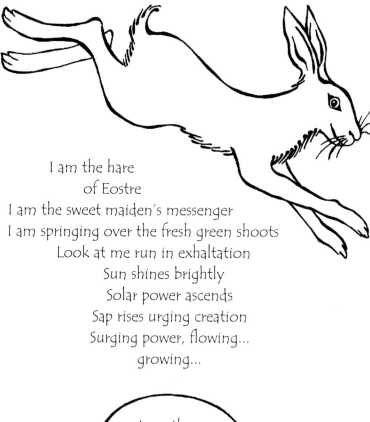

I am the hare
of Eostre
I am the sweet maiden's messenger
I am springing over the fresh green shoots
Look at me run in exhaltation
Sun shines brightly
Solar power ascends
Sap rises urging creation
Surging power, flowing...
growing...

I am the egg
Potent power
protected

Nicky Martin

PREPARATIONS FOR
SPRING EQUINOX

SPRING FLOWERS ◇ DECORATED EGGS ◇ MAKING FLAGS ◇
SYMBOLS OF BALANCE ◇ DRAGONS ◇
MAKING A DRAGON ◇ THINGS TO FLY IN THE WIND ◇
HERBS: NETTLE ◇ CLEAVERS ◇ HYSSOP
TREES: ASH AND ALDER

θ Decide whether to celebrate with friends or on your own
and where you might go which will enhance your connection to Earth energies - a
place where you can make contact with the newly awakened nature spirits,
commune with the trees and feel the pulse of the Earth as it hums with new life.

θ Create a shrine which reflects your spiritual and sacred
connection. It may be in a room or in the garden. Bring together things which will
help you focus on balance, awakening and new life. This is a very uplifting and
peaceful thing to do and will bring a sense of direction as you work. Perfectly in
harmony with the time, you actively bring out into the world what you are
connected to within. Sing while you create, and see what insights this may bring.
This could provide inspiration for a chant for your celebration and ceremony.

θ If you already have a shrine, then give everything a
spring clean and a change-around. Clear out your five elemental areas in the
garden. Re-plan, re-plant, activate the energy, manifest the new understandings
and insights you have gained during the Winter's incubation period.

θ Plant new seeds of herbs and flowers, especially
those which you can dry in the later months for ceremony,
medicine and cooking.

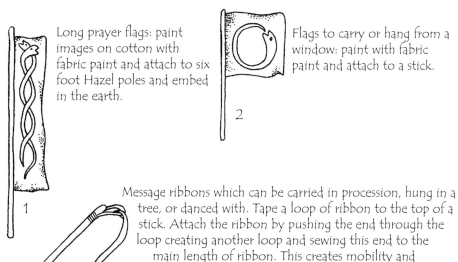

θ Decorate hen's eggs

Hardboiled eggs are easiest for young children. Paint them with acrylics or felt tip pens. Blown eggs can be hung in the window with Spring flowers, or as part of your Spring Equinox shrine. To blow an egg, simply make a hole with a pin at each end, and blow the contents out through the other. Blown eggs can be decorated by dipping them in coloured candlewax and scratching off a pattern, or by glueing straw, string or embroidery threads to them. Blown eggs can be hung up by tying a piece of string to half a matchstick, then sliding it into the hole at the top to wedge against the inside of the egg. Alternatively, tie a bead to a piece of thread and thread through the egg with a long needle so the bead is at the bottom.

There are many traditional folk designs to be found in countries all over Europe along with many customs concerning eggs at this time.

θ Flags

Make flags to fly in the wind, to carry your prayers and your wishes - flags of vision, flags to carry symbols and to invoke energy. There are many different shapes and ways to do this.

Long prayer flags: paint images on cotton with fabric paint and attach to six foot Hazel poles and embed in the earth.

Flags to carry or hang from a window: paint with fabric paint and attach to a stick.

2

1

Message ribbons which can be carried in procession, hung in a tree, or danced with. Tape a loop of ribbon to the top of a stick. Attach the ribbon by pushing the end through the loop creating another loop and sewing this end to the main length of ribbon. This creates mobility and facilitates using the ribbon for dancing and whirling around in the air.

3

θ Symbols of balance

Celtic Cross

This symbol is common to almost every shamanic tradition in the world and appears on stones throughout the Celtic lands. It represents the natural order: the two Equinoxes crossed by the two Solstices, the four seasons, the four directions and the five elements. The circumference represents the cycle of the year, Spirit, the circle of existence, and the still point of balance at its centre.

The Caduceus

This is the symbol of the medical profession and healing, the symbol of Hermes/Mercury. It symbolises the volatile and fixed principles: mercury and sulphur, male and female, light and dark.

Entwined serpent

Representing the balancing of the self and the awareness of the male and female energies which exist within each person.

The Spiral

Unfolding growth within and without, Spirit and Matter, Spirit into Matter and Matter into Spirit ascending and descending. At the centre is the place of perfect balance.

Triple Spiral or Triskelion

This represents the three circles of existence. The Triple Goddess. Spiritual, mental and physical. Past, present and future.

Six Pointed Star

Originating in Tantric Hinduism and adopted as a Judaic symbol. This represents the sexual union between male and female. The downward pointing triangle was the primordial female image, Yoni Yantra, existing before the universe was created. The upward pointing triangle was the male, the Lingam, and is called Fire (Vahni).

Yin and Yang
Chinese symbol of light and dark, male and female, Sun and Moon. Each of its equal sides contains the seed of the other.

A similar pattern found on standing stones and in Celtic design.

θ Dragons

Dragon Day was celebrated twice yearly at the Equinoxes. Dragon images were paraded through the streets and symbolically killed or staked in fertility and Earth-stimulating rituals and celebrations. Many processions had a St George whose name means 'tiller of the Earth'. He may, in fact, have been a geomancer rather than a dragon-slayer. St Michael was the Church's champion at destroying dragons which seems to be synonymous with destroying the old religion. Some dragon paths or paths of Earth energy can be traced by following St Michael's churches which were built on hilltops over sacred sites of the old religion.

The ancient trackways, the ridgeways, were said to be the backbone of the dragon. The ancient burial mounds were known as dragon hills and guarded by dragons. New research suggests that these mounds are built over areas of intense underground radiation. The energy of the dragon paths meander from side to side (sometimes called the Mary line as its path follows churches dedicated to St Mary, springs, wells, and other places associated with the female principle). But the straight line of the leyline or St Michael line seems to direct the energy from point to point across the landscape.

It is now beginning to be understood that in the past the dragon wasn't killed but staked, and that this may have been a form of Earth acupuncture such as is practised today by modern dowsers who can detect black radiation, black streams or black water. These are found directly above certain underground water-bearing fissures and badly affect the health of the people, animals and crops who live above them. Modern-day dowsers can redirect this harmful energy by 'staking' it with metal pipes. In light of this, the dragon paths or Earth energy is controlled and re-balanced in areas where it has become stuck or 'poisoned' (the noxious breath of the dragon), and the local hero sorted it out, sword (stake) in hand.

From Spring Equinox to St George's Day (23rd April, almost Beltain) many dragon rituals and processions took place. The fertile Earth energy is activated and runs strongly through the land, so Spring was given a good welcome in with music and dancing in the streets. It is said that Druids made a journey to the seashore to look for the red egg of the serpent which symbolised the entry of the seed or germ of life into the Earth.

θ Higher vital energy is sometimes called dragonfire. This comes from spiritual devotion and can be seen as a flame burning brightly from within. It has been found that the pineal gland, when stimulated by natural sunlight (not artificial light), will bring a natural enthusiasm akin to a spiritual connection. The more time you spend outside with nature, the more you consciously connect to your spiritual path, the more enthusiasm you will draw into your life.

θ Herbs of Spring Equinox

Nettle - *urtica dioica* and *urtica urens*

A famed Spring tonic, regular cups of nettle tea will tone up the whole system and cleanse the blood. Use the nettle tops in soup or as a vegetable (once cooked, it loses its sting). It is rich in iron. Nettle has a fiery energy so drink every day to break free of stagnant emotional states and to contact the warrior within. Make an infusion in the usual way.

Cleavers - *galium aparine*

Cleavers is a prime blood purifying herb and an important Spring tonic. It was added to beer in the Spring (probably because it tastes so bitter). Make an infusion with between ½ and 1 ounce (15-25g) of the dried herb to one pint (570ml) of water. (Two to three times more of the fresh herb is needed). Pour on boiling water and cover. Leave to infuse for ten minutes. Strain off the herb. I find that cleavers is best kept in the fridge and drank cold by the wine glass or add to beer in the old tradition.

Hyssop - *hyssopus officinalis*

Hyssop is a herb of purification previously used for cleansing temples and holy places. It can be used for washing all your special things on your shrine or sacred space. It has an association with dragons and serpents and the raising of the kundalini from the base of the spine.

It will help balance the emotions. Drink as a tea, burn as an incense or throw on ritual fires. It is a blood cleanser and will help build up the system after illness. It is a cleansing lung remedy and liver tonic. It is a herb of Jupiter, warming and strengthening.

θ Trees of Spring Equinox

Ash - *faxinus excelsior*

The Ash is the fifth tree of the Celtic Tree Ogham N. NION and is associated with understanding universal truths. It appears in Norse mythology as Yggdrasil, the great Ash of Odin or Woden who hung from it to obtain enlightenment and the secret of the runes. Ash teaches us that all of life is interconnected on all levels of existence - past, present and future, spiritual, mental and physical. Whatever happens on one level, happens on all levels. Your actions and your thoughts form an endless chain of events and whatever you do in the physical world, will affect all levels of your being.

Due to its straightness of growth, it is an excellent wood for making walking sticks and staffs. It carves easily. In woods where it grows with honeysuckle, it is possible to find sticks which have been spiralled by the honeysuckle binds. These are particularly potent for wands and talking sticks.

Alder - *alnus glutinosa*

The Alder grows alongside rivers where it can be seen easily in the Spring as it shimmers in a red haze formed by its reddish brown catkins. The third tree of the Celtic Tree Ogham F. FEARN, it represents the balance of Fire and Water. It brings a powerful direct energy which will help you to take up challenges and face things previously avoided, balanced with a receptive understanding and awareness of what is going on below the surface.

Spending time with the Alder will help you to know when to move forward with courage and strength, challenging everything which doesn't ring true, and when to find inner stillness and receptivity to divine inspiration. These are the challenges of a spiritual warrior.

Alder leaves are cooling and soothing and can be pulped to form a poultice for sores and swellings. Use the fresh leaves inside your boots to soothe aching or burning feet when travelling long distances.

The Alder yields three powerful dyes: the catkins make a strong green dye, associated with Faerie's clothes, to help them hide from humans (also used by the outlaws and forresters in medieval times). The bark yields a red dye, used by the Celts, and the twigs yield a brown dye. The wood is oily and water-resistant - good for outdoor use. It is easy to carve by hand.

θ Dragon making

Prepare to have a dragon procession in the age-old folk tradition of Equinox. Making the dragon head is of course quite a big undertaking and could be done as a group project. There are various ways it could be done:

1. Make a shape of a dragon's head with basket maker's Willow or cane. Use masking tape to secure the places where several whips cross each other, and binding over the joins. Cover the whole thing with torn strips of cotton sheeting dipped in watered-down PVA glue or torn strips of newspaper, also soaked in PVA. When it is dry, paint with emulsion. When this is dry, paint and decorate in all its splendour. Red and gold are traditional dragon colours.

2. Use a cardboard box as a base for the head, cutting and shaping it, and using strong parcel tape to add other cardboard-shaped pieces for nostrils etc. Cover with material or paper which has been soaked in PVA and mould it around the shapes underneath. Paint with emulsion and when dry, decorate with coloured material or paint.

3. Make a large hoop from a fresh Hazel pole. Secure it well by binding the ends together with strong garden twine. Using a piece of material, cut large enough to be able to wrap over the Hazel hoop, sewing it into place. Sew and appliqué dragon features onto the material and sew ribbons around the edge of the hoop.

The body is joined on to the top of the head and is made using a series of Willow or Hazel hoops to which a long piece of material is attached. The head will need one or two people to carry it and each hoop will need one person. Two people inside the 'body' can each carry a wing. This can be made using a long stick to which a fabric wing has been attached. This can be stiffened with Willow whips inside it, or attached to the back.

θ Theatre, plays or dance theatre can be prepared to perform at the Equinox. Explore themes of dragons and Earth energy. Include a dragon procession at the beginning or at the end.

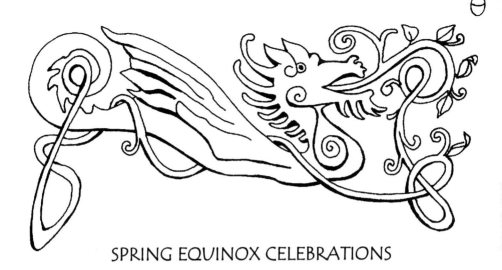

SPRING EQUINOX CELEBRATIONS

Θ Be outside today, wrap up warm if it is cold, enjoy the elements, the wind and the rain and the sunshine. Rejoice in them! Celebrate the end of Winter. Be a mad March hare, run wild and be expansive. Look for the arrival of Spring everywhere.

Θ Whether you are celebrating with friends or on your own, choose a wild and powerful place to go today, somewhere where the Earth's energy runs strong, where the serpent or dragon paths can be felt. Experiment with your ability to dowse these energies.

Θ Share a special breakfast together before setting out to spend the day outside.

Θ Make a shrine to honour the awakening Earth. Place on it Spring flowers, bulbs growing in pots, blossom, catkins and pussy willow. Represent the five elements in ways which reflect the Equinox. Burn lavender to welcome the Spring. Hang cloths of yellow and green.

Θ Make time to meditate with the trees, especially if a particular tree draws you towards it. Put your back against its trunk, feel its life-force energy, and be open to receiving impressions and inner understanding from the tree. Greet the Dryad, the Spirit of the tree.

ϴ Greet the nature Spirits of flowers and herbs. Communication is greatly enhanced if you are open to their existence. Be open to communication from Faerie and you may have a surprise. This ancient race, far from the Victorian image of pretty winged nymphs, are a shape-shifting people, rarely seen but sometimes felt, often near.

ϴ If you are gathered with a group, begin by making a circle holding hands and then walk a spiral inwards to the centre, chanting an easy meditative walking chant. When you get to the centre and are tight together, share with each other what the Spring Equinox means to you by calling out your awareness, understanding and feelings: 'may the Spring Equinox bring...' When this has reached its natural end and all has been said, take up each other's hands and the chant, and the person leading the spiral turns its direction outwards again to bring the group back into a circle. (see page 78)

ϴ The group can be led to honour the five elements which had previously been marked with coloured ribbons on sticks. A similar process can happen here with members of the group saying their own understanding of them. Thank each Element in turn for its gifts.

Air in the East
Spring Equinox belongs here. Give thanks for opening the way, life renewal, birth, birds, dawn, inspiration, smells, germination, breath of life, the return of Spring, balance of light and dark, clouds, spirals, awakening, communication, inner voice, inner wisdom, balance in the mind, conscious and unconscious.

Fire in the South
Give thanks for fertility, sexuality, expansion, new growth, dragon and serpent energy, balanced power, transformation, the Sun, fertility on many levels, Fire within, Fire without, expression, movement.

Water in the West
Give thanks for compassion, caring, nurturing, balancing emotions, inner knowing, trusting the intuition, mysticism, enchantment, dreams, poetry, cleansing, following your heart, flowing within and without, spirals, receptivity in action bringing balance.

Earth in the North

Give thanks for the Mother, for fertility, sexuality, abundance of growth, Spring flowers, eggs, seeds, germination, roots, buds, shoots, nature Spirits, Faerie, Green Man, Earth energy, dragon and serpent paths, herbs, medicine, manifestation from within.

Spirit

Give thanks for Spirit, for Unconditional Love and for this essential part of ourselves which we long for. Reach out and in, connecting to your source and the guidance from within. Touch the sacred, the still point of power at the centre of your being. Feel yourself part of all life and all existence.

θ Seed meditation for renewal and self-healing

Imagine you are a seed full of life. Plant the seed of yourself in the warm Earth and water it gently until it begins to open. Feel your roots growing and reaching down into the Earth, drinking all the nutrients. Feel the shoot unfold into the air, your leaves unfold soaking up the Sun's rays. All that you need is given - for growing, for your wellbeing. You are in radiant health.

θ Plant the seeds of yourself and look at where you are going now. Affirm your most positive wishes. Connect to your life-force. Ask your Spirit guides and helpers for direction and remain open to receiving these messages.

θ Honour the Earth and the fertility of all life, the animals, the birds, fish and the insect world, the great abundance of plants and flowers, the herbs for medicine, and all the food growing for us to eat. Honour the balance of the Sun and the Moon, the male and the female, and the power of their union.

θ Pass an imaginary egg around the circle, each focusing on what they have been incubating since the Autumn and wish to bring out into the world. This is the fertile time. Being aware of your direction will greatly enhance the outcome. Share your thoughts with each other if you want to, before passing the egg to the next person. At the end, place the imaginary egg on the shrine.

θ The fertility which the merging of the unconscious with the conscious brings, will manifest on many levels, through the arts, dreams, emotions, gardening, whatever project you undertake at this time. Begin new ventures which enhance your understanding of this fertility and balance. Break away from old outworn ideas. If you are a man, find ways to embrace your inner woman. If you are a woman, find ways to embrace your inner man.

Θ Positive affirmations are positive repetitive statements (said in the present tense). They act like a meditative mantra, and will break negative thought patterns which are no longer serving you. These may have been built up over the years and can actually begin to manifest as physical illnesses. Use the Equinox to look at areas of imbalance in yourself and use positive affirmations to help rebuild positive thought patterns for the future.

Θ Decorate eggs, either hard-boiled or blown. Hard-boiled eggs can be rolled down a hill or eaten for breakfast. Special decorated eggs can be given as gifts to each other.

Θ Plant seeds of herbs and flowers for medicine. Each bring a packet of seeds and a tray of compost. Share the seeds around so each will have a variety of useful plants.

Θ There is a tradition of decorating hats with ribbons and Spring flowers at the Spring Equinox (Easter bonnets).

Θ Flying things
Make all kinds of things to fly in the wind. Using basket-maker's Willow, streamers of crepe paper, ribbons and wool, create shapes which you can run with in the wind.

1. Make a circle of Willow and tie or tape on coloured streamers, the string at three points to balance at the centre, and then tie on a piece of string. It looks great flying along behind you as you run.

2. Sew together two circles of felt (about 7cms in diameter). Leave a small gap and fill with medium brown lentils. Sew in several long ribbons and then sew

the whole thing up. This is great thrown up high into the air, streamers flying as it falls to Earth.

3. Make prayer flags or prayer sticks, writing your positive affirmations onto material and attaching them to sticks to stand in the wind. Send your prayers and messages out into the wind and out into the world. Fly dragon flags, dragon kites. Make dragon masks which can be attached to a long stick with streamers flying from the mask.

θ As part of theatre, plays or dance-theatre, have a dragon procession led by the dragon you have made. If this is done at night, everyone can carry candle lanterns and nightlights in jars as part of a spectacular and memorable evening. Weave the path of the dragon's meandering path, activate and energise, dance and celebrate the return of the dragon or serpent energy.

θ Other plays and theatre can be performed in the round, exploring other Equinox themes of balance, birth and life awakening.

θ Dance to celebrate the first day of Spring. Begin by imagining yourself curled up inside an egg or a seed. You are your egg or seed space. This is your world in the dark, growing life, incubating your plans, waiting. Feel the life-force growing within you. Feel the new you who is waiting to be born into the light, into action, who will become manifest. As you begin to move outwards and break out of your shell or seed case, take with you your most positive intent, breathe new life into yourself as you break through into a new phase of your life. Celebrate and dance this power and energy. Celebrate being alive. Celebrate the balance of the world within and the world without. Celebrate yourself as you seek to balance this within yourself.

θ Bring the group back into a circle for the closing ceremony, holding hands and humming to attune and blend the energies which have been released. If you are celebrating on your own, return to the centre of your circle created by the five elements. Thank the energy of the Earth, Air, Fire, Water, Spirit. Thank the Guardians and Spirit guides. Thank the nature spirits and elementals, and thank each other.

θ Bless the food and drink to share.

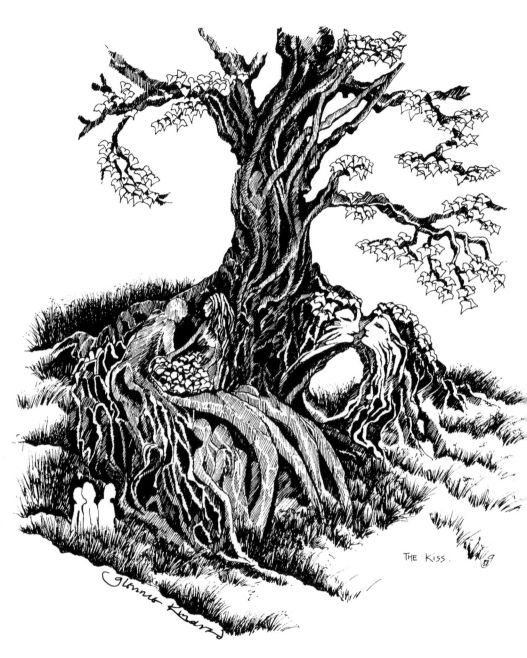

THE KISS.

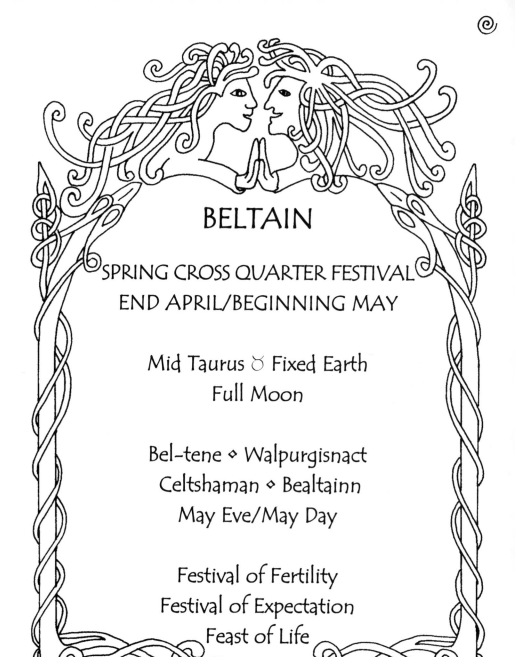

BELTAIN

SPRING CROSS QUARTER FESTIVAL
END APRIL/BEGINNING MAY

Mid Taurus ♉ Fixed Earth
Full Moon

Bel-tene ◇ Walpurgisnact
Celtshaman ◇ Bealtainn
May Eve/May Day

Festival of Fertility
Festival of Expectation
Feast of Life

BELTAIN

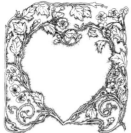

Beltain is a celebration of the fertility and rampant potency of the life-force. All of nature is growing and manifesting now in a wild whirl of creative energy. This is the time to celebrate unions of all kinds, fertility and manifestation on many different levels, love, sexuality and fruitfulness.

It is a time to be in touch with the instinctive wild forces within and without, to be aware of the potency of the life-force and its power on the physical, spiritual and mystical levels.

In the Celtic Pagan past, this was the night of the 'greenwood marriage' where the union between the Horned God and the fertile Goddess was re-enacted by the men and the women to ensure the fertility of the land. It was a night to spend in the woods, to make love under the trees, stay up all night and watch the sunrise, and bathe in the early morning dew. On this night, people walked the mazes and labyrinths and sat all night by sacred wells and healing springs whose waters were said to be especially potent at this time. This was the 'merry month' when people dressed in green in honour of the Earth's new Spring colours and the Faerie folk, elementals and nature Spirits, who are easier to meet at this time.

The Horned God, Herne the Hunter, untameable instinctive wild man of the forest, becomes a white stag and chases the fertile Goddess who becomes a white deer. The legend tells us he becomes the prey he hunts, and is magically transformed by his union with the Goddess. Since prehistoric times there have been many images of horned Gods: Actaeon the Stag, Pan the Goat, Dionysus or Zeus the Bull, Amen the Ram. There is a connection between horns and male vitality through an ancient tantric belief that by the transformation of ejaculation, a mystic energy mounts up the spine, made visible by horns, and brings mystical power and wisdom. A composite of all these horned Gods of the Pagan religions became the the Christian version of the Devil. His lustful nature gives rise to the modern slang word 'horny', but the word lust in old German meant 'religious joy' and holds a clue to the transformation which takes place in the horned God as he releases his seed and brings fertility to the land.

The Goddess is Grain, and Creiddylad, who rides her horse across the sky as Epona, Rhiannon and Macha. A free and powerful Spirit of womanhood, she knows the power of love and the power of her own sexuality. She too is transformed by their union, becoming the Grain-Mother, carrying the fruit of their union.

Together the God and Goddess represent the great circle of life and death through the seasons. Through their union at Beltain, their knowledge and power is shared. Through the blending of these opposite forces, they become the fertile force of manifest energy. Through their love and sacred union, they become transformed both physically and beyond the physical. Beltain is the celebration of this mystical and spiritual transformation inherent in this sexual union.

May Day celebrations included dancing around the maypole, symbolising the interweaving and joining of the male and female energies to bring fertility to all unions. This creates a web of energy in a living matrix of power and energy. It was common practice to bring a new pole into the village every year, representing the year's incarnation of the vegetation or nature Spirit. Incorporated into the maypole dance was the Green Man who danced around the edge and represented the Spirit of vegetation. All this is linked to a much older ceremony of fetching a living tree into the village every year (possibly a May or Hawthorn tree). This living tree would still have its resident Dryad within the tree who would be central to the ceremony and danced around. It would have been asked for its help to ensure fertility of the land and a good harvest. Garlands of May blossom ('knots' of May, not 'here we go gathering nuts in May' as the song goes, as it is entirely the wrong month for nuts) were used to decorate houses, doorways and each other.

Another folklore custom of this time is the tying of ribbons and shreds of clothing to the May trees, especially where they grow by sacred wells. They were said to be gifts for the Faeries who choose to live here.

'Cast ne'er a clout before May is out' may not refer to the uncertainty of the weather (they have a similar expression in Northern Spain where the weather is very settled by this time), but may bear some reference to the woodland revelries as it is no good wearing new clothes to go for a frolick in the woods. Old clothes can be torn and hung in the May trees.

Beltain is one of the four great Cross Quarter Fire festivals. A bel-tene means a goodly fire. A special fire was kindled after all the other fires in the community had been put out. This was the Tein-eigin, the need fire. People jumped the fire to purify, cleanse, and to bring fertility. Couples jumped the fire together to pledge themselves to each other. Cattle and other animals were driven through the smoke as a protection from disease and to bring fertility. At the end of the evening, the villagers would take some of the Tein-eigin to start their fires at home anew.

The Church changed the focus of Beltain eve from a night of revelry and sexual potency, to the May Day celebration whose May queen was a symbol of virginity, purity and chastity, transforming the image of the wild sexually potent fertile Goddess into her opposite. Of all the things that the Church repressed, sexual expression and the sexuality of women was one of the greatest. Sexual pleasure and overt sexuality were serious offences, while killing and Holy Wars continued. With generations of deep disapproval influencing us, Beltain is one of the hardest ceremonies to connect to without causing embarrassment and offence.

At Beltain we can also direct our focus to the fertility of the Earth, especially now when there are large areas of land all over the world dying from man's mismanagement, pollution, and intensive farming methods.

Beltain energy is one of reverence for all of life, celebrating and honouring the fertility which grows from the union of opposites. It is about the sacredness and spirituality of love and sexual pleasure, and deep connections of the heart. These life-changing forces are not just the focus of sexual union, but unions of all kinds. Integrity of Spirit and power brings the physical and spiritual into balance. This creates a strong life-force energy which becomes the light and eternal love of spiritual ecstasy.

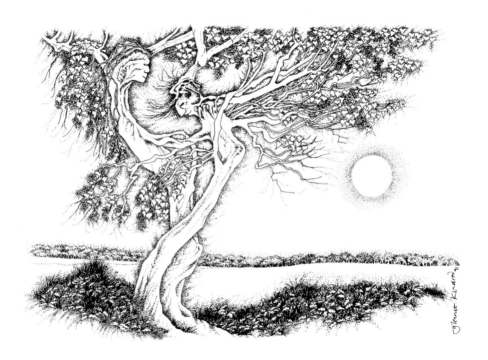

THE UNDERLYING ENERGY OF BELTAIN

This is the beginning of the final and most actively potent of the waxing phase of the Sun's cycle. All of life is bursting with fertility and the power of its own potential. Everything is in the process of becoming. This is the peak of the Spring season and the beginning of Summer, the onset of the growing season when the Earth is clothed in green, the vibration of love and the heart chakra. Flowers are everywhere, birds and animals are having their young, the sounds of birdsong fill the air. It is a time of sunshine and rain, swelling and bursting, rising sap and fresh new growth.

The Earth's energies are at their most active. The dragon paths can be intuitively sensed or dowsed. This is the perfect time for walking these ancient energy paths.

Beltain, like its opposite on the wheel of the year, Samhain, marks a particularly potent transition in the yearly cycle. At dawn and dusk especially, the boundaries between the worlds are thin, and we may find ourselves 'spellbound' by the power of the moment, touch the Faerie realms or experience the paranormal. This will bring insights and understanding which will greatly expand our consciousness.

From here to Summer Solstice is the peak of the sunlight and the conscious outward expression of ourselves. During this high energy time, we need to be aware of where we are and what we want and need. Create the most fertile and positive environment in which to grow the seeds of yourself. Reach out for what it is that you want and let the energy of growth whisk you along. It is a time to honour sex in its raw state, to see this as part of the cycle, to allow the extreme to exist which is part of nature and the expansive energy.

Beltain brings the union of opposites: the rational and the intuitive, the active and the receptive, Fire and Water. Fertility comes from the blending of these two energies, regardless of gender. Fertility is inherent in everything, everything is possible. Manifestation is reaching the height of its power.

Look at you – Father Sky
all puffed up proud and swollen
Clouds float dazzling
in sunshine and sapphire blue
piercing and penetrating...

Look at you – Mother Earth
so soft and wet, squelching and sucking
Juicy sap rising
in every lip and bud
swelling and bursting
into frothy flower and frond
How you glow in your new bright green!

Look at me, your child, a little animal
surrendered to the sweet sex of spring,
my pulse races with the urgent breath
rising and falling in the soft silk tummy
of the sleeping newborn lamb...

My heart sings fit to burst
and flies with the busy birds
flashing feathers flutter
as they lift into the blue...
and I'm buzzing with it all,
lazily meandering among bluebells and primroses
gulping down the sweetness,
poking my nose in moss, stone, bark, mud...

I walk, and a thousand blades of fresh new grass
vibrate
trembling diamond drops
catch rainbows from the sun
and my dreams of you and me
spiral up and up and up
– away we go –
a pair of buzzards soaring
with gliding outstretched wings.

Nicky Martin

PREPARATIONS
FOR BELTAIN

PRIMROSES ⬦ BLUEBELLS ⬦ MAY BLOSSOM ⬦
THE GREEN MAN ⬦ SHEILA-NA-GIG ⬦ MAYPOLE ⬦
HEADDRESSES ⬦ SACRED SPRINGS ⬦ DRAGON PATHS ⬦
MASKS ⬦ FOLK-DANCING ⬦ CEILIDH ⬦ FIRE ⬦ CANDLES ⬦
WEARING THE GREEN ⬦ HAND-FASTING ⬦ LABYRINTHS ⬦
BELTAIN TREE: HAWTHORN
BELTAIN HERBS: COWSLIP, ROSEMARY

Beltain should be celebrated on the night of the full Moon which is nearest to the end of April and the beginning of May. If possible, stay up all night, have a fire outside and enjoy being out under the moonlight. If it is clear, watch the Sun come up and wash your face in the early morning dew.

Leading up to Beltain or on the actual night, visit sacred wells and springs in your locality. If there are Hawthorn trees growing nearby, sit with these beautiful friendly trees and learn from them. Hang ribbons in the trees in an age-old custom to honour the tree and the Faerie folk who may live there. It is quite possible that this will inspire other people to do the same, and before long there will be many things hanging in the tree.

If you want to meet with Faerie or connect to nature spirits and tree spirits, find wild places where you feel their presence and make your intentions known. Feel your heart and mind open with love for the Earth. Dress in green to signify your allegiance to the Earth. Sing to them, meditate, and see what connections you make. Follow your intuition, but do not be lulled into vulnerability. These are powerful and sometimes mischievous creatures. Remember your folk stories!

Walk the dragon paths of activated Earth energies. Dowse for these paths using either Hazel or Rowan twigs. Cut a new forked twig, grip each fork in each hand, pull them apart until you feel the pressure 'bite'. As the twig passes over underground water, it twists and twitches in the hand. Alternatively, you can use a pendulum of any kind, state clearly your intent to chart the dragon paths. If you sense any areas where the energy is stuck or congested, you may place crystals here or stake the Earth with a metal rod. Meditate and dance for healing and harmony.

Make a pilgrimage or sacred journey, perhaps walking from one sacred spot to another. Tune into the energy of the Earth. Some ancient sites may contain the memories of previous times and may have Guardians attached to them. Strange coincidences, phenomena of the natural world, seeing sudden images in rocks, trees and clouds, omens and impressions, should all be noted as significant when on a pilgrimage or sacred journey. Take food and drink with you, perhaps a wooden whistle, notebook or sketchbook, and make a day of it. The ancient sites still retain a power which can shift our perceptions outside of time. Mystical and spiritual experiences bring an inner alignment and a deep sense of the sacred as we connect to the Earth and her energies.

Making your own flower essences

If you are drawn towards a particular flower, you can explore your relationship with that plant by making your own flower essence.

Pick the flowers gently, or cut them and let them fall straight into a glass dish of spring water. The petals and flowers should lie face down in the water, if possible. Stand it next to the plant or tree and leave in the sunshine for at least three hours. When you feel that the essence and Spirit of the plant has entered the water, scoop off the flowers using a stalk or leaf from the same plant, and mix the water with equal parts of brandy to preserve it. This is the mother essence and should be treated with great respect. After a few days, this mother essence can be made into a stock essence by adding seven drops to a 10ml bottle containing half brandy and half spring water. Keep the stock and the mother essence together for a few days. This makes a happier and more effective remedy. Take four drops from your stock bottle three times a day in a little water or straight on to the tongue, and note the subtle changes in your emotions, perceptions and life-force energy which the plant can bring. These remedies will keep for years, ready to be used when needed.

The Maypole

If you are going to have a maypole, this of course will take some preparation. This usually consists of a pole with an equal number of alternate contrasting ribbons attached to the top, and a base to hold the pole.

The dancers each have a ribbon and their interweaving dances produce a pattern of ribbons around the pole, representing the union of the male and the female.

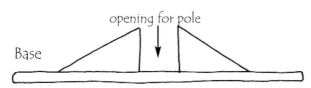

opening for pole

Base

Prepare a staff to take with you to the Beltain celebration. Either cut a new stick from Hazel, Ash, Blackthorn or Hawthorn, or decorate an old stick. Wrap bells and ribbons around it. Great to dance with, shake and brandish! Wrap small bells around your ankles and legs so that when you dance, you also make music

A talisman is a form of contagious magic, carried on the person. If you wish to cut a piece of wood for this purpose, sit with a tree you are drawn towards and ask it to guide you to a piece of wood you can cut. Thank the tree for its gift. As you whittle your talisman, state why you are making it and what for. This will help focus its use. As this is the fertile time, what do you wish to bring fertility to? Be clear in your intent. When you have finished carving and shaping your piece of wood, sand it to a smooth finish using first a coarse, then a medium, and then fine sandpaper. Hang it round your neck or carry it in your pocket as a 'touch-wood'.

The Green Man

Throughout the Celtic lands are many images and stories of Green Men and Green Women. They represent the Spirit of nature or the Spirit of vegetation and they usually consist of the head only, surrounded in leaves, or sprouting leaves like horns, or pouring vegetation from their mouths, eyes, ears, horns. Old churches were built on the sites of Pagan worship and the early churches incorporated Pagan images to encourage the people to worship there. Many of the images displayed from the Pagan religions contrived to be touched for luck and had offerings made to them, despite the Church's desire to demonize them. Many Green Men look distinctly female or androgynous - a nature Spirit being neither male nor female, both aspects honoured. There are hundreds of these carved foliated heads hidden in our old churches, surviving from a time when the Green Man was of great significance and importance to the people of these lands. It is an interesting archetype to work with, either through visualisation or meditation. Honour this energy by making a Green Man out of Willow. Weave the Willow whips into a basic head framework and on Beltain eve, weave it with fresh greenery of all kinds pouring from its mouth and eyes. Using Oak leaves and Oak twigs is a potent reference to the Sun King who reaches the height of his power between now and the Summer Solstice, returning back into the Earth at Lammas.

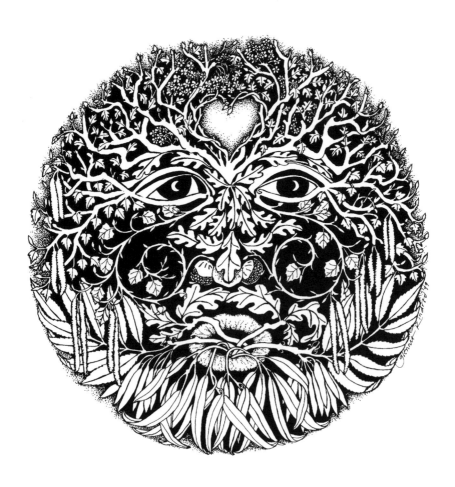

◉ Sheila-na-gig

Also to be found hidden in the old churches are the Sheila-na-gigs, a carved naked woman squatting with knees apart, displaying her vulva. Her vulva is most often carved as a double-pointed oval, a common genital/yonic symbol known as the vesica piscis (the vessel of the fish). This fish symbol is found worldwide to represent female genitals, the Great Mother, the Creatress. Sheila-na-gig means vulva-woman. Most Sheila-na-gigs have one or both hands drawing open the vulva, emphasising the sexuality she is offering. Many have deeply furrowed ribcages, perhaps linking their potent sexuality with the Death Goddess and the cyclic nature of fertility, life and death. Her open vulva is an invitation to her potent dark womb. Many have been destroyed, especially when Victorian prudery was at its height. Many were defaced or removed and have been found buried near the church. The ones that remain can be found hidden behind fonts, and in dark corners. In the past her vulva was touched for luck and many are worn smooth from much touching.

◉ Our view of sex is still influenced by a male conception of what sexuality is. Use this time to explore sexuality as sacred union. Love, intimacy, tenderness and sensitivity towards another's emotional needs, are all areas which help focus the deep integration of the erotic, the sexual and the emotional. These elements touch and inspire a deeply spiritual experience of sexual ecstasy.

◉ Trees of Beltain

Hawthorn - *crataegus mongyna*
The May tree, Whitethorn, Quickthorn, Haegthorn - brings the Spirit of wild places with it, even when growing in a town. Said to be the haunt of Faeries, of love, fertility and sexual abandonment. Later, as the Christian religion took hold, it was said to be an unlucky tree, representing chastity, sexual abstinence and misfortune. Once again it is being understood as a positive symbol of the heart through its ability on the subtle levels to open the heart to spiritul growth and Love. It is particularly potent for healing affairs of the heart and can be given as a token of friendship and Love. It will help release blocked energy, release stress and fears, and open the flow for healing and open-hearted loving communication.

The flowers, leaves, and particularly the berries, are prized as a cardiac tonic which acts in a normalizing way upon the heart by either stimulating or depressing its activity, depending on the need. It may be used safely for long periods of time, for heart weakness, palpitations, high blood pressure and angina. Use

133

to strengthen the body in old age by drinking an infusion of the berries daily. Also in times of stress. Pour one cup of boiling water onto two teaspoons of the dried berries. Leave covered for twenty minutes. Drink three times a day for long periods.

In the Spring, drink the blossom as a tea for a Spring tonic which helps the heart and circulation. If you want to collect and dry the flowers yourself, pick them on a dry sunny morning and hang them to dry in brown paper bags in a warm airy place. When they are completely dry, seal them in a dark, airtight container or jar. Gather them fresh every year. Use the fresh flowers in salads and fruit salads. Eat the young leaf shoots straight from the tree (known as bread and cheese) or toss those into salads too.

Herbs of Beltain

Cowslip - *primula veris*
On May morning, posies of cowslips would be given as a token of friendship and Love. Associated with the Norse Goddess Freya and the Roman Goddess Venus, both linked to love and sexuality, it used to grow freely everywhere, but in the UK is now a protected plant, so grow it yourself and then re-introduce it into the wild.

It is a safe herb to use with babies, children and the elderly. Use for mild insomnia and headaches, and as a general nerve tonic. It is also beneficial to the lungs and can be used at night to calm a dry irritating cough. It will help clear the body of poisons.

Make an infusion using ½ an ounce (15g) of dried flowers to 1 pint (600ml) of boiling water. Cover and leave for ten minutes. Strain and keep in the fridge. Drink one wineglassful three times a day. Drink when you want to lift the spirits and move on emotionally. A prime ingredient in love potions.

Rosemary - *rosmarinus officinalis*
Rosemary has a long association with magical use. A sprig carried or worn would protect the wearer from magic, but was itself an ingredient of magical charms. Ruled by the Sun, it has a vibrant stimulating energy. It was a symbol of fertility and used in marriage and hand-fasting ceremonies. It can be burnt as an incense and has an uplifting energy.

Make a herb tea in the usual way, pour 1 pint of boiling water onto ½-1 ounce of the dried herb (two to three times more of the fresh herb is needed). Cover and leave for ten minutes. Strain off the herb and drink a wineglassful three times a day. This same liquid can be used as an antiseptic on wounds, to ease muscular pains, neuralgia, and for bites and stings. Drink the herb tea as well. It is a stimulant for the whole system and will strengthen the heart and increase circulation. Use whenever the body is sluggish and the limbs are cold. It will raise low blood pressure. It will lift the spirits, chase away lethargy, anger, hatred, grief and bitterness. It increases blood flow to the head and can be used as a mental stimulant instead of caffeine. It will improve memory and aid concentration.

Warning! Do not use as a herb if there is a history of high blood pressure and you are pregnant.

Hand-fasting

This is an old form of sacred marriage between two people, a ceremony, a pledge to last a year and a day and then be renewed every year. The couple join right hands to unite their male souls and then join left hands to unite their female souls. This forms the figure of eight infinity sign with their arms crossed. This can be enacted outside under the trees, under the stars, as part of a larger ceremony of marriage.

Labyrinths

Building a simple labyrinth is not as difficult as you might think. The first considerations are availability of materials and where to build it. It need not be enormous as long as it can be walked. Ten feet across is enough for a small one, you may have room in your garden or on some land you may have access to. Stones can be used if you build it in a wild place where there are lots of stones lying around. For a more permanent site, it may be cut from the turf, or as gravel or mosaic paths. Hoops of Hazel or Willow can define it, with herbs along its pathways. Indoors its pattern may be laid down in free-flowing cooking salt, or a dry potting compost. Both can be swept up easily afterwards.

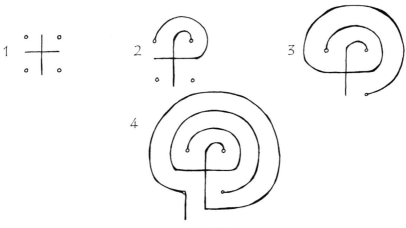

This is a classical seven coil labyrinth. Larger and more complex (about 16ft in diameter) but good for a permanent site, see below:

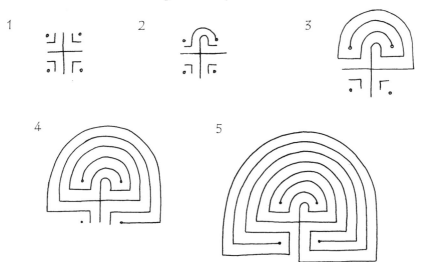

or try this unusual labyrinth which retains a continuous flow, while offering a choice of direction at the beginning.

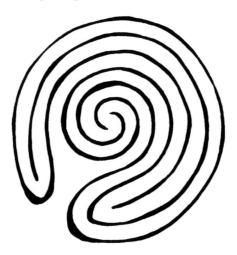

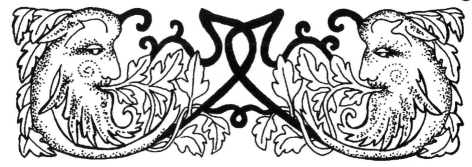

BELTAIN CELEBRATIONS

◎ If possible, choose a venue which allows for the greatest freedom of expression.

◎ The fire is central to Beltain eve. Ask everyone to bring firewood so that you can have a really good fire. Build the fire beforehand so that within whatever ceremony you devise, the fire can be lit with impact and certainty. Carefully make the sacred fire using special woods. This is the bel-tene, the good fire, bringing healing purifying energies and fertility, and should be lit with invocation and blessings.

◎ Make a beautiful shrine area with Spring flowers, May blossom and greenery. Light a candle for each element and represent each of them here. Represent the Horned God and the fertile Goddess in some way, either with figures of clay or bone, or by suggestion, using materials such as horn, flowers, greenery and muslin.

◎ Wear green in honour of the Earth and her new colour.

◎ Ask everyone to wear a head-dress of greenery. This can be made by creating a base for the head by weaving a circle of Willow and then wrapping other greenery around it (see page 47). Weave the power of your new direction as you work. Sing a chant which enhances this energy.

◎ Have a masked ceremony with everyone wearing greenery masks. These can easily be made by glueing green leaves onto a cardboard or leather base. Masks which only cover the top half of the face are the most practical as they leave the mouth free to speak, eat and drink.

Ask everyone to bring food and drink to share, and after the ceremony, have a great feast.

 Make the most use of drumbeat and other music. Dancing will energise and relax and can bring emotions out into the open. It is a good way to begin a ceremony as it brings the group together. Let a peak be reached and then bring the energy down again, and gather the group into a circle.

 Focus the five elements. Outside in the dark, each representative of the elements (adults only) could carry a lighted brand (a rag soaked in paraffin or wax and tied to the end of a stout stick or a garden candle on a stick). These can then be used to light the Beltain fire to great effect.

Air in the East

Thank the element of Air and thought. Our thoughts bring manifestation. Heed them. Direct communication between our minds, our hearts and our speech. All thought is manifest. Meditation stills our thoughts. Use your intuition, follow inspiring paths. Breath of life. Song. Words have power. Invocation has power.

Fire in the South

We thank the element of Fire for transformation and creativity. Focus on your intent at this time. The active principle is powerful now as the Sun is reaching the peak of its power. Spontaneity, passion, expansion, sexuality, growth, self-expression. The Sun which warms the seed and creates abundant growth.

Water in the West

Be conscious of your emotions and where they lead you, especially now at the high point of manifestation in the physical. Follow your heart's most positive and loving intent. Be receptive to the subtle energies deep within you and within the natural world. Express your emotions and deepest feelings. Bring them outwards and find creative ways for release.

Earth in the North

Our love and thanks to the Earth for all its gifts, fertility, and the power of the life-force. Celebrate all growth: flowers, trees, the abundance of nature and the way this manifests in our lives right now. Give thanks to the Earth for the food we eat.

Spirit

Within and without and ever-present, we give thanks for this timeless connection with this part of us which cannot be seen and cannot be named. We reach out and in, connecting to our source and the guidance from within. We touch the sacred, the still point of power at the centre of our being. Universal Love guide us, bring us inner peace and harmony.

 Use the mesmerising effect of Fire, candles and drumbeat to evoke a trance-like atmosphere. Altered states of consciousness bring deep insights and help us slip between the worlds and into a timeless state.

 Meditation is another aid. Meditate on the fertility of the Earth and the plants which are growing to become the food we eat.

 Celebrate the fertility of the land and the fertility of manifestation within us all.

 Explore ways to connect to the wild man and wild woman energy. Openly express this wild energy through dress, dance, voice and the power of your sexuality.

 Pass around a sacred marriage basket. Let each person use it as a focus for their hopes, gifts and blessings for their relationships.

 Focus on the heart chakra which is green, the colour of life and love, and the throat chakra which is blue, the colour of communication. The energy between the heart and the voice brings communication from the heart. Use this fertile time to talk your talk, and to express yourself from your inner truth. Use this potent time between now and the Summer Solstice to say what you want to say, and to focus your direction. Pass round a piece of turquoise and let each person speak from the heart.

 Walk a labyrinth or path of Earth energy. Journey into the centre to seek an answer. Journey out to bring it with you into the world.

 Whistling women were believed to conjure up destructive storms. Therefore, during the centuries of witch hunts, girls and women were not allowed to whistle. It was used in sympathetic magic to raise a wind and there was a deep link between a bird call, a magic formula, and singing. Find ways to explore the possibilities hidden here. Focus a low whistle first, making it resonate with the base chakra. When the group has found a harmony which resonates well together, move on up the chakras finding the notes which resonate for each one. Learn to whistle the calls of birds. There are many possibilities here for exploring these channels of shamanic communication.

139

@ Look at what you are currently manifesting. Will it lead to the harvest you wish for? If it does, then find further ways to help the flow of this energy. If it doesn't, then now is the time to plant new seeds and nurture them so that they can grow strong and well. Envision what it is you want. Believe you deserve it and that it will come to you. This is the power of positive manifestation and prosperity consciousness.

@ If it is a clear night, find Venus, the wishing star, and make a wish as you align yourself to her.

@ To dance a maypole dance successfully, you really need to find someone to teach you and a folk band to play the tunes (a simple 'scratch' band is enough). A few practices beforehand really helps too as even the simplest of dances can result in the ribbons getting tangled. The interweaving of the two colours of ribbon form a pattern down the length of the pole which is undone as the direction of the dance is reversed.

@ A simple interweaving circle dance without a maypole can be fun to do and it doesn't matter so much if you get mixed up. Begin by making a circle of equal pairs who face each other. Decide who is the man or woman, 'A' or 'B'. All of the 'A's and 'B's face each other. Additionally all of the 'A's face one way and all of the 'B's face the other way. Taking right hands, pass on the right shoulder and reach for the next person's left hand. Pass on the left shoulder and reach for the next person's right hand, and so on. This pattern of interweaving can be continued until the couples reach their starting partner and they can then dance together, spinning off to dance with others as well.

@ Another simple dance ritual, known as the wolf-dance, consists of men and women separating and making a line on opposite sides of a room or dance area. They then advance towards each other dancing, slinking, swirling until they pass each other and then they reach out to twirl around together before moving back into their line. This can be repeated many times.

@ Create your own dance rituals which reflect unions, courtship, the chase, and the blending of energies which signify Beltain. Use the Green Man you have made for interaction with nature Spirits within the dance, or have the Green Man lead the ritual dance.

@ Jumping the fire is an age-old Beltain tradition. Jump and say what you leave behind in the fire. Jump as a couple and pledge yourselves to each other.

 Many folk dances can be learnt with the help of a good caller and a barn dance band. Learn the simple dances which enable you to forget about watching and counting, and allow you to slip into the pattern of movement which is the inner ritual of the dance.

 Dance around a favourite tree or use a tree in a pot placed in the centre of the circle. Light candles to honour the tree kingdom and the Dryads. Thank them for their help to humankind. Make a circle around a tree you are drawn towards. Link to the tree's energy, hug the tree together and feel its presence and powerful life-force. Tone with the tree, chanting the sacred Om or Aum for at least ten minutes or more while you align and harmonize in spiritual union with the Spirit of the tree.

 Come together in a circle for the closing ceremony, holding hands and feeling your connection to each other, the love and the friendship which celebrating together brings. If you are celebrating on your own, return to the centre of the circle. Thank the elements for their gifts, thank the nature Spirits, the Guardians and the Spirit helpers for their presence, and thank each other. End on a chant to energise and enhance the power of Beltain.

 Bless the food and drink which everyone brought to share. Have a feast.

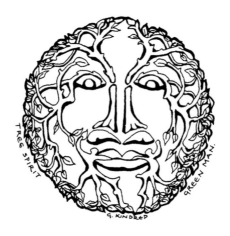

G. KINDRED

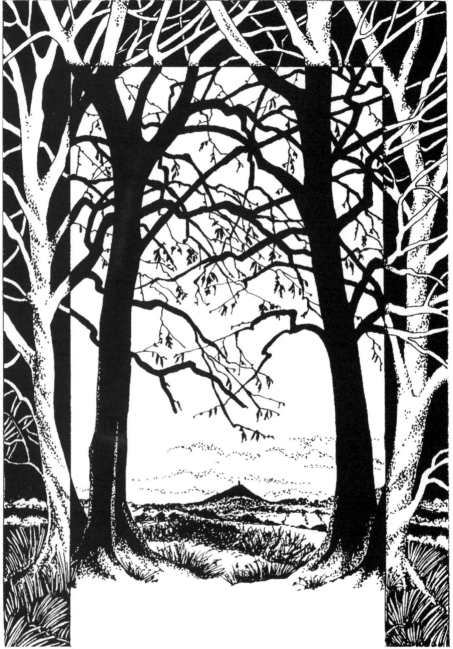

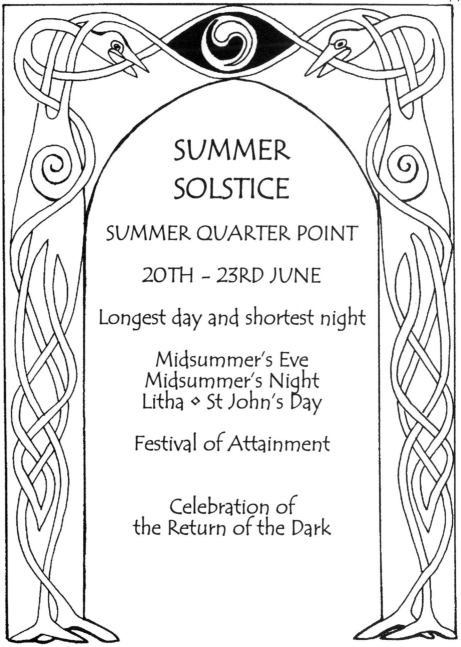

SUMMER SOLSTICE

SUMMER QUARTER POINT

20TH - 23RD JUNE

Longest day and shortest night

Midsummer's Eve
Midsummer's Night
Litha ◇ St John's Day

Festival of Attainment

Celebration of
the Return of the Dark

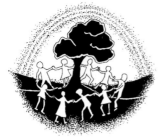

SUMMER SOLSTICE

The Sun enters the sign of Cancer ♋ as her rays shine down on Earth directly at the furthest point North in the annual cycle (the Tropic of Cancer). In the Northern Hemisphere it is the longest day (24 hours of sunshine North of the Arctic circle). The Sun is at the height of its power, but now is the second great turning point in the solar year, where the cosmic wheel stops and starts again. This is the longest day, but from now on the days will shorten.

On Midsummer's eve people stayed up all night to watch the sunrise and celebrate the longest day. Bonfires of Oak were lit on the hilltops and aromatic herbs thrown into them. Cattle, and the sick were passed through the smoke for healing and good health. People leaped the fires to rid themselves of misfortune and to assure abundance in love and the fertility of the land. The wheel is an important symbol of this festival but, unlike at the Winter Solstice, when all wheels were stopped, here wheels are kept in motion. Cartwheels swathed in straw and lighted were rolled down the hillsides. They were called fate wheels and the abundance of the harvest depended on how well and how far these blazed.

Midsummer's eve was a night of candlelit and torchlit processions which usually took a circular route, known as a carousel, or wheel of chariots. This is the origin of the carnival procession celebrating the great cosmic wheel of the year, she who turns the year, Fortuna, Goddess of the wheel, the wheel of karma, the wheel of Fate, Lady Luck, Dame Fortune, the Ferris wheel (a form of Faeries' wheel ridden by Faerie folk whose souls were involved in karmic cycles). Cycles of death and rebirth are celebrated here. Giant effigies of the Corn Mother, the Green Man and dragons made of wicker (Willow) were carried through the town and later burnt on the Midsummer fires. This was a form of sympathetic magic ensuring their continuance by giving them Fire. Ships were wheeled through the towns and villages (the origins of the carnival float) as a symbol of the burial mounds and long barrows, and a celebration of the dark inner world beginning now.

Both the ship and the ark were symbols of the germ of life, the womb of the Earth, fertility and wisdom. With the new cycle of the Sun begins the journey to the Summerlands within. The outer energy begins to wane. The inner energy begins to expand. Farmers would circle their crops three times with lighted torches in celebration of the Earth Mother and the harvest which was to come.

This is a dual celebration. On the one hand, it is a celebration of all which has become manifest during the outward cycle of the Sun, and on the other hand, it is a celebration of the return to the dark side of the year, the exploration of the inner world, inner wisdom and inner development. Sometimes two fires were lit to express this duality. It was a time of dancing and joyful abandonment, a celebration of the Corn Mother Goddess, Ceridwen, Cerealia, Ceres, Demeter, and the magical transformation of the power of the active principle. At this point of fulfilment and power, the Sun becomes one with the swelling of the grain and the darkness within. This is a celebration of the sacred marriage of Jupiter and Juno (Roman) and Zeus and Hera (Greek) symbolizing the joining of the active and receptive principles. It was an important occasion in the Old Calendar, and many stone circles are aligned to the Solstice sunrise so that this peak of the solar year could be acknowledged. But more than this, they acknowledged and celebrated the return of the Dark. They valued the power of the inner realms, the wisdom from within. They celebrated its rich potency, its vital, dynamic nature, and saw it as a necessary part of the whole, as active and expansive as the outer world of manifestation.

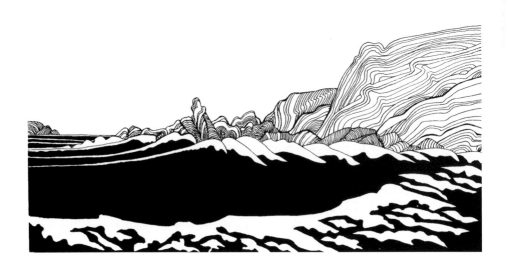

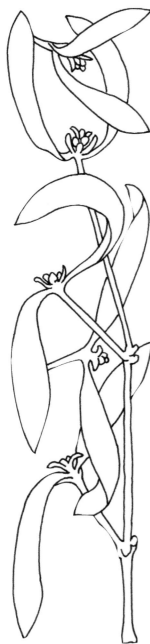

THE UNDERLYING ENERGY
OF SUMMER SOLSTICE

In all of nature the rampant growth period of the year has reached its peak and the natural world is in total manifestation. The trees are in full leaf and blossom, herbs and flowers are flourishing. There begins to be an abundance of vegetables and the fruit and grain are ripening. Everywhere there is a sense of completeness and abundance.

The Summer Solstice is the peak of our expressive and expansive selves. Celebrate what you have achieved and manifested. It is the festival of attainment and the fulfilment of the individual. It is a time for the enjoyment of what you have and what and who you are. Use this special day to focus and charge with healing and positive intent all you wish to be. Add the strength and power of the Sun to enhance and activate. Abandon yourself to expressive dance, song, joy and a sense of your own uniqueness.

Here at the peak of this active solar energy, the cosmic wheel is turning, and within this point a transformation is taking place. The active principle now begins to ripen these achievements on the inner levels. Our achievements will now continue to grow within, bringing spiritual strength and awareness to all we have manifest. This transformation brings spiritual rebirth and completion of our whole selves. Celebrate the death and rebirth of the great cycle of the year. As the power of the outer realms wane, the power of the inner realms expand, and we are made whole.

Come out Dancing

Get on your gladrags, sniff out the clues
It's a warm summer night for blue suede shoes
Someone, somewhere is playing the blues
So tune in, turn on, step out and

Come out dancing
Free the spirit
Find the laugh in your heart and beam it out

Come out dancing
Find the energy
Loosen limbs and limber up

Come out dancing
Defy gravity
Scatter inertia to the four winds

Come out dancing
Like a wild one
Dancing
Like a wild one
Dance like a wild one
Write your name in the sky

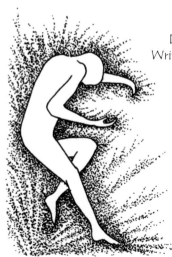

Brian Boothby
Tomorrows Ancestor

PREPARATIONS FOR
SUMMER SOLSTICE

FIRE ◇ PROCESSION ◇ CARNIVAL ◇ FEAST ◇ CANDLES ◇
SUN-SHRINE ◇ SUN CLOTH ◇
COLLECTING AND DRYING HERBS ◇ HERB PILLOW ◇
HERB SACHETS ◇ MEDICINE BAGS OR SHAMAN'S POUCH ◇
CREATING A WHEEL OF POWER ◇ SWEAT LODGE ◇
THE ROSE ◇ MISTLETOE
HERBS OF SUMMER SOLSTICE: ELDERFLOWER ◇ LAVENDER ◇
LEMON BALM ◇ ST JOHN'S WORT
TREE OF SUMMER SOLSTICE: THE OAK

☼ Summer Solstice, like Winter Solstice, is a time for gathering together with like-minded people. Many people go to the stone circles on Midsummer's eve to watch the Solstice sunrise. If you are celebrating on your own, this is an opportunity to meet and be with fellow kindred spirits. If you are organising a Midsummer celebration, try to find somewhere to be outside where you can have a fire, make music and dance, where there is enough outdoor space for a procession and for camping out. Ask everyone to bring firewood and food and drink for a feast.

☼ Because it is the longest day, it will not get dark until late. If the Moon is full and the night clear, it will not really get dark at all, but if the Moon is new, you will need some candle lanterns and nightlights in jars for those few hours between dark and dawn.

☼ A procession can be as elaborate as you have the time and energy to make it. Traditionally wicker dragons and Corn Mothers were carried or wheeled along in a cart.

☼ Making large effigies for procession may take weeks of preparation, but will create a memorable occasion for all. Create the shapes you wish to make using basket maker's Willow, weaving and binding over the joins with masking tape. When you are happy with the shape, soak strips of cotton sheeting in watered-down PVA glue and lay the strips over the wicker base. Later other coloured material can be glued over the top of this base, or it can be papered and painted.

☼ Make an area where you will have the feast. You will need tables to put the food on, haybales for sitting on, flowers and herbs in pots. Hang up Sun images, either painted on wood, in hoops or as flags. Make streamers, hang ribbons to fly in the wind and find a way to hang up lanterns. Forked sticks cut from the Hazel and pushed into holes in the ground, are effective. All this helps to make this a dynamic socializing area, where people can relax and chat. It is always a good idea to create an area here where children can get into sleeping bags safe and secure, with parents nearby. Ask everyone to bring rugs to put down for this purpose.

☼ This area can also be transformed for theatre and sacred drama performed in the round. Explore themes of transformation and changing cycles, the light and the dark. Masks for the play or procession will need to be made beforehand. Use lots of gold paint and any shiny gold material which will catch the light of the fire and candles.

☼ Make a shrine to the Sun, preferably on a circular surface, either painted as a Sun or covered with a cloth painted with a Sun. Make an appliqué Sun cloth for a lasting treasure which can be brought out and used whenever the Sun's energy needs to be invoked. Alternatively, use gold, orange and red scarves and any sparkly gold materials. Place the Sun shrine where it will get the most sunlight. There are many different things you can charge with sunlight. Bring Fire to Water by placing a glass of spring water in the Sun and after a few hours, drink the solar-charged water. You can add specific herbs and gemstones of your choice to the water to bring their unique properties to the solar-charged elixir. Wash all your crystals and leave them to dry and charge in the Midsummer Sun.

☼ Mandalas are circular patterns which have a centre and

movement within and without from this still point. They can be used as a meditation aid. Explore the cyclic patterns of light and dark to help you understand the cycle of the year, the benefits of both the light and the dark sides of yourself, and the way the changing year brings changes and transformation. Drawing patterns can take your mind out of time and place, bringing new awareness and inner peace.

☼ Harvesting and using Herbs

There are many herbs which are ready to be picked at this time, useful in cooking, salads, teas, and for medicine. Leaves are at the peak of their potency just before the flowers open, and flowers are at their peak of potency just as they are opening. If possible, pick aerial parts of the plant as the Moon is waxing to full. Do not overpick and thank the plants as you pick them. It is best to collect herbs into a basket or paper bags on a sunny day, when the dew has dried. Choose only the best quality plants growing in big clumps away from roads or sprayed cultivated land. Use secateurs or scissors and do as little damage as possible. Hang the herbs up as quickly as possible by tying them in bunches, away from direct sunlight, in a dry airy place, or lay them out on clean sheets of paper, turning them frequently. You can also hang them with the flower heads in brown paper bags.

When they are fully dry, the leaves and flowers will crumble and the stems snap cleanly. Store the dried herbs in brown paper bags or dark jars, as it is sunlight which reduces their properties. Keep them away from damp and label them at the time. Dried herbs should smell and taste as good as the fresh herbs. Leaves and flowers should be replaced every year.

The dried herb is twice as potent as the fresh herb, so if you wish to use the fresh herb, you need twice as much. Generally the proportions remain the same: around ½ - 1 ounce (15g - 25g) of the dried herb to 1 pint of water/½ litre (570ml). The proportions do not need to be exact. A single dose can be made with one teaspoonful of the dried herb covered in the usual way. For the very young or the very old, make a weaker solution. For applying externally, make a stronger solution. Pour the boiling water over the herbs and cover to keep in the essential oils. Leave to stand for ten minutes, then strain off the herb. The herbal liquid is usually drunk by the wineglassful three times a day. Some prefer it hot, sweetened with honey (you can re-heat the liquid, but do not boil). Some prefer it cold, straight from the fridge. Alternatively, pour your wineglassful in a mug and top up with hot water. **Herbs need to be taken regularly over a period of time, but generally do not use any herb for more than twelve weeks because of the danger of certain chemicals building up in the body. Most minor conditions will improve within a few days, chronic problems within several weeks. As soon as the condition shows signs of improvement, gradually reduce the amount of herb until you feel** you no longer need the remedy. Professional advice should be sought if there is no improvement after eight to twelve weeks, or if there is a deterioration in the condition.

☀ Herb Pillows

Use your dried herbs to make herb pillows, herb sachets and herb tea bags. Herb pillows need to be about a 10-20cms rectangle and flat. They slip in the pillowcase and help a person sleep.

Sew a material rectangle, turn it inside out, fill with herbs but keep flat. Re-sew around the outside edge with small running stitches to keep the herbs evenly distributed.

☀ Herb Sachets

Cut a circle of fine muslin, place the herbs in the centre and gather the edges up to form a sachet. Tie embroidery thread or thin ribbon around the top. Place one or two sachets in a jug. Pour on boiling water. Cover and leave for ten minutes. Pour the solution into the bath. Herbs can be absorbed through the skin as well as drunk.

☀ Medicine Bag, Shaman's Pouch

Medicine and charm bags are small and contain herbs or a crystal for healing. They are hung round the neck and worn next to the skin. The crane bag or Shaman's pouch is much larger and is hung from the belt. The old shaman believed that some items contained Spirit helpers and would draw you to be attracted to pick them up. These items include stones, shells, bone, crystals, feathers, any small items which have potent and personal power to you. If you later decide that they are no longer potent to you, pass them on, leave them in a special place, or lay them back on or in the Earth with honour and thanks. Keep herbs, roots and bark which may be useful to you in your pouch. The Shaman's pouch is a record of your spiritual journey and each thing you place in it will have significance, power and meaning to you, and may serve to remind you of an insight or healing gained. The best material to use is soft leather. Vegans can use a fine woollen scarf or a leather substitute. A good piece of chamois leather is easy to obtain from car accessory shops. The size of your bag will depend on its use. Experiment with a piece of old material or paper napkin. Generally the diameter of a medicine bag will be approximately 8-10cms and a shaman's pouch will be 25-30cms.

1. Draw a circle using a compass or cup or plate of approximately the right size. Make holes in the leather all the

way round about 1cm in from the edge and about 1cm apart. To make the holes, fold the leather and snip across the fold.

2. Either thread one long thong or two shorter thongs (40cms each for Shaman's pouch) through opposite directions, completing the circle at opposite sides. Experiment with a piece of string before cutting leather strips or buying leather thong. Use a bead as a fastening.

snip here➤

☼ Wheel of Power

Create a circle or wheel of power to fix the eight points of the year. Stones can be embedded in the Earth with due ceremony and ritual. Begin with the centre pole or stone and establish its still point of power. Then, using a compass, turn it until the red arrow is on North. This establishes the four directions and each of the quarter points, the Winter and Summer Solstices, North to South, and the Spring and Autumn Equinoxes, East to West. This also establishes the five elements with Spirit at the centre and around the circumference. Then establish the Cross Quarter Points, the four great Fire festivals of Imbolc, Beltain, Lammas and Samhain. This provides a framework for working with and understanding the patterns and cosmology of the cycles of the Earth.

Many other systems can be woven into your wheel. Around the circle you might put the thirteen stones for each of the Moons of the year. The Tree Ogham, the Runes, planets and totem animals may also be represented. The sacred wheel will mean many things to you on many different levels as you work with it over the years. This is why a permanent placing of the stones will build up power and significance both on the physical wheel that you establish and within your own cosmology. It becomes a place where the passage of time and your understanding of the underlying energy of its passing can be reviewed and experienced. At the centre is the still point where time stops. Here you can meditate and orient yourself to face the directions. It need not be a large circle and could easily be made in a garden, with appropriate plants and herbs growing in each area.

If it is not possible to make a permanent sacred wheel, then collect nine special stones or special pieces of wood or sticks, and make a temporary circle in a room or outside somewhere where you feel comfortable and relaxed. Place the first stone or stick in the centre and focus the still point of timelessness. Then, using a compass, place a stone on each of the Quarter Points, focussing on what you understand each to represent. Finally place the stones or sticks for each of the four great Fire festivals, considering what they mean and how their passing is affecting you. Working in this way helps to understand the underlying energy and patterns of the solar year.

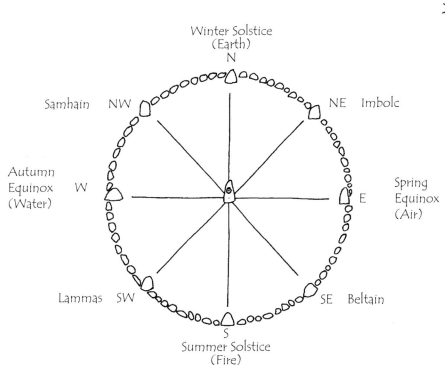

Winter Solstice
(Earth)
N

Samhain   NW

NE   Imbolc

Autumn
Equinox   W
(Water)

E   Spring
Equinox
(Air)

Lammas   SW

SE   Beltain

S
Summer Solstice
(Fire)

☀ Sweat Lodge

The sweat lodge is a shamanic tradition which has survived from many tribal cultures around the world, and has become a growing tradition in recent years amongst people who celebrate the passing of the solar year, or the passage of the Moon (held at full Moon or new Moon). It is a process of physical and spiritual cleansing. Volcanic stones (Basalt) are heated in a fire which is lit beforehand to heat the stones. These are placed on top of the fire. Once the fire has died down, some of the stones are carried on a shovel into a pit inside the sweat lodge and water is gently poured onto the hot rocks to make steam. This is a sacred space and involves ritual and ceremony which have many traditions. The simplest is to go in and out five times, dowsing yourself in cold water each time you come out, and bringing fresh hot stones in each time. Each time of entering the sweat lodge, a new element and direction is honoured, and your truth within that element is shared with each other. There is often one person who will keep the focus of the ritual. The fifth and final time is a space for meditation and inner journeying. At the end when everyone has come out, the last hot stones are put in, water is poured on for the Ancestors, and the door is closed.

☀Building a sweat lodge

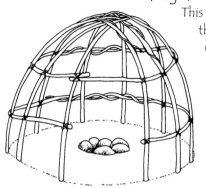

This shows the framework of Hazel rods with the pit in the centre for the hot stones. (Everyone sits around the edge.) The whole thing is covered with old blankets to make a good thick covering. A blanket is hung over the doorway. Secure the blankets with rope thrown over the top and with stones around the bottom. A piece of canvas can be thrown over the top of the blankets for added strength and insulation, but it is not essential.

You will need:

a) 12-16 lengths of flexible, fresh Hazel rods 3-4 metres long (9-15 feet). The rod diameter = approx 3cms (1 inch) at the thick end.

b) A metal spike and a lump hammer.

c) Garden string.

d) Old blankets, rope, canvas, stones for weighing down the edges.

e) About 25 volcanic rocks (Basalt) which will not explode in the fire.

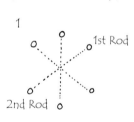

1. Decide on the size of the floor circle. 4½-5½ metres (15-18 feet) diameter is a good size. Pair up the rods, choosing the thickest rods for the main structure. Make a 15cm (6 inch) hole with the metal spike and lump hammer and put in the first rod thick end down. Then make the hole for the second rod opposite the first rod with a diameter of about 4.5 metres (15 feet).

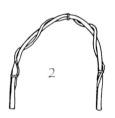

2. Bring the thin ends of Hazel together to form an arch the height you wish your sweat lodge to be. Bend the ends round each other and tie it with string to make it strong. (2)

3. Continue making the archways opposite each other using the strongest rods and tie them securely at the centre. Three pairs of rods are enough for a sweat lodge of this size. More pairs are needed for a bigger structure.

4. Use the thinner rods for horizontal weaving. Wedge the thick end in, and use the thin end of the rod for the weaving around the thick upright rods to make it strong.

154

Tie over where they join. Leave a door space.

5. In the centre, dig a pit for the hot stones, leaving enough space around for people to sit. Cover the whole thing with old blankets, with a blanket for the door. Weigh them down with stones. The whole structure can then be covered with a piece of canvas and ropes to hold it down. Reed or marsh grass can be strewn over the floor, coconut matting, old canvas, old carpet, or simply sit on the earth (although it can get very slippery and muddy as the sweat pours off you!)

6. Make a separate area with a hose, a cold shower or watering cans filled with water. Rebuild the fire after the first stones have been taken out so that each time of re-entering the sweat lodge, there are fresh hot stones. At the end, rebuild the fire so that everyone can come together around the fire to relax, eat, drink and socialize. It is good if someone is willing to take on the role of staying outside, heating the stones, building up the fire, refilling watering cans, organising the food and hot drinks.

☀A Midsummer tradition was to grow flowers and herbs in pots and to put cloth, paste or grass dolls in the pots representing the Corn Mother. This was later forbidden by the Church. Windowsills were draped with rich coloured cloths and decorated with crimson and blue ribbons. Here the pots were placed. They were also given as tokens of love and friendship.

☀The Rose

The Rose had special significance at this time and was used to decorate the sacred groves and the Midsummer's eve dancers. The wild rose (dog rose, *rosa canina*) has five petals and was a symbol of the Goddess, Venus, Aphrodite, motherhood, regeneration and eternal life. It related to the five-pointed pentacle, a symbol of power and protection used since earliest times. It was used in ancient writing and poetry as a symbol of sexuality. The red rose related to mature or maternal sexuality while the white rose belonged to the virgin. The rose garden, the rose bush, the rose garland, the rose wreath were all part of this symbolism of sexuality and the Goddess. The chant 'ring around the rose wreath' referred to a traditional mummer's dance known as the Rose, which was so popular, the Church found it hard to suppress. It has been said that a pocket full of posies referred to the cave of flowers, an old symbol of underground fairyland, and 'all fall down' referred to the end of the fertile season. Five dancers with swords formed a five-pointed star over a victim called the Fool who was symbolically slain and resurrected with an elixir called the dewdrop of the rose. The dance seems to hold within it a key to the rites of Midsummer Solstice.

☀Herbs of the summer solstice

So many herbs are reaching their peak at this time of the year. Weave them into wreaths with grasses, reed or Willow. Dry them for use during the rest of the year.

Elderflower - *sambucus nigra*

The flowers make an excellent daily tonic tea. Use 3 ounces (75g) fresh flowers or ½ - 1 ounce dried flowers (15-25g) to 1 pint of boiling water (570ml). Cover for ten minutes and drink sweetened with a little honey. This same infusion can be used as a skin tonic and a lotion for wounds, burns and rashes. Drink as a sedative to promote a peaceful sleep, for any catarrhal inflammations, coughs, sinusitis and hayfever. Useful for moving stuck emotionally congested states.

Make elderflower cordial for a wonderful Summer Solstice drink which is quick and easy to make. Put ten large flowerheads in a large bowl with 1½ pounds (600g) of sugar, two chopped lemons, and 1 ounce (25g) of tartaric acid. Pour on 4 pints (2.28lts) of boiling water and stir well. Cover with a clean tea towel and leave for twenty four hours, stirring occasionally. Strain through muslin or a tea towel, and bottle. It will keep for a week (or freeze it in plastic bottles (do not overfill) for later use). Dilute with still or carbonated water.

Lavender - *lavendula officinalis*

Lavender is a herb of the solar plexus, the area above the navel through which we assimilate and receive external stimuli. For some people this can be a problem as they pick up all kinds of vibrations and can be at the mercy of other people's emotions and feelings. By drinking lavender tea regularly, inner equilibrium and peace is restored and it will help to strengthen the inner discriminating faculties. Lavender is most useful in relieving stress and for all states of nervous debility, exhaustion, insomnia, physical and mental tension, and for migraines and headaches caused by stress or too much Sun. It will clear the blood of toxins, strengthen the liver, and will lower blood pressure. Make an infusion in the usual way. Pour a solution into your bath at the end of a hard day's work to relieve aching limbs and exhaustion. Lavender was traditionally thrown into the Midsummer fires and burnt as an incense to bring clarity, visions for focusing the mind, and trance work.

Lemon Balm - *melissa officinalis*

Make an infusion in the usual way and use as a tonic for the circulatory system and the heart, helping to lower blood pressure. It is also a good digestive tonic, helping to assimilate fatty foods. A useful herb for the menopause, helping to ease hot flushes, depression, anxiety and palpitations. It will also ease period pains and help regulate menstruation. It is safe to use in pregnancy for headaches, dizziness and morning sickness. Useful for colds and flu, it lowers fevers and promotes sweating. Rub the leaves directly onto insect bites. Lemon balm drives away all troubles and cares, lifts the spirits and eases depression. It is soothing, expansive, and opens the heart to giving and receiving Love.

St John's Wort - *hypericum*

The entire plant above ground is a valuable pain-reducing anti-inflammatory and general healing remedy. Make the infusion in the usual way and use internally and externally for wounds, ulcers, blisters, burns, rashes, bruises and sunburn. It will clear congestion from the lungs, is good for irritating coughs, for any nerve pains such as neuralgia, and for menopausal changes of anxiety or irritability. An excellent massage oil can be made to help relieve tension, sciatica and rheumatic pains. Mix together 3 ounces (75g) of the fresh herb bruised between two stones, or 1 ounce (25g) of the dried herb, with ½ pint (285ml) of grapeseed oil or almond oil. Leave in a covered glass jar in a sunny position, shaking daily. After one month, strain off the herb. When rubbed onto the skin, the properties of the herb are absorbed into the bloodstream and act in the usual way.

☼ Tree of Summer Solstice

The Oak - *quercus robur*

The Oak is sacred to the Druids and represents the doorway into the second half of the year at Solstice. It is the seventh tree in the Celtic Tree Ogham. Its Celtic name 'Duir' means doorway. Find an old Oak tree to sit with and enter the Spirit realms within you. The Oak is the Sun king whose attributes are strength, courage, inner peace, and the endurance to survive. Sit with the Oak when you need to find the strength to face difficulties and sort out complicated problems. It will bring deep calm, restore the will and self-determination. It is the doorway to your inner spirituality and the power of Love within. The Oak is dedicated to the Gods of Thunder: Zeus (Greek), Jupiter (Roman), Thor (Norse) - regarded as the great fertilizing power who sent rain and caused the Earth to bear fruit. The Druids made a distilled water from the flowerbuds to cleanse the internal body. The water, found in the hollows of the tree, was used ritually to cleanse the external body in readiness for the Summer Solstice.

☀ Mistletoe – *viscus quercus*

Mistletoe was traditionally gathered on Midsummer's eve or Midsummer's day. To the Druids it was particularly potent when it grew on the Oak. It must have appeared to be a very magical plant. It didn't have its roots in the Earth, but appeared high in the tree and therefore had a life-force of its own, perhaps sent as a gift from the Gods. Wands of Mistletoe wood were gathered at Midsummer when the Mistletoe, like the Sun, was at the height of its power. These wands were placed under the pillow to induce dreams and omens.

☀ Take advantage of the good weather to make sacred journeys to visit wells, springs, stone circles, burial mounds, clusters of trees which may once have been a sacred grove. Visit big old trees of Oak and Yew which have stood in the same spot for centuries. Walk the dragon paths, now fully activated, the ridgeways, and the old tracks. As you walk in these places, open yourself to understanding the atmosphere and pulse of energy they have. Write your impressions down, write poetry, draw and paint, experience a sense of oneness and communion with the natural world. Look for 'places of increase' marked by a spring or a rock or other natural feature which may suggest its power. Meditate here, enter the dreamtime which these places can open to us.

☀ Celebrate the solar Goddess Rhiannon (Albion), Epona (Gaul), Macha (Erin). She was known as Mother Time and is found on many Pictish stones riding a horse and carrying the orb of the Sun. She was associated with the dark half of the year which begins here at Summer Solstice.

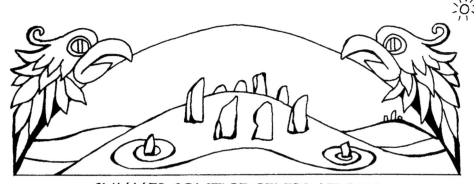

SUMMER SOLSTICE CELEBRATIONS

☀ Prepare and decorate with pots of herbs and flowers and with Sun images, an area for feasting, performance and rest. Decide where to have the fire and where to pile up the firewood. If it is Solstice eve, get the lanterns ready for when it gets dark later.

☀ Create a shrine to honour the Sun. Place Oak leaves, flowers, herbs, candles and ways to represent the five elements. Place images of the Sun made with painted salt dough.

☀ Pick lots of grasses, reeds, flowers, herbs, Oak leaves, Mistletoe, Willow, and with ribbons and wool, people can weave them into garlands, girdles or head-dresses for the celebration.

☀ Light the Need-fire using twigs of Oak. The old tradition would be to light it using friction by rubbing Oak sticks together and feeding in dry grass and small dry tinder as it begins to smoulder. Once the fire has a good base of heat, burn Oak which will burn hot but slowly. Throw in herbs such as lavender and rosemary.

☀ Begin by gathering into a circle to celebrate the fulfilment of power, the Sun and the changing cycle as we celebrate the return of the dark. A circle dance, a chant, a round will help the flow of energy. Build up the power and feel yourself as part of the cycle of the solar year reaching a peak of intensity like the Sun. Pass round a crystal and focus on the dark within as the wheel turns and the new cycle begins. Lead the circle into a procession. Begin by circling the area three times.

☀ The five elements can be honoured in turn.

Fire in the South

Honour the Sun which will swell the grain. Fire, the vital energy, has reached its peak with the Summer Solstice Sun. Transformation and change occur as the power spills over from outward expression. Honour spontaneity and celebration of the self. Salute the Sun. The active principle is transformed bringing fire within as well as without. The spiritual world is activated. Use the power of Fire to express and purify. Creativity is at its height.

Water in the West

Give thanks for Water. Bless the rain which is needed to swell the grain. Trust in the oncoming changes and cycles of flow. Patterns of spirals are changing direction at the centre. The tide turns. The life-force energy turns within to activate the inner levels. The unconscious receptive principle becomes activated. Feelings run strong. Let them out so that you can move on.

Earth in the North

The material world is manifest in an abundance of fertile growth. Herbs, flowers and food are everywhere. We too express ourselves to our fullest power in the outer world. From here this manifestation will ripen on the inner levels as we turn again towards the dark and the wisdom within. Celebrate the ripening of seeds both within and without.

Air in the East

With the peak of expressive energy, the mind and the intellect reach their full potential. Share your knowledge and the experiences you have gained. Sing and make sounds to express yourself. Communicate with each other now before you turn inwards again. Think about what you must do to use what you have gained.

Spirit

Within and without and ever-present, we give thanks for this vital conection to this essential part of ourselves which cannot be seen and cannot be named. We reach out and in, connecting to our source and the all encompassing Divine essence. We seek Truth within and without, connecting to Universal Wisdom and inner peace.

☼ Celebrate this peak of fulfilment. Each share what they have gained from the outward active phase of the Sun, and what they hope for as the energy turns inward. This helps to honour and prepare for the change. Focus on what still needs to be achieved before the changes fully take hold.

☼ Celebrate the cycle of death and rebirth of the Sun. Celebrate the new phase of the year, the descent into the mysteries, the Summerlands. Understand that something must die in order to be reborn. This is the power of the dark, bringing transformation and renewal. It ripens on the inner levels all the things we are manifesting now. Dark is not to be feared, but celebrated.

☼ Celebrate the Sun and the rain, Fire and Water, the conscious and the unconscious. This is the energy which will complete the harvest, the Earth's as well as ours. Weave coloured ribbons of red and blue in a dance of power, and focus on your direction.

☼ Collect wool of blues and black and wool of yellow, orange and red. Make a circle of people and on one side give the blue wools, on the other give the sunny coloured wools. Each person with a ball of wool ties it loosely around their waist and then throws it across the circle to someone else who wraps it around their waist once, and then throws it to someone else in the circle, and so on. The interwoven colours created thus, symbolize the merging of energies. At the end, everyone can carefully step out of the web and it can be lain on the ground with nightlights in jars, placed around the outside.

☼ Pass round a cup of honeymead, considered by the Druids to be a divine solar drink. Elderflower cordial or any fruit cup may be used. Salute the Sun and her gifts. Each say what you thank the Sun for as the Spirit moves you.

☼ Carry effigies of the Corn Mother, the Spirit of vegetation, or fire dragons in a carnival procession. Wear masks and bright clothes. Dance, drum, celebrate! Take circular paths, spiralling in and out. Carry lanterns. Celebrate yourself at the height of power and potential. Celebrate the dark. Welcome the change in direction.

☼ Circle the fire three times and leap the fire to leave behind what is holding you back. Call out 'I leave behind...' as you jump the flames. Use the power of the fire to cleanse and purify. This will help you move into the new phase. Express yourself fully that you may move on.

☀ Place aromatic herbs in the fire and expose yourself to the smoke. Traditionally, fennel, lavender, geranium, rue, rosemary, and chamomile were used. Swirl and dance in the smoke.

☀ Burn the effigies from the procession to give them the power of Fire, if you want to. Otherwise, honour their manifest power by placing them central to the feasting and drama area. People may like to place posies of flowers by them, light candles for them. This way they are taken into the heart, becoming assimilated and understood.

☀ Have a fireshow if you know anyone who can give one. Light fireworks, especially catherine wheels, or any fiery wheels which can be safely lit.

☀ The Midsummer feast is a great social occasion which brings a community together. Now is your moment to shine, express your own uniqueness, and enjoy each other's attributes and qualities.

☀ This is the time for marriages. Couples who pledged themselves at Beltain, now become joined. An old custom was to hold a stick either side of the fire, each holding one end, and passing back and forth through the fire three times. 'Hand-fasting' joins the couple for a year and a day as they pledge themselves to each other. It is open to renewal every year. Gifts are exchanged and friends gather to witness and bless the occasion.

☀ All drama began as sacred drama or magical drama, and was performed for understanding great truths and to bring enlightenment. They followed seasonal themes. The myths, legends and folk stories which have been handed down to us, provide a wealth of material and inspiration. Here at the Summer Solstice, explore the themes of the solar wheel, the mystery of renewal, death and rebirth. Perform in the round. Use masks and make good use of candlelight and fire. Weave a spell of colour, sound and movement, allowing the audience to enter into the sacred dream world where perceptions change and reality shifts.

☀ Celebrate the stopping and starting of the great cosmic wheel of the year through music and dance. There are many old country dances from many traditions. If possible, have a live band and a 'caller' (someone who is experienced in teaching the dances). Failing that, make up your own circular dance patterns. It helps to keep it very simple in units of two or three repeated sequences. Establish the pace with one main drummer. There are always people who want to play percussion and the rhythm quickly swells with sound and energy. The Antic-Hey was an old dance danced at the Midsummer Solstice. 'Antic' meaning ancient, of the old religion, venerable, and 'Hey' meaning a figure of eight pattern on the ground – the infinity symbol of the Hindu/Arabic numeral system. 'Hey nonny nonny' was the call for the dance.

☀ Tugs of war were a tradition of this time. You will need a long stout rope. On one side, all the people who were born in the Summer, and on the other side, all the people who were born in the Winter. This was the battle of Summer and Winter.

☀ A sacred sweat lodge can be done at the beginning or the end of the celebration.

☀ The ashes of the fire can be taken and used for any ceremonial purposes, or sprinkled around plants and herbs. Traditionally pieces of half burnt Oakwood were put in the ground for fertility of the crops and also kept in the home to ward off lightning.

☀ If possible, find a hill or high point from which to watch the Solstice Sunrise. It begins to get light quite a while before the Sun actually comes up, and it's a good time to walk, listen to the birds and watch the colours come back into the world. Salute the Sun as its first rays appear. Focus on your hopes and aspirations.

☀ Whatever ceremony you began with to celebrate the Summer Solstice, you will need to bring the occasion to its conclusion with a closing ceremony. Thank the five elements for their energy. Thank the Sun, thank the Moon. Thank all of nature and all the Guardians and Spirit guides, the Ancestors, and each other.

☀ Bless the food and drink. Feast and party.

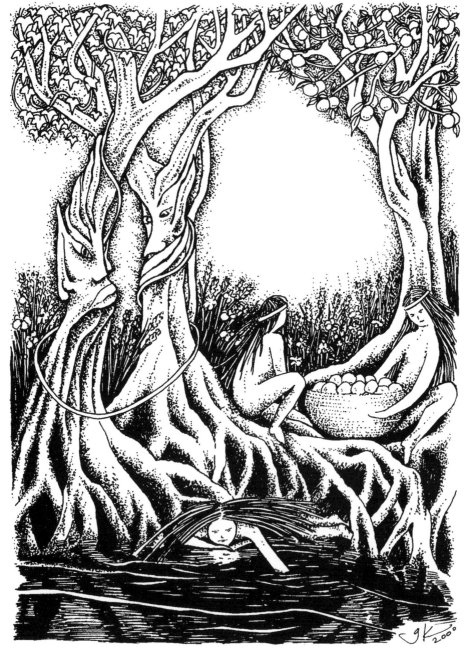

LAMMAS

SUMMER CROSS QUARTER FESTIVAL

END JULY/BEGINNING AUGUST

Mid-Leo ♌ fixed fire

Lammas Eve ◇ Lughnasadh ◇
Lugnnasa ◇ Feast of Lug ◇
The Feast of Bread ◇ Loaf Mass

Celebration of the Grain Mother

Festival of First Fruits
and Reminder

The Festival of Gathering in

LAMMAS

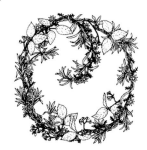

This is the Summer's height and the celebration of the grain harvest when the Corn or Grain Mother was honoured. After all the hard work of getting the grain crop cut, threshed, stored and stacked, there came a time for feasting, celebration and assessment. Lammas is a Saxon name meaning 'Loaf-mass'.

On Lammas Eve or Lughnasadh (pronounced Loo-nas-a), fires were lit on Lammas mounds such as Silbury Hill at Avebury, to honour the Corn Mother as she gives birth to her harvest child, the Grain. This is the seed which will bring next year's harvest as well as the grain which will sustain life throughout the Winter. The month of August was the month of the Grain Mother. An 'august' was a person filled with the Spirit of the Goddess. An 'augur' is an old word for seer and meant 'Increaser'.

The Grain Mother, Barley Mother, Corn Mother, Demeter, Ceres, Cerealia, Grain, Solar Goddess, the Wise One of the Earth, the Increaser - all symbolized the abundance of the Earth Mother, the aspect of the Triple Goddess who brings forth manifest life. She who is the seed, who is the womb, who is the soil, the Great Provider, the Preserver of Life, the regenerative power, was never more manifest than now as the harvest is gathered in.

The regenerative cauldron was central to Celtic spiritual understanding. We are renewed by death, sleep and darkness, and by the sacrifice of our outer lives. Here at Lammas, the doorway to the inner realms is opening. This is the symbolism behind the Demeter/Kore/Persephone story. Demeter, the Corn Mother, represents the ripe corn of this year's harvest, and Kore or Persephone represents the grain-seed who lives in the dark throughout the winter and reappears in the Spring. Persephone's descent into the Underworld is a mythical interpretation of the seed lying in the ground during the dark Winter months, and her reappearance as the young maid, or the new sprouting seed, in the Spring. This depicts the Triple Goddess in all her aspects, as Earth Mother, the abundant provider; as the Crone, the wisdom found within; and as the Maiden who returns renewed in the Spring. Pluto/Hades' abduction of Persephone is a later reworking of this older myth.

After all the manifest energy and activity of the Summer, we thankfully turn inwards for regeneration and renewal of our Spirit, that we may rest and assimilate all that has happened to us during the Sun's active phase.

The main cereal crops would have been wheat, barley, rye and oats. Cutting the 'corn' seems to be a general term for all cereal crops. There were many customs and rituals throughout Europe to honour the first and the last sheaf of corn to be cut. The last sheaf was often cut by the youngest girl present and fashioned into a Corn Maiden, a baby or an old woman. It was carried joyfully back to the village, sometimes plaited and decked with ribbons, and usually hung over the fireplace. Sometimes it was dressed in women's clothes, and ritually burnt on the Lammas Fire. Sometimes these Corn Maidens were kept until Yule when they were divided up amongst the cattle or kept until the Spring. Sometimes they were kept with the date tied to them. Many Corn Maidens would be seen hanging above the fireplace. In Scotland the 'young maid' was made out of the last stalks cut, and kept. The 'old wife' was made out of the first stalks cut and was passed on to the nearest farmer who had not finished bringing in the corn. This was then passed round until it ended up at the last farm to be cut. Another old European custom was to weave the last sheaf into a large Corn Mother with a smaller corn doll inside it, representing next year's unborn harvest.

Lammas eve was a night to honour the Corn Mother and the cauldron of regeneration inherent within this moment of harvest and gathering in. Celebrations may have begun with the cutting of the last sheaf of corn, or the harvest full Moon. August 2nd is a traditional date, but the Lammas fairs and feasts lasted for a period of one month, fifteen days before August 1st and fifteen days after. Once the grain had been safely gathered in and the men returned from their hunting trips, it was a time for feasting, dancing and merry-making, a celebration of the first harvest. Beer, wine, cider and whisky made from the previous year's harvest, were ritually drunk, celebrating the transformative power of Fire and Water. Cooking fires were honoured as they too embodied the power of Fire and Water. Bread was made from the new grain and thanks were given to the Sun's life energy reborn as the bread of life.

Lammas was a tribal gathering, a traditional time for travelling fairs, horse fairs (in honour of Rhiannon, the horse Goddess of the Underworld), trading fairs of all kinds, markets, business transactions of all kinds, ritual games, horseracing, trial marriages (hand-fasting). The choosing of a new tribal leader would have taken place now as assessment and review of the active part of the year (and success of the crop) was undertaken. In the North of England these fairs are known as the 'Wakes'. They are still celebrated today, although they have lost touch with their roots which included mourning for the death of the Sun's power.

Lugh or Lug was a Celtic God, a Sun King who, according to the myth, dies now with the waning year. He is John Barleycorn whose energy has gone into the grain, is cut down and sacrificed back to the land. This is the key to understanding Lammas, through the death and transformation of the Sun. We too, like the Sun, must sacrifice ourselves and the active outer energy of the year, and welcome the inner journey. In the Pagan tradition this is often interpreted as the sacrifice of the male ego giving way to the feminine power. But we must look beyond this to understand the energy shift we must all make from the potential of the active (referred to in the past as male) phase, to the potential of the receptive and regenerative (referred to in the past as female) phase, irrespective of our gender.

As we are becoming more whole and learn to balance both sides of ourselves, the sacrifice of the active outer energy at this time is crucial to our wellbeing. The Western lifestyle has forgotten the power and necessity of the cauldron of regeneration which the Celts understood as so important. Here at Lammas, we can make the necessary adjustments to turn and face our inner selves. We will now carry our harvest through the darkness of Winter, understanding it further on the deeper levels, until it is reborn and becomes manifest again in the Spring.

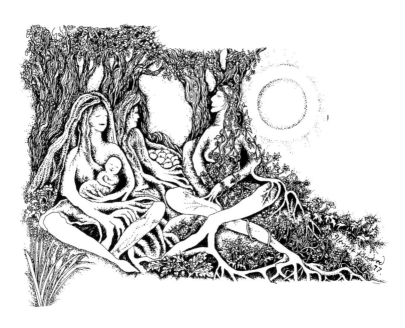

THE UNDERLYING ENERGY OF LAMMAS

Lammas is the seasonal peak of high Summer,
but as with all Cross Quarter festivals, it
represents a change in the manifest energy. Summer
feels as if it will last forever, but from this peak of
growth onwards, we see the first signs of change and
death. In the fields the cereal crops have turned from
green to gold and are gathered in. The first fruits are
ripening, the first nuts are falling and we must think
about laying in stores ready for Winter. It is the time to
gather seeds which can be saved and planted in the
Spring. It is a time of making the most of the
remaining sunshine, getting about while we still can.

Here we begin to assimilate and
gather in our own harvest, the first fruits of our active
phase now manifest in the outer world, the harvest of our
heart's desires, and the fruits of our labours. This is a period
of assessment as we begin to understand on the inner levels
what we have manifest on the outer levels. We begin to gather
ourselves together again after much scattering of energy. Now we
must change from the outward-looking expansive energy and begin
to take a reflective look at ourselves. In the Spring we planted the seeds
of our desires and ourselves. We now begin to reap what we have sown.
We need to return to the inner spiritual world now to bring a deeper
understanding of ourselves and our actions.

It is a time to give thanks for all the rewards we are
harvesting. Being aware of them will help you to see ways
to use them in the future.

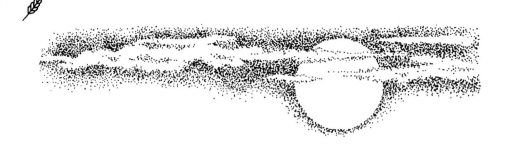

Full Moon in Aquarius

What is this coming through the Fire?
What is this spell in the song?
What is this star burning brighter?
What is this? What is this?

There's a rise in the eyes of the Gods of the forest,
There's a swell in the heart of the Gods of the sea
Sky-fliers swim in the winds of the wanting
And the Goddess flame burns ready
Inviting footprints on a path to the dawn
Bewitching steps across a leaping fire
Arms outstretched in the love of the moment
In the yell of the yelling and the breath of desire.

It's a rising tide of a new generation
Swelling sea of a storm to come
Shiver in the leaves on a fine Summer dawn
Echo of the future in the tribal drum

Full Moon in Aquarius

Brian Boothby
Tomorrows Ancestor

PREPARATIONS FOR LAMMAS

FIRE ◇ FEAST ◇ BREAD MAKING ◇ RATTLES ◇
CORN DOLLIES ◇ SEEDS ◇
THE GRAIN MOTHER ◇ CERES ◇ DEMETER ◇
MOTHER ◇ FATHER ◇
MAKING A MOON GARDEN ◇ HEALING WANDS ◇
BASKET OF ABUNDANCE ◇ BOWER ◇ CROP CIRCLES ◇
TREES AND SHRUBS OF LAMMAS: HAZEL ◇ GORSE
HERBS OF LAMMAS: CHAMOMILE ◇ MARIGOLD

Lammas is traditionally a tribal gathering, bringing the tribe together for work and play, for enjoyment and assessment. It may last over a period of many days and therefore camping space would help with this influx of visitors. It is a good time to harness many people's energy for a community project such as clearing a piece of land, building work or a garden project.

Prepare a place for the Lammas fire, with space around it for dancing and some seating. Moveable benches can be made easily with a plank of wood nailed to two rounds of treetrunk. You will need several 4 or 6 inch nails for each. Give them a coat of wood preserver and they will last for years. They are very versatile and can be used for tables as well as seating and for creating a theatre space. Ask everyone to bring firewood.

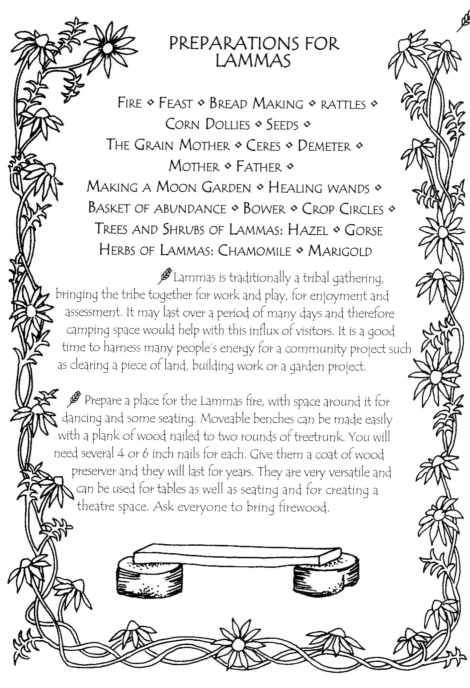

🌾 Prepare an area for the Lammas feast. Some tables are needed for people to put the food they bring to share, sleeping mats/carpets/rugs for the children to lay their sleeping bags. An outdoor feast is very central to this celebration. Decorate the area with sheaves of wheat, oats, rye or barley tied up with red ribbon.

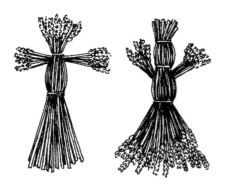

🌾 Weave and fashion a Grain Mother, starting with a sheaf of wheat. Tie the bundles with red ribbon. As you weave and plait the corn stalks, focus on the harvest of the Earth. If you cannot get a bundle of wheat, then use long dry grass or reed.

🌾 Weave and plait smaller corn dollies from wheat or grass stalks. A single plait or concertina can be used to create simple shapes which can be hung up.

As you plait and weave, focus on your own harvest which

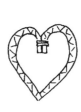 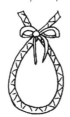 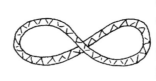

can be seen in the outer world and understood in the inner world. Look in your heart and find all you have to be grateful for.

There are many traditional corn dollies and corn weaving which can be learnt from an experienced teacher.

🌾 Create a shrine dedicated to the Corn Mother Goddess and the Sun God. Ask everyone to bring something for it. If you have enough space, you can place this within an area created for contemplation and meditation. A circle of stones 15 feet across or a circle of bent Willow or Hazel rods is enough to define a space. Use a lump hammer and a metal spike to make holes in the ground and push in the thick end of the rod. Space the rods 1 - 2 ft apart, bending them over and weaving the tops in the usual way. This could easily be created on a lawn, as it is impermanent and leaves just a circle of small holes. If you use fresh Willow-rods, water them well and leave them over the Winter. By the Spring they will be growing well. This quiet meditation space is a much valued area, especially at a larger gathering. Place the shrine in the middle, or to one side, in the West for Lammas.

🌾 Finish off the projects you began this Summer while you still have the energy and the light, especially outdoor projects.

🌾 Take a long walk in the country, walk one of the dragon paths you have discovered in your area. Walk to a local power spot, a stone circle, barrow, well, woods, or high point. Make a day of it. Take some bread, spring water and some fruit. Experience the changes in the Earth and in yourself. Look at the ripening grain, the seeds, the first blackberries and the first hazelnuts; bring them back for your shrine. Contemplate and assess your own harvest. Did the seeds that you planted at Imbolc grow as you had hoped? Are they the same dreams to take with you through the incubation period of Winter? Do not be disappointed if they have not yet materialised. Keep the vision strong and all things will come when you least expect it and in ways which also may not be apparent at first. Perhaps there is a sacrifice to be made in order to achieve your heart's desire? True sacrifice is not giving up yourself for others, but the sacrifice of a lower ideal for a higher one.

🌾 Meditate on the seed inherent within your harvest. Make time for meditation. State your readiness to receive inspired guidance, and let your intuition guide you. Take time to look at your life. What is its purpose or reason? How can you best serve humanity? How can you be of service to help the Earth? Much damage has been done. Industry and intensive farming has brought much pollution and destruction to natural resources, environments and the climate. Now we have a new threat with genetically modified crops which bear no seed and are the product of a world which has lost touch with nature and the natural cycles of the Earth.

Rattles

Make a rattle filled with seeds, representing new life, which can be used in any ceremony for renewing energy. Different seeds make different sounds. Make sure they are perfectly dry or they will go mouldy. Join two clean dry yogurt pots or tin cans together with tape, first adding some rice or lentils. Experiment with the sound. The sound will become dull if you put too many seeds in, and will stay 'lively' with less. It depends on what sound you like. When you are satisfied with the sound,

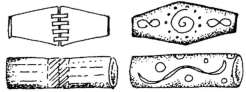

sellotape it together well and cover the whole thing with a couple of layers of newspaper strips glued on with watered-down PVA glue. When it is dry, paint with a base coat of household emulsion and then a design of your choice.

Look for seeds in the countryside or in friend's gardens that you can collect and dry now ready for sowing in the Spring. Put them on paper to dry in the Sun, then store them in envelopes, labelling them carefully.

Moon Garden

Make a Moon garden now that the energy is turning within. This is a place to sit in outside especially at the full Moon and the new Moon. It need only be a small area but, with planning and intent, it will become a very special place in your garden to sit outside under the stars, a place for contemplation and meditation. It needs to be a sheltered spot, but the Moon's place in the sky changes throughout the year and the night, so it also needs to be kept open to the sky, possibly raised. A small seat in each of the four directions will help your orientation to the Moon's place in the sky. A large flat stone in the centre can be used to put special things on, and as a place to put crystals to charge in the moonlight. Place a mirror face upwards at full Moon. Place a glass bowl filled with spring water on the mirror and let it stand out all night under the full Moon. In the morning add a ¼ - ½ part brandy to your Moon water to preserve it. Take drops as needed to invoke full Moon qualities. Plant white flowers, scented night flowers, aromatic herbs and plants associated with the Moon.

Ceres ♀ and Demeter ∇

Ceres or Cerealia was the Latin (Roman) form of the Great Mother Goddess, the

Grain Mother, Mother Earth, the dispenser of natural law. She was called 'Ceres Legifera', Ceres the lawgiver, and was the founder of the Roman legal system. The Greeks called her Demeter. 'Meter' means Mother, and 'De' is delta or triangle, the female genital sign. She was known as the abundant Mother, the Barley Mother, the wise one of the Earth, she who is the Mother of the seed. The Goddess was worshipped before the patriarchal religions began to supplant her 3,500 years ago. Country people, especially, continued to honour her despite the desperate measures the Church took to stop them during the witchhunt years.

Demeter's spirit was believed to be in the first and last sheaves of the corn to be cut. It was called the Demeter, the Corn Mother, the old woman. Kore, Ker or Persephone was the aspect of the Triple Goddess who descended into the Underworld for renewal and is reborn in the Spring.

The Mother

In ancient times all temples were dedicated to the Mother. The Earth was seen as a womb and our relationship to the unseen part of ourselves, our inner world, was seen to be just as important as our relationship to the outer world. The Mother aspect of the Triple Goddess was seen as a bridge which linked the active manifest energy and the unknown inner world. The Mother was 'the Great Provider' bringing fertility, growth, nurturing abundance, harvest and community. Mother Earth, mother love, mother instinct – all reflect this link. Her colours are red, orange, gold. The other aspects of her trinity are the Maid in Spring representing rebirth, and the Crone in the Winter representing the regenerative wisdom within.

In ancient times, when it was your birthday, you honoured your mother who gave birth to you. Motherhood is a sacred gift. We need to reclaim its power and its worth, to see it as an important time for nurturing and teaching your own and other people's children. Here at Lammas when the Earth Mother is honoured, we can use it to celebrate the mother within ourselves and our own mothers, whether they are alive or not. If you have no children of your own to mother, then help another mother. Build up relationships with children which are lasting and meaningful. We have much to teach them. Sharing time together brings pleasure and benefits beyond the time spent.

The Father

Here at Lammas the Sun King or Sun God is honoured before he too sacrifices his outer attributes and turns inwards. Logical and rational thought is now balanced by its complementary opposite, intuition and inner wisdom. Our present day western culture is in a state of imbalance because a majority of people do not listen to their inner voice, nor acknowledge their intuition. Here at Lammas we can reclaim this side of ourselves. There is a great opportunity now for all those who operate mostly in linear and logical ways, to remember the value of connecting to the dark, the hidden aspects of themselves, their emotions, their intuition and their inner knowing. Many people claim a disconnection from their fathers, lacking a deep and meaningful emotional relationship. It is generally agreed that there is much healing work to be done here. So much damage has been done by the patriarchal religions which have not encouraged men to follow their emotions or to acknowledge their deepest feelings, thereby denying men a true relationship with their women and children, and also other men. Here at Lammas, honour your father, whether he is alive or not, and fatherhood. Honour your relationship with your children and with other people's children, if you do not have children of your own. Honour the children. If you are male, pledge to open your hearts and emotions to fatherhood or surrogate fatherhood. Forgiveness and compassion open the doors to the heart. Here at Lammas, let us share in a vision, a process of discovery, assessment and positive affirmations towards a more balanced male of the future.

Trees of Lammas

Hazel - *corylus avellana*

This is the ninth tree of the Celtic Tree Ogham C. COLL and is linked to inner wisdom. In Celtic legend nine nuts of wisdom fell from the Hazel tree into the river. They were eaten by a magical salmon who absorbed all the wisdom and changed into a young girl. The transformation inherent at Lammas is hidden in this story. The visions we act upon now will change our future and transform our present. Our dreams can become our reality through creative life-enhancing solutions in areas of our lives which we intuitively feel need changing. The Hazel will help us find inspired solutions and to follow an intuitive path rather than a well-thought-out plan. It is an easy tree to communicate with and is used to sharing its long straight poles with humankind since ancient times.

Cut yourself a Hazel stick or staff, asking the tree first and choosing intuitively. Thank the tree for its gift. Leave the bark on or strip it off.

When it has dried out, sand it down until it is smooth, beginning with a rough sandpaper and ending with a fine one. Oil your stick with teak oil or linseed oil, or a beeswax polish. Hazel makes a fine walking stick and companion which will enhance other communication with non-verbal beings such as minerals, stones, trees, plants and animals. You can make a small healing wand in the same way, which can be carried in your pocket and placed under the pillow. Go to the Hazel when you need to overcome any creative blocks and when you need to find inner wisdom. Gather the nuts before the squirrels have stored them all away for the Winter.

Gorse - *ulex europaeus*

Although not a tree, the Gorse is the seventeenth tree of the Celtic Tree Ogham O. ONN. In Celtic legend it is linked to wisdom which comes as a result of hard work, linking fruitfulness and fulfilment on the inner levels as well as in the outer world. The Gorse is linked to Lammas as we harness the last energy of the waning year and reap the harvest of our hard work. For those who feel their harvest has not been a good one, the Bach flower remedy, Gorse, will restore hope and faith in the future. It will also help you see ways to use them in the future. Gorse is found on moorland and common land and flowers for most of the year. Lay down near a Gorse bush and assimilate its vibration. Cut yourself a healing wand, carry it with you to help you focus on your harvest.

🌾 Healing Wands

Sometimes a branch or twig of a tree will 'call out' to you, wanting to come with you. This means the Dryad, the tree spirit, is willing to subdivide to come with you. This subdivision is a complete Dryad in itself, contains all the wisdom of the bigger Dryad and will live in the piece of wood, gaining mobility which the tree doesn't have. By meditating with the Dryad, you can learn to communicate with it and work together for healing. A healing wand can be used for energy balancing on the chakras or the acupuncture meridian points and meditation. You may find a completely new way to work with tree spirits. Keep your intuition flowing and your heart open. Do not underestimate the power and abilities of the trees. In the past they were revered for their sacred connection to humankind. They still wish to work

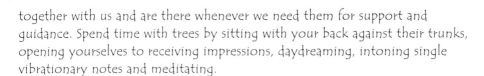

together with us and are there whenever we need them for support and guidance. Spend time with trees by sitting with your back against their trunks, opening yourselves to receiving impressions, daydreaming, intoning single vibrationary notes and meditating.

🌿 Herbs of Lammas

This is a busy time for harvesting herbs and collecting herb seeds to sow in the Spring. Give thanks and blessings as you pick them, dry them and store them. Review what you know about them and ways you can use them medicinally, psychically and magically.

Sage - *salvia officinalis*

Sage is a herb associated with wisdom and releasing blocks in expression. It is connected to the throat chakra and is for those who have something to say but cannot let it out. It will help you express your emotions. Harvest sage at the end of July, before the flowers have come out. Make the herb tea in the usual way. The infusion is a useful antiseptic herb for sore throats, laryngitis, tonsillitis, mouth ulcers and mouth infections. It can be used as a gargle, for bathing wounds, sores, and to stop bleeding. Use the tea infusion externally and then drink afterwards as well. It will dry up excess secretions such as catarrh or sinusitis. It contains oestrogen and is useful in the menopause and for delayed menstruation. Burn as an incense to cleanse and purify. Waft the smoke around a person to cleanse their aura (called 'smudging'). This is a good way to begin any ritual or ceremony. **It must not be taken if pregnant, and because of its drying action, it must not be taken for long periods of time. It will dry up mother's milk. Care must be taken by those who are insulin-dependent, and to be avoided by epileptics.**

Meadowsweet - *filipendula ulmaria*

Garlands of meadowsweet were traditionally worn for the Lammas celebrations. Its heady perfume expands the psyche, and builds inner strength and connection to the source. It enhances flexibility and connection to the inner levels. It is a mild sedative and painkiller containing salicylic acid (aspirin) which affects the rate at which blood clots. It is a good digestive tonic which

178

reduces excess acidity and is useful for heartburn, hyperacidity, gastritis and peptic ulcers. As it cleanses the body of harmful acids, it is useful for any inflammatory conditions such as rheumatoid arthritis. It is a strong diuretic (increases urine) and can be used for any bladder or kidney complaint including cystitis. It reduces stagnation in the liver and therefore will help the immune system function more effectively. Its harvest time is July and August when the flowers are just beginning to open. An infusion is made in the usual way with ½ –1 ounce of the dried herb to one pint of water. Two to three times more of the fresh herb is needed. **Avoid if on anti-coagulant drugs.**

Crop Circles

Patterns in cereal crops have been appearing every summer in the South of England since the early 1970s and continue to defy acceptable explanation and logic. Since those early simple circles and concentric rings, the designs have evolved and developed. Each year new patterns appear, symbols of keys, pendulums, insectograms, mandalas, Moons, spinners, and many other complex and perfectly formed geometric shapes, symbols and patterns. Many are huge and seemed to appear in a very short space of time. The pattern's appearance is often accompanied by electrical disturbances reported locally and other unexplained phenomena. The patterns are formed by the stems of the cereal crop being bent at the base (the crop continues to grow and ripen despite being horizontal) and is found lying in swathes all facing the same direction and in spirals. For those lucky enough to get to the crop circles early, their perfection is awe-inspiring, lying perfectly straight and untrampled. Many people have told of physical and emotional phenomena connected to their experiences in these crop circles.

Research and speculation continue as crop circles move us to mystery and delight, helping us to find new levels of understanding beyond words and the rational. Perfectly in harmony with Lammas, they provide a catalyst for change and transformation.

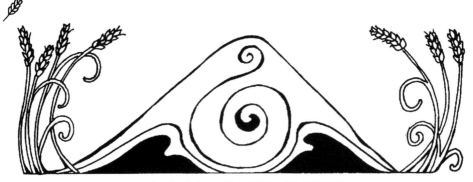

LAMMAS CELEBRATIONS

🌾 Make time to be outside and appreciate the peak of Summer. Sense the changes that are coming. Prepare yourself for the waning energy of the Sun and how this will affect you. Gather grasses, herbs and flowers for weaving into garlands and headbands for the Lammas celebration. Give thanks for the harvest enhancing a state of gratitude in your heart. Think about your own harvest which you begin to reap now, and how you can facilitate this further. Look beyond the outer harvest which is manifested, to the harvest within. Every cloud has a silver lining. Everything that happens to you can be seen in a positive light. Count your blessings.

🌾 Ask a local farmer for a sheaf of oats, wheat, barley or rye. Failing that, gather armfuls of long grasses. Use this for weaving a Corn Mother and for smaller corn dollies and other woven corn mementoes. Weave in flowers and herbs and decorate with red, orange and gold ribbons. This could be something to help bring focus to the Lammas theme, as people arrive.

🌾 Weave a headband or garland of grasses and flowers to wear at the Lammas ceremony. Bind a circle of grass together and tie with grass or a pale coloured garden string. Weave in flowers and herbs.

🌾 Bread Making and Seed Biscuits

Bake your own bread and biscuits with seeds and nuts in them. As you do this, give thanks for the grain harvest that makes this possible and focus on the seed within the harvest. Celebrate the Earth's abundance. Focus on ways you can support organic farming which respects the Earth. Making bread is very relaxing and easy. The 'quick' yeasts in sachets require only one ten minute knead. Mix with 1½ pounds (600g) flour and 1 pint (570ml) lukewarm water. To make plaited loaves, make three long rolls of dough and plait in the usual way. Place the plaited loaf on a warm greased baking tray. Cover with a clean tea towel and leave in a warm place to rise (about one hour). Bake in a hot oven for 15 - 20 minutes. Small rolls can be made in the same way and only need baking for ten minutes. Just before baking, brush with milk and sprinkle with poppy seeds or sesame seeds. Experiment with different shapes and added extras such as dried fruit, nuts, olives, sunflower seeds.

🌾 Create a four-way archway with four Hazel poles joined in the middle. Each pole can be orientated to each of the four directions. Each pole can be decorated by tying on bunches of flowers and grasses. The children love helping to do this. In the centre on a golden cloth, place the Corn Mother you have made and all around, place the food which represents the grain harvest: bread, cakes, biscuits. Include vases of flowers, hedgerow fruit and nuts, and any edible fungi you may have found. Hang red ribbons from the top and any other corn creations. Make it look beautiful, a true celebration of the grain harvest and first fruits.

🌾 Bring the group together into a circle round the bower. Light a candle at each of the directions, place something at each one representing each element. Honour Spirit at the centre and around the outside of your circle. 'Smudge' the bower with burning sage, coltsfoot, or lavender. As you smudge, state clearly your intent for cleansing the space and raising awareness during the ceremony.

🌾 In the centre of the bower, place three large candles: one green to represent the Earth in her Spring green colour, one gold to represent the Earth in her harvest colour, and one purple or black to represent the Earth as she moves inwards for the Winter. Light these with ceremony, honouring the three aspects of the Earth as you light them. Bring the group together with a chant to honour the Earth Mother.

Make a circle around the bower by holding hands. Walk or dance around it, first clockwise to the right, and then widdershins to the left. Focus on the turning direction of the year as you dance. If you are celebrating on your own, dance around the bower and honour the five elements in turn.

Ask five people beforehand to represent the five elements. Towards the end of the dance, they can take up their positions by the direction they are going to speak for. Each person should be dressed in the colours of that element, easily achieved with coloured scarves. As the dance comes to an end, let each welcome the spirit of the element into our understanding. Speak from the heart and keep the vision of the words strongly in your mind as you speak so that your words have strength and power. Agree on the order beforehand so that the ceremony flows.

Fire in the South

Honour and give thanks for the power of the Sun which has brought the harvest to fruition. The creative outer world is manifest in growth and abundance. Give thanks for the harvest of your own creativity. Now we must take the Sun within and expand on the inner levels. Now we can understand this harvest on the spiritual level, prepare for change and transformation as the outer growth is sacrificed and the inner Fire is activated.

Water in the West

Honour and give thanks for Water, the rain which has swelled the grain. Give thanks for the expansive flow and currents of the heart and emotions, which have been brought out into the light. The energy begins now to flow back within for renewal and regeneration. The outward spiral turns inward. Trust the changes. Welcome the chance to rest again, to dream, to be cleansed. Give thanks for the inner harvest which is to come.

Earth in the North

The material world is manifest in the harvest. Give thanks for the grain which will sustain life throughout the winter. Give thanks to the Earth Mother, the support of the Earth, sustainability. Honour the Earth's gifts and the seeds which will bring next year's harvest. Give thanks for the abundance of food, the grain, for bread, for nurturing, for our mothers, our fathers, our friendships, our family, for the children, for our experiences and achievements this year. With assessment, the cycle is complete, and we can turn to face the inner journey ready to internalise our experiences.

Air in the East

Give thanks for the abundance of communication, information, experiences, and for the manifestation of our desires and thoughts. Now we take a reflective look at ourselves, assessing our harvest, learning from our experiences. New beginnings, a new journey, new seeds, as we turn inwards once again for renewal.

Spirit

Give thanks for Spirit which sustains and nurtures us. Give thanks for this essential part of ourselves which cannot be seen and cannot be named. We reach out and in, connecting to our source, guidance and inner nourishment. We touch the sacred, the still point of power at the centre of our being. Through it we are a part of all life and all existence on this Earth and beyond it.

🌾 Honour the Grain Mother and the harvest of the Earth. Give everyone an ear of wheat and let each one add it to the Grain Mother in the centre, in a ritual where each person gives thanks to the Earth and her abundance as the Great Provider. We gather the seeds which the Earth has provided for its own continuation. We take this for our food. Remember the people in the world who are hungry. How can we share our abundance with others? There is no need for anyone in the world to be starving. Focus now on healing this imbalance. A simple drumbeat or hum will help to focus this moment.

🌾 Feel yourself to be part of the abundance and fullness of the season. Share with each other what your personal harvest is. Lammas is the moment to assess where you are on your path. Give thanks for what you have gained in the outer world, and what you will take with you into the inner realms.

Count your blessings. Being thankful for the things you have, open the doorway to your own abundance.

 Welcome the changes which are coming and the journey we must make into the dark. See what we can take with us as we carry our outer Sun within. Storing our blessings in our hearts means we can access them in the Winter.

 Look within to see what negative thoughts you may be nurturing. Look beyond them to the fear which lies behind them, and then beyond this to a loving positive solution. Acknowledging negativity and understanding its purpose in your life, is the beginning of transforming it for your greater good.

 Make a 'Basket of Abundance'. Put something in from your Summer harvest, and take out something which someone else has put in. Ask everyone to bring something for this purpose.

 Honour your father and your mother or the people whom you acknowledge as being a father or mother to you, even if they are no longer alive. Ask everyone to bring a photograph of them. Pin them to the Corn Mother, thanking them for their positive qualities and forgiving them their negative qualities. Honour yourselves as mothers and fathers, or surrogate mothers and fathers. Honour the energy that you give to the children. Forgive yourself the mistakes you have made.

 Dance a sacred dance of Summer. Express the energy that the season has given you. Let the drums bring a focus for the Sun and your creativity, and then let the mood of the dance change as you gather yourself together to welcome the changes and the dark. End the dance with a connection to the source of all things. Meditate, breathing deeply, and focus on the seeds of your heart.

🌾 Holding hands, dance the mystic spiral, with one person leading the group into a large circle and then spiralling evenly into the centre. Lead everyone into a tight cluster. When everyone has stopped and can go no further, intone the sacred harmony of Om. (The Celts called their Moon mother Omh - 'she who is'.) Let the sound flow in one continuous sound bath lasting for at least ten minutes. As everyone is very close, the sound resonates and vibrates through everyone's bodies and is very powerful. After it is over, let each say "thank you for..." as the spirit moves them. This facilitates a state of gratitude and radiance from within. Now would be a good moment for a hand-fasting or baby's naming ceremony.

🌾 Bless the food and drink brought to share. Feast and party.

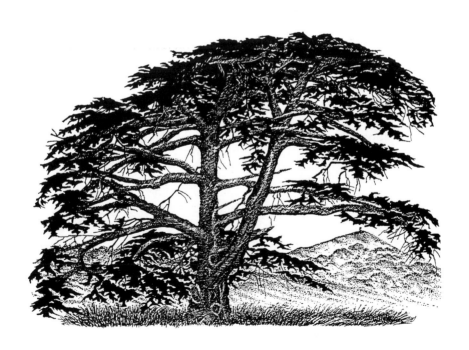

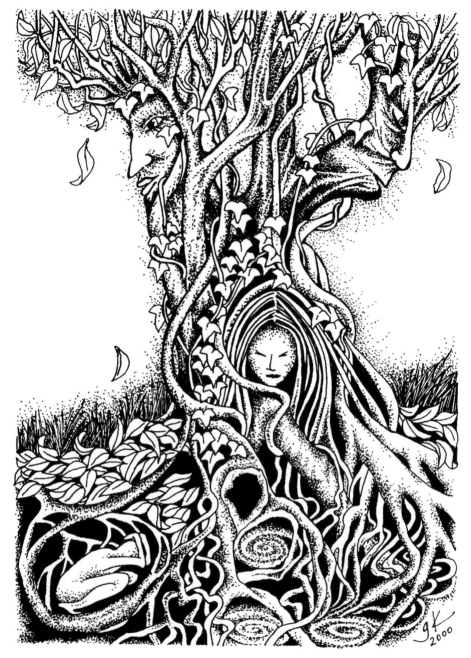

186

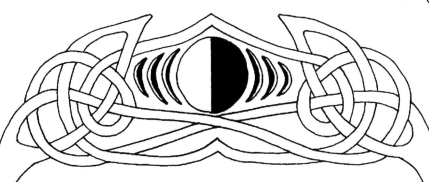

AUTUMN EQUINOX

AUTUMN QUARTER POINT

20TH - 23RD SEPTEMBER

SUN ENTERS LIBRA ♎

Mabon ◇ Alban Elued ◇

Harvest Festival

Festival of Thanksgiving

Festival of Restored Balance
and Integration

AUTUMN EQUINOX

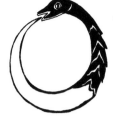

Day and night are in perfect balance again all over the world. The Sun enters the sign of Libra, bringing balance and harmony and, by necessity, change and transformation. It is time to take action and move into a new energy phase to balance the outer world with the inner world. It is a time to release the past and move forwards, a chance to be clear about what it is you want to do now and prepare for Winter.

After all is gathered in, and the outside jobs are completed, we can celebrate the harvest. It is the family gathering of Autumn's end, Thanksgiving, the big harvest party, a feast and a celebration of the year's abundance. Here we can celebrate the Earth and all her gifts, friendships, family, our produce, our creations and achievements, our own personal harvest. Autumn Equinox is the doorway to Winter. Summer is over and a new phase will begin. Here we can share with each other what we have gained and completed during the Summer and make our plans for the coming Winter. From now on the days will get noticeably shorter and colder. The Sun's power is waning fast. This is the time of ripening fruits, nuts, mushrooms and berries. It is a busy time if you want to lay in stores for the Winter.

It is a time for balancing and reconciling opposites and to see them as part of the whole. Everything co-exists together and we need both sides in order to be balanced and whole: the seen and the unseen, the known and the unknown, creation and destruction, death and rebirth, materialism and spirituality. Here at the Autumn Equinox, celebrate your whole selves, your masculine and feminine aspects, your conscious and unconscious, the active and the receptive, your light and dark sides, your fortunes and your misfortunes, your young self and your old self – and all aspects of the cycle of life. Celebrate it all, the good and the bad. Honour the changing season which brings a chance to start again.

Dragon Day was celebrated at the Spring and Autumn Equinoxes. Here the dragon is invoked to carry the Fire energy into the inner realms, to activate the Fire within. The dragon goes underground now for the Winter. The dragon is an ancient energy symbol representing Earth energy, dynamism, Fire, will and courage. This we take with us now as we turn to face the dark inner realms. This is not a place to fear as we have been taught, but a place to get in touch with your power, strength, inner focus, spiritual path and a reconnection to your inner wisdom. We are part of this whole, not separate from it.

THE UNDERLYING ENERGY OF THE AUTUMN EQUINOX

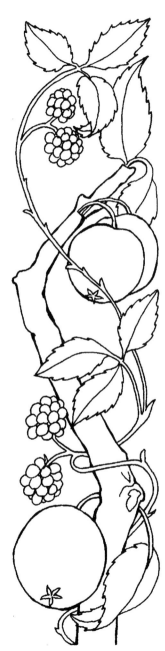

The Equinoxes prepare us for change in the Earth's energy. This is the transition into the Winter season which we must all respond to. Things are moving fast now. Preparations and intentions for the coming Winter months must be made now. The days are shortening and the increasing cold are here to remind us that change is coming. The leaves are changing colour and falling from the trees; the fruit is ripening and needs to be gathered in. Outside jobs need to be completed.

The sap in the trees and plants is moving down now. This is the beginning of root energy and brings sleep, rest and renewal. It is a chance for all of life to go within and re-enter the dark womb of the spiritual world. This is the balance between the outer journey and the inner journey, which provides a strong foundation for our lives. It is a time for long-term planning and incubation. The seed ideas we plant now will re-emerge in the Spring changed, transformed and strengthened by their time in the unconscious. We have become disconnected from the source of our inner knowing. Use the Autumn Equinox to reclaim this imbalance. Listen to the wisdom and intuitions which come from within, trust your inner journey, value its path as much as you value the path of your outer knowing and outer journey.

Give thanks for your harvest. A state of gratitude opens your heart and increases the flow of love and abundance in your life. Give thanks for the inner rewards you are beginning to harvest and look for ways to use them in the future. Ask for guidance, be open to a change in focus, or a change in direction in your life. State your intent to find inner wisdom and to follow your spiritual path.

At this moment, when we appreciate all that the Earth has provided for us, ask yourself what you can give back, to help the healing of the Earth, to undo the damage of our industrial/scientific age. The gift you have is your inspired vision and enlightenment, your love, compassion and higher ideals which will affect all those you speak to, and will bring changes in the world. Welcome your awakening intuitive creative faculties which will help heal our imbalanced rational world. Share the wisdom and power this brings you. Manifest the goodness of your Spirit in all you do.

The double spiral is the symbol of Autumn Equinox. It illustrates the inbreath and the outbreath, the point of balance between the worlds, the inner and outer journey. The endless cycle of change brings renewal and new opportunities to explore and understand ourselves. Your harvest is the starting point of this understanding. At the Autumn Equinox, look back with thanks and blessings to the gifts and help given, to the expansion which began in the Spring. Welcome the turning, the change of energy flowing towards the dark, the power within. Connect to your inner pathways, your spiritual path. Rest, re-charge, find the source of your inner world. Slip out of time. Dream a new dream.

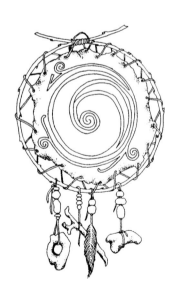

Love for Life

I am so small and yet I'm always cared for,
My share of abundance awaits.
And your life is yours just for the cost of living it,
And even that is up to you.

Counting blessings
Thanking the land
Connecting to the source of Life

Opening hearts
In simple gratitude
Returning love for life

So sit on the hill, and watch the Sunrise,
Forget your hardships, break your bread.
We give so much - we give so little
The balance settles with gratitude.

Counting blessings
Thanking the land
Connecting to the source of Life

Opening hearts
In simple gratitude
Returning love for life

Returning love for life returning
Love for life returning
for life Love
Returning love
For life

Brian Boothby
Tomorrows Ancestor

PREPARATIONS FOR AUTUMN EQUINOX

THANKSGIVING FEAST ◇ FRUITS ◇ BERRIES ◇ NUTS ◇
FLOWERS ◇ HARVEST PARTY ◇ SPACE–CLEARING ◇
SEEDS ◇ BULBS ◇
PREPARE FOR WINTER ◇ CRYSTALS ◇ MEDITATION ◇
TALKING STICK ◇ BINDING ◇ DRAGONS ◇
HERB SACHETS ◇ INCENSE ◇ BALANCE ◇
HERMES/MERCURY
TREES AND SHRUBS: APPLE ◇ HEATHER
HERBS: FENNEL ◇ MARIGOLD ◇
HAWTHORN BERRIES

This is the harvest party of Summer's end, a time for getting together with friends and family to celebrate the harvest and for thanksgiving. This can be a great occasion for a feast with everyone seated around a table sharing food and drink.

Get out and about and taste the Equinox on the day (the exact time and day can be found in any astrological diary). Celebrate the abundance of the Earth, apples, damsons, sloes, rosehips, haws, elderberries, blackberries, the flowers and fungi, the ripening seeds on all the plants. There is so much to appreciate now before the rain and the cold begin the period of disintegration and decay. The energy of the Earth is turning inward now. The sap in the trees and plants is returning into the roots. Young trees and plants will become stronger through the Winter months as their roots grow deeper. Here, in this moment, feel the same energy within you turn and seek strength in the roots of your deepest being. Sit with your back against a favourite tree, tune into its descending energy. Rest and sleep is the completion of the cycle of growth which began in the Spring. Bring back treasures from your walk to put on your Autumn Equinox shrine.

℃ Collect Autumn leaves and make a celebratory basket of different colours and shapes. In another basket collect nuts and seeds, seed-heads, fungi; and in another basket collect fruits and berries. They can be displayed and honoured in any creative way you wish. Hang coloured muslin cloths to create an area for their display.

℃ Plant tree seeds such as acorns, horsechestnut, hazelnuts, almonds, spindle, rowan berries, pine seeds, alder cones, hips and haws. Label them and leave them outside without a saucer under them. The frost and snow will not harm them, but the roots must not stand in water and become waterlogged. After two years, you will need to find permanent homes for them. Plant them in the ground when the leaves have fallen and root energy begins.

℃ Finish off any garden projects you may have started. Move trees, bushes and perennials to their new positions. Split herb plants and share them with your friends or replant in new positions. Clear the garden, cut back, weed and compost. Collect seeds for growing in the Spring. Give thanks for the abundance you have enjoyed in your garden. Give thanks to the nature spirits who are retreating now. Give thanks to the flowers, herbs and the medicines you have harvested.

℃ Plant bulbs in the ground where they will stay hidden until the Spring. Plant mixed bulbs in large pots and stand them outside your door. This way you will see and appreciate their re-emergence as the light returns after the Winter Solstice.

℃ Prepare food for the feast which reflects the abundance of the season. As you make the food, give thanks from your heart for the Earth's

193

abundance. There is much to do at this time, gathering fruit, making fruit wines, jams and preserves, collecting and drying mushrooms, and harvesting the last of the vegetables. It is a time for fruit pies and savoury pies which can be eaten hot or cold. This is a busy time in the kitchen which once again becomes the heart of the home.

 Decorations for Autumn Equinox can be quickly prepared. Make the most of coloured cloths of brown, yellow, orange and red. Let the abundance of the Earth speak for itself and use coloured leaves, herbs, flowers, seed-heads, hops, dried grasses.

 This is the time to clean out and clear your space ready for the coming new season. Throw out or give away unwanted things which are no longer relevant, or hold emotional associations which may be holding you back. Move forward into the new season with greater clarity, uncluttered by psychic dross. Creating light and harmony in your living space will greatly affect how you feel and what you achieve in your space. As you are about to move indoors now, the importance of a clean uncluttered space for yourself cannot be over-emphasised. Give everything a wash, getting rid of all the dust. Burn sage to cleanse the space. Create a special area or shrine to focus your spiritual journey. Light candles there. Put appropriate Bach flower remedies into water and, using a plant spray, spray the room to enliven and enhance its energy and your energy within it. Ring bells in all the high corners to clear out the psychic dust. State clearly, as you work, your intent for clarity and harmony. It is a wonderfully uplifting thing to do and afterwards your room feels very different.

 Dedicate an area of your room to your spiritual growth: a window ledge, a table, a shelf. On it, place a coloured cloth, a vase of fresh flowers, crystals, anything of significance which will help you keep connected to your spiritual path and the insights you are gaining. Light the candle here whenever you make this connection.

 Wash all your crystals and put them under the harvest full Moon to recharge. Thank them for all their help, for their energy, power and healing. Crystals are very powerful living things, acting directly on the energy field of the body. They respond to vibrations of respect, care and love, like all living things. They can help us to become balanced and to communicate with all of nature. This helps us see all life as sacred.

cx/cy Make time for meditation and connection to your inner self. Meditate with the spiral, the double spiral, the inner and outer breath. Seek to balance the busy outer world with the peace within. Nurture a sense of gratitude for all you have. This will open your heart to love and inner peace. Meditation will facilitate positivity, hope, and internal synthesis when it becomes a part of your daily life, providing balance between our active and receptive selves. Practise mindfulness meditation. This means staying present, watching what comes up from the unconscious, and being aware of it, but not distracted by it.

Talking Stick

Make a talking stick which can be passed around the group to facilitate discussion, sharing deep thoughts and feelings. The person who holds the stick is the only one who can speak and must not be interrupted. When she or he has finished speaking, it is passed on to the next person who wishes to speak. It is a power stick and can greatly focus and aid communication. It can take many forms. It may be a piece of wood you find, or one you cut, with thanks and intent. A good size is 40-60cms long and 2-3cms in diameter. But there are no fixed rules. Your stick can be stripped of its bark, sanded smooth and polished with beeswax polish or oil. You may prefer to leave the bark on, or cut a pattern into the bark. Oiling it will keep the wood strong and stop it from drying out and cracking. You can also bind coloured threads on to it. You can use embroidery threads or coloured wool.

1. Tie on a length of thread with one long thread which runs the length of the stick and stays inside the binding.

2. Wrap the wrapping thread around the stick carefully laying each wrap snuggly against the last and keeping the long thread inside the binding. Change colours by tying on a new colour to the wrapping thread, carefully binding the knots inside and continue to keep the inner thread running along inside the binding.

3. Tie off by tying the wrapping thread to the thread which ran inside. Tie on bells, shells, stones with holes in, feathers, beads, and other special things.

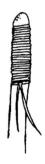

❧ Herbs

Sort out your dried herbs, throwing away last year's unused leaves and flowers. (Roots may be kept for two years if they still smell good.) Make sure that this year's herbs are properly dried, labelled and stored in dark jamjars or brown paper bags. Sunlight and damp will destroy their properties. Using circles of muslin and coloured threads, tie herbs into herb teabags or herb bath sachets (see page 151). Pour boiling water over the bags or use for sleep pillows. Make a note of the herbs used, store them and label them. Give some to friends as gifts.

❧ Experiment with different incense mixtures of dried herbs, berries and flowers. Keep a note of what you put into the different mixtures. Choose herbs for their psychic and magical properties as well as their sweet smells. Burn the dried mixture in a special dish. You have to keep blowing it to keep it glowing.

❧ Balance the male and female within yourself. Take a look at your life and perhaps notice areas where you are still responding to your conditioning and what society is expecting of you. Find ways to change so that you feel more balanced within.

❧ Trees of Autumn Equinox

Apple

The cultivated apple tree (*malus pumila domestica*), and the crab apple (*malus pumila*), both have similar properties and a long history of myths and legends, cures and uses. In every country it is regarded as sacred, magical, a symbol of fruitfulness and abundance, a means to immortality, a cure for all ills, and a gift of love. It is the tenth tree of the Celtic Tree Ogham. Q. QUERT. From Greece to the British Isles, it is connected to the fabled Western Isles of immortality, and has strong links to the Underworld and inner journeying. Here at Autumn Equinox, it is a symbol of abundance. It shows us how to give all, in total trust that all will be replenished. It teaches us to open our hearts to the abundance in our lives. By affirming and feeling thankful for what you have in the present, you open up the channels for your own abundance. Apple is a powerful cleanser. The Bach flower remedy can be taken internally by those who have a poor self-image, and used externally, a few drops in the washing water to cleanse your outer body, room, utensils, or wherever you feel the need of its cleansing energy. It is used for psychic cleansing as well as physical. Verjuice, the ancient magical drink of the Druids, is made by laying ripe crab apples in a heap until they begin to sweat. Remove the stalks and the rotten fruit, beat the remainder to a mash in a large bowl. Press this through a coarse cloth or muslin. Bottle the juice and leave for one month.

Heather - *Calluna vulgaris*

Heather is another plant associated with the Autumn Equinox, seen as a gateway between the inner world of spirit and the manifest outer world. It is number eighteen in the Celtic Tree Ogham. U. UR. How you go about your life is very much a reflection of your inner world, and demonstrates a loyalty to one's true self. If you are at peace with yourself, you will do what is right without ulterior thought of reward or advantage. This is the message of heather. Spending time with heather will lift the spirits and bring a calming soothing energy. Heather inspires us to go about our lives with this same lightness of spirit, which we can then pass on to others. Seek out any areas of your life which are causing you stress and find inspiring ways to increase your inner peace. Walk the wild places, spend time with heather and soak up its inspiring energy.

❧ Herbs of Autumn Equinox

Fennel - *foeniculum vulgare*

Use the leaves and seeds, harvesting the seeds in the Autumn. Make an infusion in the usual way and use for all gastric disturbances, for stimulating digestion, reducing bloating and helping to expel wind. Fennel is a hot dry herb and will get rid of dampness and cold. It can be safely drunk by nursing mothers to increase milk production, passing through the mother's milk to the baby to reduce wind and colic. Fennel is nourishing and sustaining. Drink whenever you feel you need nurturing. It has a soothing calming effect on the emotions. **It is a uterine stimulant, so use sparingly if pregnant.**

Hops - *humulus lupulus*

Harvest the hop flowers in September as they cascade over the hedgerows. Hang them up to dry as part of your Equinox decorations. It is a strong sedative, calming the liver and the stomach, relieving headaches and sleeplessness due to stress. Mix hop flowers and lavender flowers and fill a small cotton pillow with this mixture. Sleep with the herb pillow inside the pillowcase to ease insomnia. **Please do not use hops if you are feeling depressed, as they will make the depression worse.**

Marigold - *calendula officinalis*

A herb of the Sun to take with you into the Winter. The petals can be gathered in September and dried for Winter use as herb tea. It is a powerful blood cleanser which works on the lymphatic system and builds up the immune system. Drink the infusion whenever the immune system is lowered, and for viral and fungal infections such as candida. The fresh leaves and petals can be added to salads. The same infusion can be used to bathe wounds, and is safe to use with children and babies. Calendula will bring comfort to the Spirit. It has a soothing effect after shock, trauma or anger.

Hawthorn berries - *crataegus monogyna*

Collect and dry these from September to October. A herbal decoction, (same proportions as an infusion, but pour cold water onto the berries and let them stand overnight) is the primary remedy for all problems of the heart. It should be drunk regularly in later life to relieve and prevent angina, hardening of the arteries, palpitations of the heart, water retention and poor circulation. It will regulate high or low blood pressure, depending on the need, and gently bring the heart back to normal function, improving the general condition of the heart. It is also a useful herb for relieving stress, insomnia and any nervous condition. The berries can be burnt as an incense to help release blocked energy and open the heart to giving and receiving love. By releasing stress, it enhances a person's ability to let go and trust.

At the Spring and Autumn Equinoxes, fast for a day to help cleanse the body of harmful toxins. Drink mineral water and herb teas (fennel is good) to aid the process.

❧ Hermes (Greek)/Mercury (Roman)

Worshipped extensively in the pre-christian era as a four-fold God, his sign, the Arabic numeral 4 later became incorporated into the Christian cross. Hermes-Mercury was a God of the four elements, the four quarters of the Earth, the four winds, the four seasons, the four great Fire festivals, the four quarters of the year (Solstices and Equinoxes), the four zodiac and animal totems of the year, and later the four Archangels. Hermes-Mercury represents the blending of opposite forces, outer and inner, active and passive. His logical aspect, represented by the phallus or rod, was balanced by his intuitive aspect represented by the twin serpents (the caduceus). This gave birth to astrology, medicine, divination, magic and alchemy. The serpents, dragons or snakes of Hermes-Mercury were sometimes shown in a circle biting their own tail, representing the unending cycle of death and rebirth.

There were many temples dedicated to Hermes-Mercury, always on high places. Many of these later became dedicated to the Archangel Michael, the Angel of death. The two St Michael's Mounts, one in Cornwall and the other across the English Channel in France, were both called Mercurius in pre-christian times. (The French one still bears the name St Michel - Mont Mercure.) These mounts of Hermes-Mercury focus the hidden pathways of the dragon paths or serpent energy, rediscovered this century and referred to now as the Michael and Mary line. The hermetic power of androgyny and blended opposites is an ancient mystery whose potent symbolism has survived for us to re-examine.

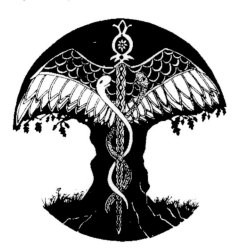

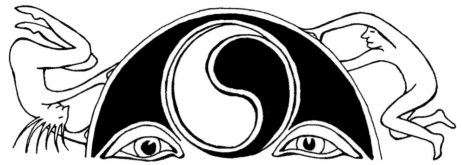

AUTUMN EQUINOX CELEBRATIONS

 Gather with friends and family for a bring and share feast. Ask everyone to bring food and drink which reflects the season. By putting tables together and covering them with sheets, it may be possible to seat everyone for a real communal feast with much toasting and dedications, thanking the Earth and each other. Decorate the tables with vases of flowers and the corn decorations you made at Lammas. Light candles with a dedication and thanks for the harvest of the year. Before you eat, bless the food. Say a simple grace together. You will need to decide whether to feast first, or have the ritual celebration first, how to balance and harmonise the two, and how to use the space available creatively.

 Thanksgiving and balance are the twin themes of the Autumn Equinox. These can be woven into the celebration to help bring clarity to the way ahead as the season changes from Autumn to Winter, and to integrate the harvest you have gained in the outer world with the path within.

 Have some baskets of yarns, seeds, shells, string, sticks, fir cones, feathers, dried grasses, dried flowers, ribbons, threads, needles, scissors. Ask everyone to bring something and then sit together, weave, thread, bind, create something which reflects the abundance of the moment. It may be a necklace to wear, a head-dress, a posie to hang, a special wand or totem. As you make it, think positively about what you are harvesting and how you can use this for your greater good and the greater good of the Earth.

 Set aside a special place for a shrine. Ask everyone to

bring something to represent harvest and balance. This quiet place can also be used for meditation and contemplation.

⊘⊘ Bring the group together to celebrate and focus the five elements. Set up each direction and its element, reflecting the abundance of the harvest in whatever way is appropriate to the space available. Wall hangings are often easiest if you are inside. Hang decorated Hazel hoops in the trees outside, or marker stones or sticks. Lead the group round in a circle, stopping at each element.

Water in the West
Give thanks for the cleansing power of Water washing away the dust of Summer, bringing renewal, mystery and inner journeys. Give thanks for the watery season about to begin as the rains replenish the Earth and sustain life. Give thanks for our emotions which show us the way and guide our actions. Give thanks for abundance of love and compassion, and the deep connection to the soul. Balance the emotions within and without. Give thanks for the gift of expression. Through tears and laughter we are made full, find inner strength and move forwards.

Earth in the North
Give thanks for the harvest of the Earth and all her gifts of food, medicines, and all the resources we take. Give thanks for all the nature spirits who cohabit this Earth and now withdraw for rest and renewal. Give thanks for the wisdom we have gained through our experiences. These we now take within for understanding and assimilation. The physical harvest is a result of all our hard work and creativity. Celebrate what has been achieved and manifested.

Air in the East
Give thanks for communication, for new ideas and realisations. Give thanks for all the opportunities to share our thoughts with each other. Give thanks for the freedom of communication and the different methods of communication available. Give thanks for communications from beyond our world, for telepathy, for our inner voice. Resolve to balance these inner communication systems with the more acceptable outer forms.

Fire in the South
Give thanks for all the beneficial changes which have manifested. Celebrate your

spontaneity and the strength of your will and courage. Celebrate your vitality and your health. If you are not well, give thanks and celebrate those days when you feel better. Celebrate and give thanks for your achievements and successes. Give thanks for your creativity and even for what has been destroyed, and pray it serves your greater good. Fire cleanses and activates. Balance its outer power with the spiritual journey within. The active power of Fire now brings expansion and light within, illumination, insights.

Spirit

Give thanks for Spirit. Within and without and ever present, Open your hearts to the abundance which this vital connection brings us. Give thanks for the power of Universal Love. Connect to our source and the guidance from within. Touch the sacred, the still point of power at the centre of our being. Embrace this energy and through it be at one with all existence on this Earth and beyond it.

Here at Autumn Equinox, the Earth's energy is balanced between the outer and the inner worlds. Now, at this point of balance, look back on what you have achieved and plant the seeds of where you wish to go. Share this with each other. Remember your vision by decorating and writing on a piece of card or wood which can be placed in your special sacred area at home.

Focus your vision using sound and words, saying what you need to express. Let sounds or notes out from deep within. Begin with a simple harmony of hums, then let out any words you wish to express. Help each other by echoing words, notes, or humming back. Weave together an expression of sound harmonising the power of the moment. Feel the power of expression as the unconscious and the conscious become balanced. Let yourself go, release your inhibitions, celebrate your freedom to be yourself.

Go around the circle, each in turn, saying "I love and approve of myself exactly the way I am". Go round several times until the energy shifts and begins to have power. Resolve to say this to yourself every day. It will bring great strength and healing.

Lay on the floor and, to a simple drumbeat, feel your breath become steady. Focus on the still point within. When you feel you are calm and connected to your inner being, make a wish, a prayer, an affirmation, and ask for an image which will help you or guide you. Know that you can do anything you want to do. Don't limit this. Your spiritual path, respect for the Earth and each other, and Love, will guide your actions. Affirm this to yourself. Make a drawing of your vision and share it with each other afterwards.

        Weave a simple circle dance which reflects the blending of the outer and inner worlds, the integration of opposite forces which blend to make the whole. Create a walking-meditation dance you can lose yourself in, and which centres your energy in the abdomen area, known as the hara. Feel your feet firmly on the Earth and your energy returning to your roots way down deep under the Earth.

        Reflect on the gains and losses of the year. Give thanks for the outer expansion and what has been possible. Look at what is no longer needed, and what it is time to let go of with thanks and blessings, as you release the past.

        Share with each other the seeds of your harvest which you take with you into the next cycle. Count your blessings. Celebrate your abundance.

        Using drums and percussion, dance your harvest dance. Let out any sounds or words from within to express this celebration. Take up each other's words to give them strength and power. Feel glad for all you have gained. Visualise the rays of the Sun being taken within, warming you from the inside. Celebrate your self, balanced and whole.

Root Meditation

Plant your feet firmly on the ground, feet apart, and let your mind relax and come to rest in your lower abdomen. Let any tensions flow down through your body, and let your weight sink into the soles of your feet. Now begin to feel your roots reaching down into the Earth and spreading out like a tree's roots. Visualise the deep dark world within yourself and feel the contact with the Earth's energy as it flows through you bringing calmness, nourishment and a strong firm foundation.

@/☉ Honour the dragon with a snake dance led by a dragon mask or dragon effigy. The dance begins with expansive expressive energy, with much noise, drumming, percussion, singing and celebration. Weave in and out and all around, and then into a wide circle. Gradually spiral the circle inwards until the energy begins to move within, quietly and slowly until the dragon is laid to sleep for the Winter.

@/☉ This is the time for reconciling opposites and bringing our whole selves into balance. Light a candle for restored balance, and to help focus an area in your life which you feel needs balancing. Balance light and dark, young and old, male and female, conscious and unconscious, emotion and detachment, active and passive, material and spiritual. State your resolve. Share with each other your intentions, hopes and fears.

@/☉ Pass the talking stick around the circle. Let each say what each person feels grateful for and what has been learnt from the active phase.

@/☉ Plant some bulbs or tree seeds in pots to place outside. Plant your own inner seeds with them. Focus on your hopes, ideas and intentions for the Spring. Plant some of the fruit, nuts, seeds and berries you have gathered for the Autumn Equinox, label them, leave them outside without saucers underneath, and see what comes up in the Spring.

@/☉ We all need to know we are loved and respected for who we are. Share what you value about each other. Celebrate and give thanks for your friendships. This too is part of your harvest. Pass the talking stick around.

@/☉ Continue the process of letting go of things, ideas, conditioning, and values which are no longer serving you. Write it down on a piece of paper and burn it in the candle flame or fire as part of a ritual of letting go.

@/☉ State your intentions for getting in touch with your intuitive wisdom, for internalising your harvest within, respecting your intuition, your dreams, your psychic abilities. Thank your higher self for all the help it has given, and resolve to listen and act on its wisdom more often in the future.

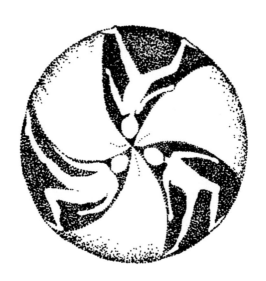 Pass some fruit round the circle and let each share with each other any blessings they know which can be said or sung before eating. Teach them to each other.

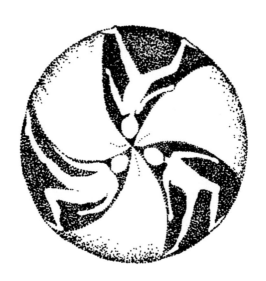 In the centre, place a basket of abundance into which everyone has put a wrapped present, a giveaway, something they no longer need. Let each in turn light a candle with thanks for your harvest and take out a present.

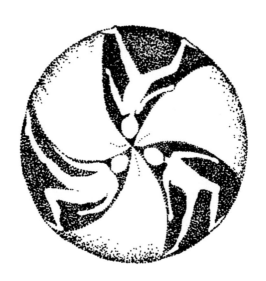 Come together for a closing ceremony. Thank the elements, the nature spirits, the Spirit guides and helpers and each other. Sing one of the blessings songs you have learnt. Bless the food and drink and have a great feast and celebratory party.

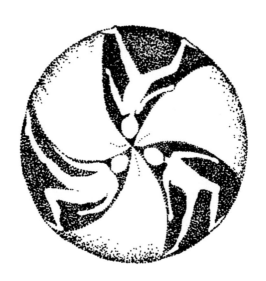

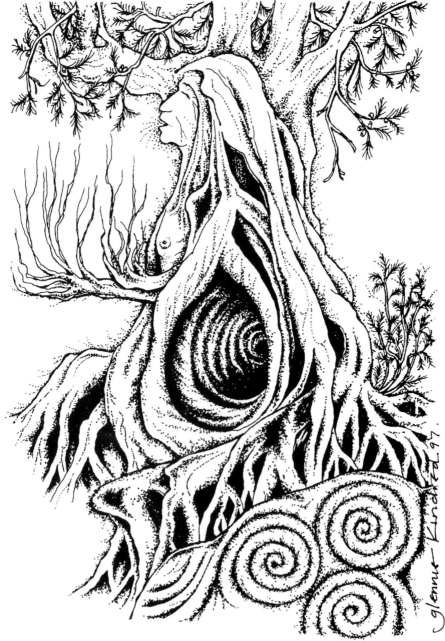

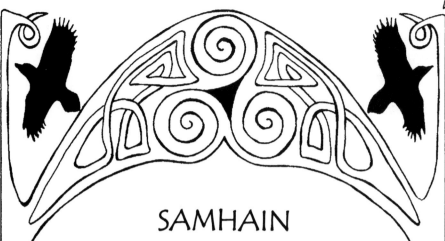

SAMHAIN

AUTUMN CROSS QUARTER FESTIVAL

END OCTOBER/BEGINNING NOVEMBER

Mid-Scorpio ♏ fixed Water

Dark of the Moon

Halloween ◇ Hallows Eve ◇

All souls Night

Night of Hecate and Cailleach

Feast of the Dead

Festival of Remembrance

SAMHAIN

This is the Summer's end and the beginning of Winter. It is the end and the beginning of the Celtic New Year, affirming rebirth in the midst of death and darkness. At Samhain, the Grain Mother becomes the Crone, the wise woman, the death aspect of her trinity, until she is reborn as her virgin aspect with the rebirth of the Sun at the Winter Solstice. The Sun King is sacrificed back into the land having swelled the seeds which now lie in the dark of the Earth until the Sun's return. He too becomes a death God and shaman, able to travel the inner realms. Celtic understanding of the year's cycle saw death and darkness as important and necessary, as a period of rest and regeneration before rebirth.

Samhain (pronounced Sow-ein), like Beltain, is a magical time. The veil between the seen world of Matter and the unseen world of Spirit becomes thin - a crack in the fabric of space-time. It is a time for communication with the Ancestors, a time for divination, omens, portents, and seeking mysteries. It is a time to drift, dream and vision, a time for inner journeys connecting to the wisdom within yourself.

Samhain is named after an Aryan lord of death, Samana or Samavurt who, along with other pre-christian male Gods, was given the title Grim Reaper, the Leveller, the Dark Lord, Leader of Ancestral Ghosts, the Judge of the Dead. Sata, the Great Serpent, was an underground aspect of the Sun found in ancient Egypt, the root of Satan, the Angel of Darkness. Pluto, Hades, Aidoneus, Saman, Sammael, Cronus, Saturn, Hermes, Samanik, were some of the old Gods associated with death and the Underworld which the Church personified as the Devil. The Underworld and darkness became a place to fear and the Celtic understanding of its regenerative aspect became lost. The Church created Hell out of the Celtic Otherworld, and every sadistic cruel fantasy man could invent, was assigned to it.

Hell was previously a Norse Queen of the Underworld, Hellenes, and 'Hel' a uterine shrine, a sacred cave of rebirth deep within the Earth. The dark regenerative power of the Goddess was honoured throughout the Celtic and ancient world. Rhea-Kronia (the female counterpart to Cronos) devoured time itself, returning to the dark elemental formless chaos before time. Kali or Kali

Ma, the Dark Mother of the Hindu Triple Goddess, devoured her own children. Rhiannon, also known as the Mother of Time, also devoured her own children and rode her horse through the regions of the dark. Morgan le Fey, Morgan the Fate, Morrigan, the Queen of Phantoms, Death Goddess, reappeared in the Arthurian legends as Morgan. Cerridwen who kept the Cauldron of rebirth and regeneration, was known as the Grandmother of Memory and the Keeper of the ancestral gateway. Cailleach, the Black Mother, made the world. Scotland was once Caledonia, the land given by Cailleach or Cale. 'Scotland' came from Scotia, a Roman Goddess known as the Dark Aphrodite, and known to the Celts as Satha or Scythia. To the Scandinavians, she was known as Skadi, personified as Old Woman, hag or veiled one. Mana and Mara were ancient Roman Goddesses whose ancestral spirits were called Manes, and ruled the Underworld. Maia was the Greek grandmother of Magic, mother of Hermes, the enlightened one, who conducted the souls of the dead to the Underworld. Hecate was one of the oldest Goddesses in her Crone aspect, found in ancient Greece. She ruled heaven, Earth, and the Underworld; she ruled magic, omens and prophecy and she was also known as Persephone, ruler of the Underworld of ancient myth. Other Goddesses of the Underworld include Minerva, Athene, Sophia and Medusa. The word 'Crone' which describes this aspect of the Goddess, may have come from Rhea Cronia, Old Mother Time, but may also be linked to 'corone', the carrion crow which was sacred to the death Goddess. Black was the colour she assumed before her re-emergence as her white virgin aspect at the Winter Solstice. Samhain can be seen as a psychic return to the dark womb before awakening once again new and rejuvenated.

In the Middle Ages, this dark aspect of the Goddess became an object of fear. She became Queen of Witches, Queen of Ghosts, black, evil, capable of bad magic and all manner of diabolical doings. Hag originally meant holy woman, wise woman, healer. Old women were originally revered for their wisdom as midwives and herbalists. But during the witch hunt years, they were tortured and killed in the most sadistic ways by the Church. It was obviously important to the Church to destroy these women who had previously held such power and respect. We cannot undo all the centuries of persecution and debasement of women which the Church brought to our land, but we can turn and acknowledge that it happened, try to understand it and work through our feelings about it.

All over the world patriarchal religions forced the female to retreat into the unconscious, but, true to her cyclic nature, after a period of rest in the dark, she is now re-emerging rejuvenated, made new, strengthened and changed.

The Celtic shaman, the wise man, also belongs here. The shamanic tradition embraced both sexes, as the early Druids did not exclude women, but recognised the differences between their energy, power and focus. Celtic shamanic traditions never completely disappeared. Death and resurrection ceremonies were part of the process which brought about enlightenment and healing. Their practices included necromancy (consultation with the ancestral dead); scrying (seeing visions in clear water, mirrors or crystal balls); reading omens in the land, in clouds, in fire, from the appearance of animals or birds; clairvoyance, interpreting dreams and visions, journeys to the Otherworld or inner world to gain a Guardian, guide, ally, or power animal; Tarot cards, Runes or Tree Ogham, and other divinatory systems. Shamans and witches were said to be able to shapeshift, the ability to transform into the spirit shape of a totem animal at will. This gave them the freedom to fly, to travel great distances, and invisibility.

Fear of magic brought about a great deal of superstition and the psychic arts became seen as demonic. Fear of punishment and even death further inhibited their progress, but also true to the cyclic nature of rest in the darkness, many of the old traditions are re-emerging now, rejuvenated by their period in the dark. They are being understood in new ways, reinterpreted in the light of a New Age - true expressions of a living tradition.

Darkness was important to the Celts. To them it was as important as the light. Darkness and death had power which they did not fear. Here at Samhain, as the Earth is plunged into its darkest time of the year, they blessed the seeds whose germination in the dark would once again bring life, when the Sun returned. They communicated with their Ancestors, believing deceased family members could visit their loved ones at this time of the year. Places were laid at the table during the feast so that the dead could be with their families and friends. Both the word ghost and the word guest have their roots in the German 'geist', originally a spirit of the dead invited to the Samhain feast. Samhain became the Christian All Souls Night, All Hallows Eve (Halloween) of 31st October and All Souls Day of 1st November.

Others could also slip through the gap in space-time: the Faerie, the Sidhe, Hobgoblins, Elves and other mischief makers. This is the root of

Halloween's 'mischief night'. Only those in disguise could venture out. Later the emissaries of the Devil were also feared along with evil ghosts and many 'horrors of hell' which were let loose on this night which all good Christian folk were led to fear.

Bonfires called 'samhnagan' were lit on the hilltops. All the other fires in the community were put out and were then rekindled from the samhnagan. The hilltops were probably the tumuli or burial mounds. Later, each village or household had bonfires (note the proximity to Bonfire night). The Church may have brought the people away from the burial mounds, but Samhain customs continued to thrive. In Wales, omens were read from white stones which were thrown into the ashes of the fire and then interpreted the next morning by the marks found there. Halloween apple games grew out of the Celtic belief in the apple as a holy fruit, sacred and magical, a means to immortality, death and rebirth. The western paradise of Avalon, known as apple-land, was ruled by Morgan, Queen of the Dead. The fabled Isles of the Western oceans, where the Greeks believed the golden apples of the Hesperides were to be found, also bestowed immortality. In Celtic myth, the apples of the Goddess, (sometimes called Hels apples, after the Underworld Goddess Hellenes) signified a sacred marriage and a journey to the land of death and rebirth. Later, Hels apples became the poisoned apples of Christian folklore which the 'wicked witch' used to kill her victims. Cutting the apple transversely reveals the hidden five pointed star in the core, the magic pentacle, sign of the dark mysteries of the Goddess. Apples continue to be used at Samhain for games and divination, often connected to revealing marriage prospects.

At Samhain, rituals were enacted at the burial mounds, tumuli and long barrows. Womb and tomb were closely linked in the Celtic mind, and this explains why so many tombs of this period and earlier, had tunnel entrances leading to a dark inner chamber. Previously it had been thought that these were places where the important dead were buried, but recent thinking suggests that they are important centres of Earth energy which can be used to enhance shamanic journeys within. This is the best time of year for this inner exploration, for meditating and connecting to the Spirit realms. Nurture your inner world, look for your own understanding of the spiritual path you walk.

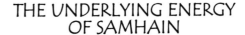

THE UNDERLYING ENERGY OF SAMHAIN

This is the Cross Quarter Festival of Autumn's end and the beginning of Winter. It is the right time to connect to root energy and for internalising the creative life force. Increasing darkness and cold means we must accept that Winter is fast approaching and we must adjust to this changing season. Leaves have fallen off the trees, birds have migrated, animals have gone into hibernation, frosts have come. It is a time of death and decay, death of the old, and within this, knowledge of rebirth. It is a time of forced adjustments which, once accepted, reveal a new set of possibilities, a new phase, a new power to life. Like its counterpart, Beltain, Samhain brings a mystical energy which we can use to explore and understand ourselves better.

This is the dark phase of the year's cycle when the mystery of transformation occurs. This process involves a descent and a death of something old in preparation for something new to be reborn. The descent into the Underworld or Otherworld can be understood as a journey into the unconscious and the Spirit realms within each of us. Here we can find renewal through meditation, trance, rest, sleep, and by sacrificing our outer selves for a while. The seeds of our ideas and future direction in life are incubated in our unconscious during the Winter months, ready for rebirth in the Spring. We can honour the cycle by being aware that each end and death of the old will bring opportunity for a new start, as each beginning holds within it an end. This endless cycle of change is necessary, bringing renewal of cells, of ourselves, our understanding and our ideas. It means there are always new opportunities to start again, to stay healthy. Many illnesses are rooted in stuck energy patterns, emotional congestion and hanging on to the past.

We have been taught to fear our inner world and to mistrust the information we may receive through insights, intuition, and our connection to our own inherent inner wisdom. Many of our actions come from our subconscious and we may not always be aware of these subtle patterns and conditioned responses that are such a part of us and which may silently rule our lives. We need to understand our unconscious selves, and to learn to listen to our inner voice. We can use the energy of the dark time of the year to explore these inner parts of ourselves. We need to face our fear of the dark mysteries, magic and our deep unwanted feelings which we may have pushed inside and not recognised as our own. We need to turn and face what these mean to us, free the energies, the potential inherent in the experience. From this courageous journey will come transformation, a balanced perspective and rebirth in the age-old tradition of Samhain.

Use this time for inner exploration, astral travel, deep meditation, contacting your deepest wisdom. Slip beyond the rational and the logical and go beyond the seen world. Use this time for collecting, sorting, memorising information and learning, so that when the time for action comes, you will have assimilated new knowledge which can be used when needed. Fear is one of our greatest teachers. Turn and look at what you fear and the understanding this brings. Seek the truth in the darkness, look for ways to find the Divine within. Out of a difficult situation comes power, hope, rebirth, inner strength, wisdom and maturity. Review and assimilate what you have learned in the active phase of the year's cycle. Prepare yourself for the new year ahead. Nurture your visions, dreams, ideas and direction, so that they may incubate in the dark Winter months ready for when the active phase begins again.

I am tomorrows ancestor
The future of yesterday
and what I am in the here and now
goes rippling out all ways
Goes rippling out
always.

You are tomorrows ancestor
The future of yesterday
and what you are in the here and now
goes rippling out all ways
Goes rippling out
always.

We are tomorrows ancestor
The future of yesterday
and what we are in the here and now
goes rippling out all ways
Goes rippling out
always.

Brian Boothby
Tomorrows Ancestor

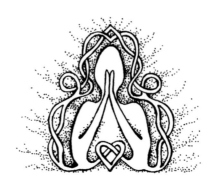

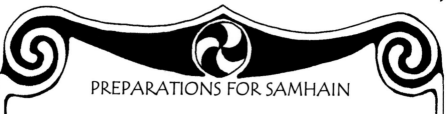

PREPARATIONS FOR SAMHAIN

Bonfire ◇ Feast ◇ Shrine to the Dark ◇
Dark of the Moon ◇ Burial Mounds ◇ Astral Travel ◇
Scrying ◇ Dreams ◇ Omens ◇ Readings ◇
Power Animals ◇ The Pentacle ◇ Persephone ◇
The Cauldron of Regeneration ◇ Masks ◇
Coppicing ◇ Besom Broom ◇
Trees: Elder ◇ Yew
Herbs: Dandelion Root ◇ Mugwort ◇ Valerian ◇ Elderberry

✫ Use the power of the dark Moon to enhance your Samhain celebrations and rituals.

✫ Prepare to have a large bonfire if you have got an outdoor space big enough. It is cold at this time of year, so the fire is important for warmth as well as focus. If you are celebrating with friends, ask everyone to bring wood for the fire and food to share. Create an area where people can put their wood when they arrive, and some tables where food can be put. Have an alternative plan for inside celebrating in case it rains. If possible, arrange to seat everyone for the Samhain feast. Buy lots of candles.

✫ Create an outside shrine area by erecting a dolmen from three flat stones. The uprights will need to be embedded in the ground. You can add a fourth stone at the back. It may be small enough to put a candle in or as large as you can physically manage. Finding the flat stones will determine the size.

☆ Alternatively, erect a standing stone in your garden or on your land where you feel the Earth's energy is strong, where you like to sit, where meditation comes easy. Choose a stone which has a good energy and embed it well into the Earth. Plant crystals beneath it.

☆ Make time to go to the long barrows, burial mounds or tumuli in your area. These can be found on any Ordnance Survey map. They are to be found in the high places connecting the ley alignments. The dragon paths link these important points of power. In the Irish tradition, the barrows were called 'the hollow hills', said to be built by the Sidhe so that mortals could enter fairyland. The same folklore reoccurs throughout Europe. Hidden in folk stories is reference to their use as gateways into another world, as places where people could communicate with the dead, journey to other lands where time stood still. Their accoustic properties are particularly interesting and worth exploring. They have an extraordinary atmosphere which will challenge and transform you through your experiences there.

☆ Astral Travel

Now is a good time for inner journeys and developing your psychic skills. Astral travel is best practised with a friend. Take it in turns to sit with each other and talk through the procedure. Be there for each other after the journey, and for assurance while journeying. Lie down comfortably and breathe deeply and calmly, focusing on the centre of your body. Feel yoursel getting smaller and smaller until you are tiny. Then feel yourself getting bigger and bigger until you fill the whole room. Repeat this again, and then feel yourself normal size but floating above your body. See the golden thread which connects your Spirit self to your body. Know with certainty that this cannot be broken in any way. When you feel ready, calmly allow yourself to float away above the room, the house, over town and countryside, moving further away until you are in space above the Earth. Look around and see if there is a guide who might speak to you or show you something, like a symbol, a picture, or a series of events like in a dream. When you feel ready, thank your guide and gently journey back through the stars to the Earth, back the way you came to your room, and come gently back into your body. Wiggle your toes and fingers, stretch yourself and take time to feel properly back before sitting up and writing down your experience. Try to remember all the details now, and

216

understand what they mean later. Alternatively, your friend could tape you talking over what happened. It is important to do this straightaway while the experience is fresh in your mind. Eat and drink afterwards to help settle yourself fully back in your body.

☆ Scrying and Seeing Auras

Scrying is another skill which you may wish to practise and spend time developing. Fill a glass bowl with mineral water. Focus on your breath as you would for meditation, and gaze towards the surface of the water. Half close your eyes to put them out of focus. Stay relaxed. Remember to breathe and let your mind also slip out of focus. Suddenly you are aware of images on the surface of the water. Use the same technique for seeing auras. Work with a friend, and gaze past them and through them, glazing the eyes until they are out of focus. Become aware of the colours and patterns of the energy field which surrounds the body. Both these techniques need practise and determination to succeed, so keep trying until you reach a breakthrough. Once achieved, it becomes easier each time you do it.

☆ Crystals come from deep inside the Earth. Use the Winter months to build up your relationship with favourite crystals. Crystals can channel energy so can be used for healing, protection, and to access your dreams. Before going to sleep, ask a crystal to help you communicate with your subconscious mind and your Spirit guides through your dreams. Place the crystal under your pillow. When you wake, while you are still half asleep, hold the crystal up to your forehead, your third eye. Keep your eyes closed and let any images, words or feelings come to you. Write these down in a dream diary. Thank your crystal for its help. Thank your Spirit guides for their communication.

☆ Divination

The Celts used this time to seek omens and portents. They would consult the Ancestors and look for signs from the natural world. They cast the knuckle bones, Tarot cards, Runes, or Ogham sticks. All the divinatory systems involve random throwing or random choosing from a system of symbols with meanings. The process of interpreting them was called 'raedan' or reading. The result was raedels or riddles as the results had to be interpreted by the reader or seer. If you wish to be able to work with a divinatory system, choose whichever system you are most drawn towards. Runes can be made by scratching the symbols onto pieces of slate, bone or wood, or made in clay which needs to be fired. If you make your own, you can take your time to learn the meanings behind each one. Similarly with the Tree Ogham, each stick can be collected after direct communication with each tree, and understanding the tree's wisdom and inherent energy. Winter is a good time to study and learn to use any of these systems. Having assimilated information in the unconscious, it can be accessed by the conscious mind in creative and inspirational ways.

⭐ Reflect on the visions which have been living on the edge of your consciousness. Make visible the invisible. Take up drawing or painting and let your unconscious speak to you through the images you produce. It doesn't matter whether you can draw or paint in the conventional sense. Let your notions of what is 'good' go, and seek the seeds of your inner world as you see what is revealed. Your 'technique' will improve the more you do, as will your confidence.

⭐ Explore every aspect of your dark side: pain, anger, loneliness, abandonment, grief, terrors, childhood disappointments, abuse, fear of death, failure, insecurities, fear of insanity, fear of rejection. We all have plenty...they are all aspects of the sacred wound which we often try to ignore and yet this affects all we do in subtle and unconscious ways. Facing these negative hidden aspects of yourself will eventually be a source of your greatest strength, power and wisdom.

⭐ There is still a great need to undo the negative propaganda surrounding the old witch woman. The Crone aspect of the Triple Goddess was once respected for being the most powerful phase of a woman's life under the matriarchal tribal system, but it became the most feared by the patriarchal Church. To the ancients this third, post-menopausal stage of a woman's life was her wisest, as she retained her wise Moon blood and, of course, the whole tribe could benefit from her wisdom gained over the years. The word 'witch' is derived from the Anglo-Saxon 'witan' meaning 'to see', to know, and a 'witea' was a seer or diviner, becoming 'wicca' (masculine seer, wise man) and 'wicce' (female seer, wise woman). 'Witch' became a convenient scapegoat for any natural disaster, disease, crop failure, or petty rivalry. Family fortunes which previously were passed down through the female line, could immediately be seized by the Church, and any woman who made trouble or was too powerful or influential, could be charged with witchcraft, tortured until 'confession' and sadistically killed. It is an appalling history. Supported by Christianised folktales, witch became synonymous with evil, black, bad magic, ugly old women, and fear. Now we no longer fear old women, but we rarely honour them either. The evil witch is still more likely to be part of children's stories than a good witch capable of wondrous magical transformations. Change the old stories, or find new stories and read them to the children. Help reverse the old images and generate respect for the power of the old ones, and the power of transformation.

Who can walk on their own at night? Who can walk alone in the dark woods, or sit alone in the dark by a sacred spring or burial mound? Who sees power in black but not evil? Dark is the womb, dark is the tomb. What does magic mean to you? Unravel what is true for you and what you fear. Turn and face the fear. Release its hold over you.

Contemplate and review your year which has ended, and where you wish to go in life. Leave behind old mental and emotional attitudes. Throw away or transform the things which are holding you back or no longer serve your higher good. Let them go and move on with freedom. Let your heart decide. Let go of the logical mind. Rebirth and transformation are constantly yours.

Trees of Samhain

Elder – *sambucus nigra*

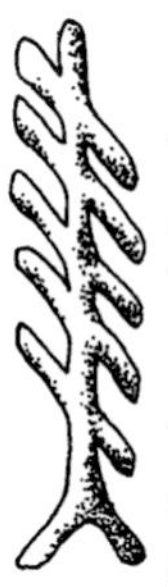

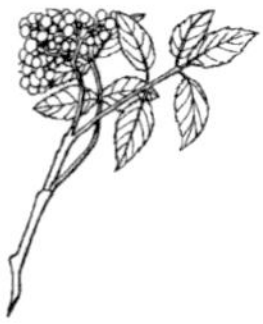

The fifteenth tree of the Celtic Tree Ogham. RUIS. R. Elder is known as a tree of regeneration and wisdom. Often called the witch's tree, the Elder Mother, the Queen of trees, it is connected to the Goddess and the Crone energy, in particular. The earliest folktales praise Elder's ability to ward off evil or malevolent spirits, and undo evil magic. But the Christianised folktales connected it to the tree from which Christ's cross was made and said a malevolent spirit dwelled within it. There are very strong superstitions about cutting the Elder, or bringing it into the house and burning it. This probably grew out of deep respect for a tree which had so many herbal and culinary uses. Later this changed to fear of releasing a malevolent spirit from within it. In early times its branches were hung in doorways of houses, cowsheds, buried in graves and its twigs carried to ward off evil. It was used to bless a person, place or object, by scattering Elder leaves and berries to the four directions and over whatever was being blessed, invoking the protection of the spirit of the Elder. At Samhain, the last of the elderberries were picked with solemn rites. The wine made from these berries was considered to be the last sacred gift of the Earth Goddess, was highly valued and drunk ritually to invoke prophecy, divination and hallucinations. Elder makes a fast-growing hedge, easily propagated by pushing small pieces of freshly cut twigs into the ground. The Elder will bring inner strength and wisdom to help deal with changes. Each ending brings a new beginning; each beginning contains within it, its end. Transformation and renewal are the fruits of wisdom the Elder brings.

Yew - *taxus baccata*

Yew is the last tree of the Celtic Tree Ogham. IDHADH or IDHO. I. Like Samhain, it represents the end of one cycle and the beginning of a new one. All races of the Northern Hemisphere have a deep respect for this remarkable tree which survived the Ice Age. A new system of dating now suggests that some of the old English Yews are 4,000 years old due to their ability to grow a new trunk from the decaying mass of the old trunk, keeping their original root bole. The Yew, therefore, is associated with immortality, renewal, regeneration, everlasting life, rebirth, transformation and access to the Otherworld and the Ancestors. Known as the death tree, **the whole tree is poisonous, apart from the fleshy part of the fruit.** Sacred to Hecate and the Crone aspect of the Triple Goddess, the wood was prized for sacred carving and votive offerings. **If you carve this beautiful wood, be aware that even the dust produced by sanding, is poisonous.** The Yew provides a link to the Guides, Guardians and Ancestors of the Otherworld, reminding us of other levels of existence beyond the material world. Spending time with the Yew will help overcome fear of death and fear of endings. We may also fear the death of our old selves, an old way of life, or old ways of looking at things. Each death can be seen as a new beginning, hope for the future, and transformation. Sometimes one thing needs to end before something new can begin.

220

✭ The Winter months, from November to early March, are the right time for planting trees and moving saplings, bushes, or splitting herbs. If you have land, you might want to plant a Celtic Tree Circle (see page 58) or create a new grove of trees for celebration and ritual. It is also the right time for coppicing (cutting a tree right back to the bole at the base of the trunk). This encourages the tree to send up many long straight poles instead of just one central trunk. Any tree can be coppiced to give a variety of straight poles for domestic use. November to March is also the traditional time for cutting Willow whips for basket-making, and Hazel poles for hurdle-making, when the sap is down and the leaves are off the trees. Hazel poles can be used for making garden screens, creative fencing, archways and garden bowers.

✭ Herbs of Samhain

Dandelion root – *taraxacum officinale*
Dig up November to March if you wish to store them. Scrub them, wash them, but do not leave to soak. Chop them up and leave them to dry in a warm airy place until brittle. Store them in a dark jar. Use ½ – 1 ounce of the dried root to 1 pint of cold water (or 3 ounces of the fresh root) and leave overnight. Put in a saucepan (not aluminium), bring to the boil and simmer for ten minutes. When cool, pour the unstrained liquid into a jug and store covered in the fridge. Drink one wine glassful three times a day for any distrubances of the liver. This is a prime lymph tonic, removing poisons from the system and cleansing the blood. It will strengthen the lungs and help the blood to circulate. It is a useful herb for emotional stagnation, turning depression into expression and self-empowerment. (Similarly with the leaves.)

Mugwort – *artemisia vulgaris*
Grows on waste grounds and roadsides and was one of the nine sacred herbs of ancient times. A powerful blood cleanser and general tonic which stimulates the action of the liver. It is an antiseptic, relaxant and astringent. Taken hot, it will bring on a delayed period, and help with painful periods. Mugwort has a long history of magical and ritual uses, enhancing clairvoyance, astral travel and dreamwork. It can be burnt as an incense or drunk as a herb tea. Use ½ – 1 ounce of the dried herb to one pint of boiling water. **Do not use if pregnant.**

221

Valerian - *valeriana officinalis*

A powerful herb which may be of use as a painkiller and for any condition which needs the whole system to relax. It is useful for grounding someone who has become overwhelmed by physical trauma, terror or fear. It is a useful herb for helping overcome fears of darkness, ghosts, demons, as well as for those wishing to work with inner mysteries, inner journeys and exploring the unconscious. It will relieve anxieties and bring courage and a calm mind. Use ½ - 1 ounce of dried herb to 1 pint of boiling water. Take one wine glassful three times a day. **It must be taken in small doses and for no longer than three days at a time.**

Elderberry - *sambucus nigra*

Elderberry wine has curative powers of established repute. Taken hot at night, it will help in the early stages of a cold or flu and is excellent for sore throats and catarrh. This is due to the viburnic acid contained in the berries which induces perspiration and helps bring the cold out. An old cure for colds, coughs and bronchitis, was to make a rob (a juice thickened by heat) of elderberries. Use five pounds of fresh ripe berries plucking them off the stalks with a fork. Crush with one pound of sugar and boil until it is the thickness of honey. One or two tablespoons mixed with hot water at night will act as a demulcent to the chest and throat. Elderberries will help move stuck emotional states, moving the energy from the surface levels to bring deeper understanding.

☆ Power Animals

There are many power animals and birds associated with Samhain. Ravens, crows, blackbirds, owls, eagles, bats, cats - were all seen as familiars (spirit friends) of witches and shamans. In fairytales it is often the raven who leads the hero into the Otherworld or gives information. Throughout the Celtic lands they were recognised as oracular birds bringing omens and foretelling the future. Owls are known for their wisdom and their oracular power and mysteries of the dark and the night. The Romans called the owl 'strix', the same word they used for 'witch'. The owl was also called Night Hag and was feared as an emissary of the witch. A witch or shaman's ability to shapeshift into the guise of an animal or bird, was greatly feared. Birds were thought to travel freely between the worlds and were seen as messengers. Crows and vultures took the souls of the dead to the Otherworld and storks brought them back. The eagle is known for transformation and rebirth. Blackbirds were said to enchant people with their song, especially at twilight, leading them into Faerie and the lands which co-exist with ours, outside of time. Faeries could change into birds which is why they are depicted with wings. The horse belongs to the Dark Goddess Rhiannon, and in folklore the horse always knew the way into the Otherworld and was often a guide and companion there.

☆ The Pentacle

This is the sign of the Gods and Goddesses of the Otherworld or Underworld. The star of knowledge, the star of life and health, it was used by Hermetic magicians to represent man the microcosm. The head, arms, and feet of a man within a pentacle touched a circle at their points, with his genitals at the exact centre (the shape of woman as well, of course!). The five-pointed star in a circle was the Egyptian hieroglyph for the underground womb of transformation. Cutting an apple transversely reveals the five-pointed star inside. Small twigs of the English Oak (the sacred tree of the Druids) also reveals a perfect five-pointed star at its heart. The point of the pentacle should always be at the top. It represents the five elements of Earth, Air, Fire, Water with Spirit at the top. The drawing of a pentacle as a single unbroken line is used as a force-field, a protection from spirits and unwanted influences or intrusion. Because of its magical associations with the old religion, in the Church's eyes it became associated with the idea of the Devil, the witch's cross, and with evil.

☆ Persephone

Persephone was the daughter of Demeter, the Corn Mother who, in classical Greek myth, was abducted by a male God Pluto and taken into the Underworld. All the vegetation died and the Earth became perpetually Winter until he agreed to release her in the Spring as long as she returned to him again in the Autumn. This is a later reworking of an older story of Persephone, the Dark Goddess, who descended into the Underworld for regeneration and rebirth. Pluto was also an earlier Goddess, a daughter of the Cretan Earth Mother Rhea, one of the Titans or older deities. Later, Pluto became masculinised and, along with other Gods and Goddesses of the Underworld, became synonymous with the Church's idea of the Devil.

☆ The Cauldron of Regeneration and the Holy Grail

In all the early traditions there is a vessel or cauldron which held the secret of life and death, the mysteries of the Underworld, the power of healing, transformation and rebirth. The Cauldron of Regeneration was central to Celtic spiritual understanding of death and rebirth as the neverending cycle of life. It appears over and over again in the folktales and legends of the Celtic lands. The year's solar cycle provides each of us with an experience of death and rebirth through a period of rest during the Winter months. This is a time of reconnection to inner wisdom and the mysteries accessed through the unconscious realms before the rebirth of the Sun heralds the return of the active phase of a new year at Winter Solstice. Later, the Cauldron of Regeneration was assimilated into Arthurian legend as the Holy Grail sought by the knights of the Round Table who looked for ways to re-interpret the old knowledge and the ways of the Goddess through the new religion of Christianity.

☆ Masks

Traditionally worn at Samhain and used in magic since earliest times. Northern shamans believed they could put on a 'Helkappe' or Hel-met (a mask of the Goddess Hellenes) which would make them invisible and help them enter the Otherworld. This same shaman's mask appeared in medieval mystery plays as the mask of Death worn by Hades, the Grim Reaper, Lord of Death, as he performed his 'dance macabre'. Masks were worn in shamanic trance-work where death and rebirth were part of transformative rites of passage. The mask can be seen to 'possess' the wearer, allowing the person behind the mask to take on a different identity. Magical masks will bring power and Spirit which must not be underestimated. When used in a ceremony, they may release an energy source within the wearer, or access deep hidden parts of themselves. Masks have been worn at Halloween as part of the fun of disguise and trickery, but they hold a deeper power if used wisely and with respect. Transformatory masks may be part of a rite of passage, healing a deep psychic scar, expressing a dual identity, or as an aid to shamanic journeying.

✫ Besom Broom

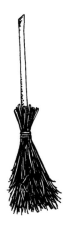

The Silver Birch is associated with purification and renewal. Birch twigs were used to drive out the spirits of the old year, re-establish tribal boundaries (beating the bounds) and drive out malevolent spirits. Birch twigs were cut now to make besom brooms for sweeping up the old year's leaves. Gather a large bunch of Birch twigs and tie them together tightly at the thick end of the twigs. Cut a Hazel or Ash broom handle, sharpen one end, and drive it into the middle of the bundle. Seen as the 'witch's broom' of folk stories, you could indeed use it as a broom for symbolic work, clean sweeps, clearing energy and boundaries.

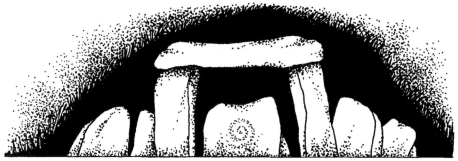

SAMHAIN CELEBRATIONS

✦ Samhain celebrations embrace the power of the dark and need to be part of the dark Moon cycle. Because of the cold, you may wish to be inside for some of the ritual, lighting the fire as a concluding ritual. But there are no rules. You may wish to light the fire at the beginning and have it as the main focus. It will depend on how much firewood and space is available. Get the fire ready to light beforehand.

✦ Make a shrine to celebrate Samhain. It may be inside or outside, or both. Hang black and purple cloths and ribbons. Place crystals, power stones, evergreens. Make patterns with white stones which can later be thrown into the ashes of the fire to be read for signs and portents for the new year. Gather sprays of dried grasses, flowers, and twigs with berries still on, such as haws, elderberries, rosehips, sloes. Make dream-catchers and hang them up. Use a Hazel hoop to make big ones to hang in the trees. Make sacred wands out of Elder wood or Yew. Ask everyone who is coming to celebrate to bring something for the shrine which is powerful to them and reflects the energy of Samhain. Light the shrine well with candles, candle lanterns or nightlights in jam jars. If possible, have the shrine in a quiet place which can be used for meditation and reflection. If you are celebrating on your own, the creation of this sacred shrine is a powerful connection to your Samhain celebration. You may wish to put a cloth down on the floor in the centre of your room or make a more permanent area on a shelf, table or window ledge.

✦ Make yourself a Samhain head-dress, weaving plants and natural things from the old year. Use Willow, Ivy or old man's beard as a base, adding any dried and dying plants, sprays of berries, dried grasses, flowers.

 Make a representation or effigy of the old year using similar things. Again, use Willow as a base shape and add the things you find. Place this in a central position to honour the old year passing. Each person may add their own sprays and posies. In doing so, they honour the year for themselves.

 Gather in a circle to a solemn drumbeat. Ask five people to represent the four directions and Spirit in the centre. If you are on your own, place something in each of the directions around your central shrine and invoke the elements in turn.

Water in the West
Give thanks for the element of Water, the ending of cycles in the West, the deep parts of ourselves which unlock the hidden door to emotional release and change, the mystical side of life which opens us to other dimensions. Water connects us to our intuition, our imagination and inner wisdom, bringing receptivity and deep knowing beyond the rational mind. Here we find inner purpose and freedom to follow our hearts.

Earth in the North
Give thanks to the Earth for its gifts of food and shelter, for the way it supports us through the seasonal changes, for the medicine it gives us. The dark Underworld aspect of the Earth at this time brings inner nourishment and holds deep secrets and wisdom. Blessings on the seeds which lie dormant in the dark Earth until the Spring, and on the root energy now beginning. Our thanks to the crystals and minerals who are willing to work with us, and to the nature spirits who rest now.

Air in the East
Give thanks for the element of Air and our ability to communicate on many levels, for inner knowing and mental skills. The element of Air brings us new thoughts, messages from other levels, the birth of new ideas and rebirth. Life-giving and life-sustaining, let our voices carry our visions through song and invocation. Speak out your truth.

Fire in the South

Our thanks for the element of Fire, the active power of the will and creativity which we take with us now into the dark. We thank its power of transformation and cleansing, for passion to learn, to expand and grow. Give thanks for keeping us warm in the Winter months and for lighting our way in the dark. Fire brings strength of purpose, courage and spontaneity, releasing old patterns and freeing energy.

Spirit

Give thanks for Spirit, and the chance to connect to this stabilizing energy. Within and without and ever present. It cannot be seen and cannot be named, and yet is part of all of us. We reach out and in, connecting to our source and inner guidance. We touch the sacred, the still point of power at the centre of our being. We ask that Universal Love guides all our thoughts and actions.

☆ Create a circle of power and protection around you, and all those gathered. If you are celebrating in a group, form a circle holding hands, creating an energy matrix by sound, chanting the sacred Om or another power chant of your choice. Burn sage for cleansing, Rowan berries for protection, mugwort for clairvoyance. State with firm intent that the circle is a protective force-field and picture an energy of light around the circle. Light candles at the four directions and in the centre. Welcome the Guardians and Spirit helpers of all present into your circle.

☆ In the centre of the circle, place a bowl of sand and let each person light a candle with thanks for the old year and what qualities they wish to take with them into the dark of the new year. This is a reflective quiet time, a time to stare into the flames and connect to your inner self.

☆ Welcome the spirits of the Ancestors and the wisdom they bring. Light a candle for family and friends who have died, honour them and welcome their presence in your circle. Do not try to call them back in any way, as this could interfere with their own journey.

☆ Enhance the moment with trance aided by drumbeat or a repetitive easy chant. Soothe the logical mind and open yourself to the inner channels. Stare into the candle flames or the fire. Seek omens in the flames, in the clouds, in shadow shapes, in anything which suddenly strikes you as revealing some message for you.

☆ Pass around a bag of small crystals and let each person take one, asking for its help and guidance through the Winter months.

☆ Release into the fire or flames what is holding you back: insecurities, fear of failure, fear of not being loved, old mental and emotional attitudes, old ways of behaving, lack of trust, lack of confidence. Leave it behind in the old year. Let each say "I leave behind..." and mentally give it to the flames to transform.

☆ Leaving behind these things will make room for new beginnings, new plans, new ways of being. Let each say what new seeds they will incubate through the Winter months, to manifest in the next growth cycle. "I plant the seed of..."

☆ Cut an apple around the middle to reveal the five-pointed star within. Each seed can be seen as a new beginning in your life. Chew each seed thoroughly to take its energy within.

☆ Shamanic Journeying

Journey to the Otherworld to meet a Guardian, Spirit guide or power animal. The sound of a steady drumbeat will greatly enhance an inner journey. If you are on your own, this could be taped. Begin with a little ceremony, like lighting a candle, some incense, an invocation of intent. Lie down, perhaps with a blanket over you. Breathe deeply and steadily. Close your eyes and drift away from physical reality, feeling completely safe and relaxed. Visualise in your mind a beautiful place in nature. When that place is strong and detailed, look around for a hole in the ground, in a tree trunk, or a tunnel, an opening which goes deep deep down into the Earth. Enter this hole and journey down it for as long as you need to, until the scenery changes and you find yourself in another place. Look around you and meet your ally, Spirit guide, Guardian or power animal who is here to help you. Observe what you see here, any visions which may be given to you, symbols or feelings. Thank the Guardian or power animal for its help and return up the tunnel into the natural world you first visualised. Relax here a while and gradually return to your physical body and the room in which you lie. Wiggle your toes and fingers, open your eyes, take time to remember what you received. Make a drawing, write a poem, or write down what happened and what you understand. Share it with each other.

✫ Share with each other what you have learnt from the old year and where this understanding brings you. Look for the direction this will lead you to, how this will serve the greater good.

✫ Honour the cycle of death and rebirth. Honour grief and loss. Honour friends and family who have died. Honour death as part of life.

✫ Put on your Samhain mask and dance a tribal dance of purification and release. Drumbeat will enhance this. Let go of your fears and your inhibitions. Touch the core of your being. Connect to your Ancestors. Express the ending of this year and the potential of this new beginning. Let out any cries or sounds you want to make.

✫ If you have made a labyrinth, walk or dance its path. Light it with nightlights in jamjars. Chant and drum as you walk its ancient pattern. Seek guidance from the still point at the centre. Bring any revelations or insights you may have there out with you.

✫ Now is the time for storytelling. Tell stories which celebrate the Crone and the shaman, traditional legends which reflect the ancient understanding; tales of Otherworld journeying, transformation, symbols of power. Seek ancient teachings hidden in the tale. Storytelling would have been an integral part of any tribe or family gathering in the past, especially through the long dark nights of Winter. Rekindle this ability by asking everyone to bring a story. Begin by reading it, tell it again at a later date and try to relate it in your own words. A story which is repeated regularly becomes rich with inner understanding on many levels.

✫ Bring the group back together into a circle for the closing ceremony. Light the Samhain Fire with ceremony and invocation. Fire will transform, cleanse and purify and can be used for any ceremony requiring its gift.

Write on paper what you wish to leave behind in the old year and offer it to the flames to transform. Burn in the fire anything you wish to finish with, perhaps from an old way of life you wish to change. Symbolically give to the fire what you wish to transform in yourself. Give to the flames what is holding you back. Do what you need to do. An act of power comes from a place of passion, from deep within your being. By empowering yourself, you bring changes, rebirth, a new beginning.

☆ Burn the effigy of the old year and your old year head-dress. Let the year go with thanks for all its gifts, for all you have learnt, for friendships, for all that you manifested for yourself, for all the opportunities, experiences and love it brought. Let it all go so that you can begin the process of incubating new seeds during the Winter months, ready for manifestation in the future. Thank the Spirit guides and helpers for their love and protection. Thank the five elements for their presence.

☆ Throw a white stone in the ashes of the fire. Retrieve it the next morning and see what signs or omens it might reveal. Honour the magical in your life. Relate and recall the magical things you have experienced, the unexplained, the synchronistic. Share these with each other.

☆ Choose three cards from the Tarot pack, or three Runes, or three Ogham sticks. The first choice represents the Underworld aspect, giving guidance to the root of a situation, something from the past, or something hidden. The second choice is laid above the first and it represents the material world, the present moment caught in time. Interpret it in the light of the first. It also represents your manifest power, your physical, mental, emotional and spiritual situation at the present moment. The third choice is the most fluid and reflects the Otherworld aspect. This is the realm where all possibilities exist and will provide you with insights into the direction you are flowing towards, and your most spiritual and positive outcome. Trust your most immediate impressions and insights. Give your intuition a chance to guide your thoughts.

☆ Bless the food and drink. Welcome the Ancestors, family and friends who have died. Leave food and space for them at the feast, in the old tradition of Samhain.

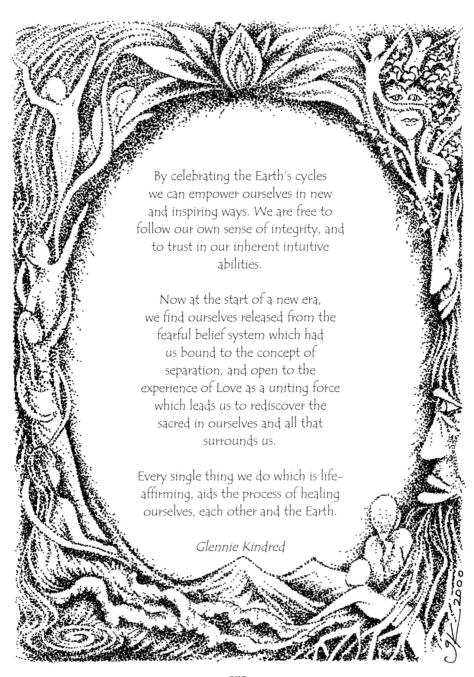

By celebrating the Earth's cycles
we can empower ourselves in new
and inspiring ways. We are free to
follow our own sense of integrity, and
to trust in our inherent intuitive
abilities.

Now at the start of a new era,
we find ourselves released from the
fearful belief system which had
us bound to the concept of
separation, and open to the
experience of Love as a uniting force
which leads us to rediscover the
sacred in ourselves and all that
surrounds us.

Every single thing we do which is life-
affirming, aids the process of healing
ourselves, each other and the Earth.

Glennie Kindred

TO WRITE TO THE AUTHOR

If you wish to write to Glennie Kindred, Gothic Image Publications will be pleased to forward your letters. Please enclose a self-addressed stamped envelope for your reply. She is happy to help you design and create sacred space, sacred gardens and labyrinths, both permanent and temporary. She is also available for workshops, talks and for facilitating sacred celebrations, rituals and rites of passage.

Please write to:-
Glennie Kindred
c/o Gothic Image Publications
PO Box 2568
Glastonbury
Somerset BA6 8XR
England

Copies of this book and other books published by Gothic Image Publications can be ordered from our website: **www.gothicimage.co.uk**
or you may order by telephone:
+44 (0) 1458 831281 or fax:+44 (0) 1458 833385
Alternatively, come and visit our bookshop at 7 High Street, Glastonbury, Somerset BA6 9DP England

BIBLIOGRAPHY

Extracts from:

Kindred, Glennie   The Earth's Cycle of Celebration. 1993
         The Sacred Tree. 1995
         The Tree Ogham. 1997
         Herbal Healers. Wooden Books 1999
         The Hedgerow Cookbook. Wooden Books 1999

It is impossible to list all the sources which have influenced me over the years. Information becomes assimilated and ideas form, reform and move on. Much of this book has grown out of my own intuitive understanding and experience working with the eight Celtic festivals by myself and with groups. It therefore includes much unique material and ideas. I would, however, like to thank the following books for their information and inspiration: -

Aburrow, Yvonne   The Enchanted Forest. Capall Bann Publishing 1994
         Sacred Grove. Capall Bann Publishing 1994

Andrews, Lynn   The Power Deck. Harper San Francisco 1991

Aziz, Peter   Working with Tree Spirits in Shamanic Healing.
         Points Press 1994

Brooke, Elizabeth   A Woman's Book of Herbs. The Women's Press 1992

Burl, Aubrey   A Guide to the Stone Circles of Britain, Ireland and Brittany.
         Yale University Press 1995

Capra, Fritjof   The Tao of Physics. Fontana/Collins 1982

Carey, Diana and Large, Judy

         Festivals, Family and Food. Hawthorn Press 1982

Cooper, Stephanie, Fynes-Clinton and Rowling, Marye

         The Children's Year. Hawthorn Press 1986

Davis, Courtney   The Celtic Art Source Book. Blandford 1988
         The Art of Celtica. Blandford 1994

Estes, Clarissa Pinkola Women who run with the Wolves. Rider 1992

Frazer, James George The Golden Bough. Macmillan London 1949

Glickman, Michael   Corn Circles. Wooden Books 1996

Graves, Robert   The White Goddess. Faber and Faber 1990

Grieve, Mrs M   A Modern Herbal. Tiger Books International 1994

Gurudas   The Spiritual Properties of Herbs. Cassandra Press 1988

Hay, Louise   You can Heal your Life. Hay House 1986

Hoffman, David   The Holistic Herbal. Findhorn Press 1983

Hoult, Janet   Dragons. Gothic Image Publications 1985

Martineau, John   Mazes and Labyrinths in Gt. Britain. Wooden Books 1996

Matthews, John   The Celtic Shaman. Element Books 1991

Meadows, Kenneth Earth Medicine. Element Books 1989

                    The Medicine Way. Element Books 1990

Michell, John   The New View over Atlantis. Thames and Hudson 1983

Noyes, Ralph   The Crop Circle Enigma. Gateway Books 1990

Purce, Jill   The Mystic Spiral. Thames and Hudson 1987

Scheffer, Mechthild Bach Flower Therapy. Thorsons 1990

Service, Alastair and Bradbery, Jean

                    The Standing Stones of Europe. Weidenfeld and Nicolson 1996

Thorsson, Edred   The Book of Ogham. Llewellyn 1994

Walker, Barbara. G   The Women's Encyclopaedia of Myths and Secrets
                       Harper and Row 1983

White Eagle   Spiritual Unfoldment. White Eagle Publishing Trust 1992

INDEX

N

R

rational mind 18, 99, 227
rational thought 175
rattles 174
ravens 222
rebirth 28, 54, 62, 64, 65, 68, 75, 76, 79,
    106, 146, 175, 208, 211, 212, 213, 219,
    220, 223, 224, 227
receptive 168, 188, 195
receptive energy 9
receptive principle 145, 160
receptivity 12, 18, 23, 30, 85, 97, 115, 118,
    227
red rose 155
regeneration 10, 87, 208, 219, 220, 223
regenerative cauldron 166
Remembrance, festival of 207
renewal 118, 161, 162, 166, 190, 201, 212,
    220, 225
Restored Balance and Integration, festival of
    187
Rhea 64, 223
Rhea Cronia 209
Rhea-Kronia 208
Rhiannon (Albion) 124, 158, 167, 209, 223
rite of passage 102, 224
ritual 15, 21, 73, 91, 101, 102, 113, 115, 140,
    141, 152, 153, 167, 178, 183, 200, 204,
    211, 220, 221, 226
ritual games 167
Roman 72, 86, 95, 145, 158, 174, 199, 209,
    222
Roman Goddess 95
root 15, 231
root energy 189, 212, 227
root meditation 203
roots 192, 193, 203
Rose 155
rosemary 58, 134, 159, 162
Rowan 57, 58, 91, 93, 102, 130, 228
rue 162
Runes 93, 98, 115, 152, 210, 217, 231

S

sacred area 23, 202
sacred circle 22
sacred dance 184
sacred drama 149, 162
sacred fire 68, 137
sacred groves 51, 155, 158
sacred hoop 24
sacred journey 130, 158
sacred marriage 135
sacred marriage basket 139
sacred shield 24
sacred shrine 74
sacred space 22, 24, 96, 114, 153
sacred springs 30, 84, 89
sacred wells 30, 52, 89 124, 129
sacred wheel 152
sacred wound 218
sacrifice 173
sage 58, 74, 99, 103, 178, 181, 194, 228
Sagittarius 17, 29
St George 113
St John's Day 143
St John's wort 58, 157
St Mary 113
St Michael 52, 113
St Michael line 113
St Michael's Mount 199
St Valentine 85, 95
salt, cooking 135
salt dough 42
Saman 208
Samana 208
Samanik 208
Samavurt 208
Samhain 6, 7, 10. 12, 58, 62, 65, 127, 152,
    207, 208, 212, 215
samhnagan 211
Sammael 208
Sata 208
Satan 63, 208
Satha 209
Saturn 17, 31, 208
Saturnalia 73
Scandinavians 209
Scorpio 6, 10, 17, 30, 207
Scotland 209
Scots Pine 72
scrying 98, 210, 217
Scythia 209
seed biscuits 180

NOTES

Other Books published by Gothic Image Publications